Raven

The Balance: Book Two

By

Nick Shamhart

Dedication

To my parents for all their love and support over the years, no matter what new vice or hobby my mania drove me to, and for the thankless task of over thirty years of constantly explaining to people, "No, you don't understand. That's just Nick."

Acknowledgements

Firstly this book is for all of those out there who said, "Vampires have been done to death. There is nothing new that can be done with vampires." Shame on you! It should be un-death and there is always another twist for any story. Especially when you bring into account human psychology, and, as Grey would say, "There ain't nothing more twisted than that, darlin'." So, enjoy my vampiric twist.

Secondly for "Omega Squadron" and all its past and present members, thank you. For Al, for Has, for Becky, for Jen, for Cyndi, for Jenny, for Kris, for the wonderfully eccentric world of social media, and most importantly for Pookey! I don't actually know a Pookey, but all my life I've wanted to say, "Pookey, this one's for you!"

Chapter 1

Have you ever wondered about what happens to you after you die? I was terrified. I didn't want to die. I didn't want many of the things that happened to me in the last few months before my death, but my not wanting them didn't mean that they didn't happen. Just like death, not wanting to die does not mean it won't happen.

By the end, my once happy life had been twisted into a state of living hell, but I'd be damned before I let either man or monster take away what was mine. It was MY life, not anyone else's to take, despite what many of those psychopaths who'd flocked to Hitler's Nazi bandwagon, like greedy fat little boys to an all-you-can-eat buffet, may have thought. Mine. Not theirs.

Heinrich Himmler, that SS coward, ordered the construction of Auschwitz II in my home village of Birkenau. You've heard horror stories about the death camps: what we were subjected to and how we were treated. Remember, those are just stories. If word of what really happened reached anyone of import it was always shrugged off as post-traumatic stress or hallucinations brought on by the chemical testing of Mengele and his crew of gleefully genocidal buddies.

I was seventeen when I watched my family torn apart by demons and I don't mean the men who raped and beat us. I mean real demons, evil given form, and not from some hallucinogenic drug making us see things that weren't there, thank you very much. You may have heard about the shower stalls where poisonous gas was pumped in to exterminate Jewish people and others the Nazis deemed a problem, but what about the barbed wire pens that my people were tossed into where demons created physical bodies? No, those didn't make it into the history books did they? I could care less if you don't believe me because I saw my six year old sister set loose in a pen like that. The demons taunted and teased her, working her into a fit of terror and tears before they ripped the life from her small body.

Have you ever been forced to watch as a loved one was dismembered before your eyes? No? So excuse me when I say fuck your post-traumatic stress.

I was the last of my neighbors, friends, and family left alive in the pens. I stood my ground, naked and beaten - ankle deep in the pieces of muscle, meat, and gore that had until so very recently been people I loved - when the demons came for me, after the men were done using me. I did not scream in fear when a red-eyed monster raked its claws across my stomach. With the limp bodies of so many people I had cared for strewn about my feet, what was a little pain in the face of that? I had nothing to defend myself with, but that did not stop me from trying. I jumped at the nearest nightmare creature, sunk my fingers into its black flesh, and bit down hard on its throat. The demon bellowed as it ripped me from its neck, tossing me to the porous concrete floor. It stomped down on my chest like I was some insect to be squashed, causing everything to go dark.

I opened my eyes to see a cowboy hero out of my uncle's dime store western novels tormenting those creatures that had so recently tormented us. Monsters who had relished in trapping us were now trying to escape their own pens. The man was flashing light about like a wizard or sorcerer casting spells. I was confused but instinct kicked back in granting me focus. When the demon I had bitten tried to sneak up behind the cowboy I ran at it, driving the monster to the ground with energy and lavender light crackling from my fingers. I rendered the beast's head from its shoulders with an unrestrained scream of released hate and agony. When I turned the grisly trophy around in my grasp, the demonic black face dissolved in my hands and I shook them to clear the oily goop. I felt no revulsion or horror at my actions, even though somewhere in the back of my mind a voice was telling me that I should.

The click of boots on concrete accompanied the rueful chuckle coming from my rescuer. In a calm country drawl he said, "Well darlin', this fight is over, but I could sure use more help like that in the future."

He crouched down to my level, then looked about with tired aged eyes at the scattered corpses around us. After a moment of silence he smiled at me, and reached out a hand to wipe a bit of black smudge from my cheek. He tilted my chin up, so I would meet his storm-cloud gray eyes and said, "How about it little raven? You want to keep fightin'?"………

***

"Damn it woman! I said put me down, right now!" Pete yelled at the Harpy sister who had scooped him up like a hawk nabbing a field mouse, then flew out into the skyscraper strewn backdrop. The sisters had been terrorizing Queens, New York for the last few years and Harmony had sent Pete to correct them as his first solo mission for the Balance. He was not supposed to do anything rash, just remind the ladies that the Balance was keeping an eye on them. But, if they pushed things much further, then the next time would not be a friendly warning or a slap on the wrist.

The sisters, Velma and Juanita, had died back in the early nineteen eighties, when the country was busy switching from disco to big hair. They had been fixtures on the street corners then, screaming at the passersby, sleeping with any man that would have them, and there were plenty who did. The sisters felt no need to change things when they were gunned down by a random drive-by shooting. Their spirits stayed, clinging to this world instead of moving on. These had always been their neighborhoods, their streets, and their way of life. They would be damned if they were supposed to let some wet-behind-the-ears, rookie hero want-to-be just waltz in, telling them what they could and could not do on their home turf. Without giving him a chance to do more than scream, the closest Harpy, Velma, had grabbed Pete by the shoulders with her sharp-clawed feet. Resembling the mythological creature she was named for, the winged woman flew about the rooftops dangling Pete from her talons. Once her sister had taken wing, joining her, they tossed Pete back and forth like a pick-up game of catch; only the ball was a black man looking to all outward appearances to be in the physical prime of his life.

Pete was dead, just like the Harpy sisters, so it was not fear of dying that had him screaming like a schoolgirl with a skinned knee. Pete, as an agent for the Balance, had stayed behind after his death to keep all of existence from spinning into chaos if either good or evil should gain too much control over the other. His body was energy now and not subject to the depredations and damage typical to human physiology. What had him scared was the idea that if these two demons were strong enough, they could take his energy thus making it their own. In essence he would be annihilated completely, without the chance to move on back to the Source of life, one of the other posthumous options he had eschewed out of fear for not knowing what that meant.

So, Pete wailed as he was lofted back and forth like a cheap *Wiffle* ball. The Harpy sisters laughed, jeered, and shouted obscenities as they played their game. When Velma caught Pete she turned him around to face her and pulled him up close, their noses almost touching. What was left of her hair was done up in high hairspray stiffened bangs, with a bright pink exercise headband wrapped around her forehead. She had matching pink legwarmers that looked at odds with her grotesquely shaped avian feet. Pete watched as those feet clawed his chest, bunching up his lightweight jacket and tee shirt. With the wind from her wings buffeting them, Velma leaned closer to Pete's ear and cooed in a slightly Hispanic accent, "Oh is the little chico scared of heights? Or are you just scared of old Velma here, hmm? I thought it was only white men who can't jump? Let's see." She punctuated her sentence by tossing him to Juanita, who let Pete fall almost to the street before swooping in at the last moment to catch him, laughing all the while.

Pete was limited in his choices. He was allowed to destroy demons and angels (people who had stayed behind after death, turning into those entities as they gained power from their good or evil deeds) if they threatened to tip the Balance of life in one direction or the other. He would know through his connection to Harmony whether the creature he was battling had crossed that point of no return and could be eliminated without threatening to sway things with his actions. It was a hard judgment for him to make at times, to act or not, even with Harmony's guidance. Pete had power, more than he had ever had in his living days. As his mentor Grey would tell him, "Power is a temptin' treat my friend, but it can turn around and bite you in the ass if you misuse it."

Grey had also taught him that just because as agents for the Balance they knew when they could strike and when they could not, that did not mean that their adversaries knew. Grey's voice echoed in Pete's head once more as he tumbled through the air, "Pete, you can call it a lie or a bluff, it don't matter none, but sometimes these evil fuckers need to be smacked around a bit to toe the line. They don't need to know you ain't authorized to finish 'em off. Just let them think you are."

When one of the sisters missed Pete, sending him to plummet ten stories down, landing in an overflowing dumpster, he had had enough. It was time to bluff. The dumpster had taken the brunt of spilled-over energy from his fall. It tipped over onto its side spilling both Pete and half a ton of greasy dripping offal onto the cracked alley blacktop.

"Alright!" Pete yelled dragging himself to his feet, "That's it! I tried to be nice and say, 'Please ladies would y'all mind taking it down a notch?' But did you listen? Were you polite? No! You had to snatch a brother up and toss him about like a damn beach ball, didn't you?"

Pete had started gathering energy about his hands in a pulsing red light as he ranted at the Harpy sisters. The demonic winged women had taken roost on the roof of a nearby broken down city bus that had yet to be repaired or towed away. Bringing forth positive energy directly from the environment, Harmony, or the Source to counter the negative voids of demons was just one of the weapons he could call upon in his defense of the Balance. As the red light glowed, dancing about his fingertips, Pete stuck his index finger straight up, wagging it back and forth in the universal symbol for, *ah ah ah, you naughty girls*. He sent a sphere of light the size of a cannonball cascading across the space between them. The nearest Harpy sister dove over the back side of the bus and the other took flight as the ball exploded where they had previously been sitting. Sounding like a flock of agitated crows they shrieked and hissed obscenities at Pete, who only raised an eyebrow at their ire, forming another crimson missile in his hand.

"So ladies, you want to play, huh?" Pete said. "Then let's play."

Before either sister had decided which direction to fly away in, Pete had started his volley. Globes of light tinted in the warm tones of the spectrum flew from his hands, coming just close enough to the demons that it would not appear to them that Pete was missing on purpose. Flashes detonated all around the bus, driving the now panicked Harpy sisters for cover as they hovered over the street. Pete ran after them and hurdled the broken down bus in a single leap. He launched a particularly large burst of energy that exploded between the sisters, sending them both flying away at full speed, one to her right, the other to her left, causing them to crash together like a pair of *Looney Tunes* characters.

They fell to the street in a heap of tangled limbs and scabby bat-like wings. Pete casually strolled over to them in his imitation of Grey's cowboy swagger and leaned down to stare the topmost demon in the eyes as he asked, "We done playing games, Velma?"

She nodded her head vigorously, sending her high stiffened bangs waggling like a sprung diving board. Pete said, "Good. That was your last warning. Do you hear me? If I have to come back here I will end you two. You got that?"

Both sisters nodded this time, having finally extracted their intertwined appendages. Pete made a shooing gesture with his right hand, sending a few red sparks dribbling off his fingertips, and turned his back on them without waiting to see if they left. It was a gamble, another bluff to see if he had driven his point home. If they attacked him then he would no longer need to bluff, and he could destroy them. *That is assuming they don't kick my ass first,* Pete thought to himself, as he walked over to a nearby car and flopped down on its hood. He was lying on his back with an arm draped over his eyes, so he did not see the Harpy sisters take flight or his fellow Balance warrior, Raven, walking up the road until her form blocked out the ambient glow of the streetlights leaking in around his arm. "You just have a way with women, don't you, Pete?" Raven asked.

"Oh yeah," Pete answered. "They can't keep their hands…well claws, or whatever, off of me. Why are you here, Raven?"

She looked down at him with piercing blue eyes that reflected the streetlights. In the night her eyes looked to be almost as black as her hair to Pete. A mock offended expression blossomed on her fine pale features as she asked, "What, a girl can't come by for a visit?"

"So you're here for a visit?"

"No, but that doesn't mean I couldn't if I wanted to, does it?"

Pete sighed before he said, "Crazy ass white woman. So, why are you here?"

"Zeus is in town with his brother and he wanted to meet up with us tomorrow. He said he needed a favor. I thought I'd come get you early. Maybe see if you needed any help with the Harpy sisters. Obviously you didn't," she said with a smirk, motioning to the overturned dumpster and reaching out to pluck a greasy brown banana peel from Pete's shoulder.

Pete slowly rolled up onto his side and swung his feet over, so he was sitting up on the hood. Feet dangling he said, "Zeus has a brother?

Great, that's what the world needs, two of those giant hairballs running around. Well it's almost morning. Where are we supposed to meet them?" he asked, rubbing the back of his neck and rolling it around to work out the kinks.

"Central Park. We have time; do you want to go grab a bite to eat first?" She asked and started walking away.

Pete jumped down from the car's hood, jogging a bit to catch up with her as she passed deeply shadowed alleys where demonic faces leered out at them. He said, "Yeah, why not, but no breakfast food okay? Grey still hasn't shown me how to do that whole charming *Jedi Mind Trick* thing to sweet talk waitresses into getting me whatever I want."

***

The end of the night took the surrounding demons with it, pulling the creatures with their natural affinity for darkness deeper into the shadows of alleys, under parked cars, down into deep dank basements, moldering caves, stuffy cloying attics, crawlspaces, or sheltering within the earth itself if their need was great enough. The sun's first rays brought forth the angels into the light, allowing them the opportunity to move about the world without fear of annihilation at the claws of their monstrous counterparts in their constant desire to acquire more power. The positive energy of life flowed onto the rolling parkland that aided in the daily joy for so many trapped among the concrete and glass, bringing with it dancing lights and glowing bipedal forms.

Pete enjoyed every dawn more and more as he grew into his new vocation. He marveled at the human connection to the sunrise. The poets tried to do it justice, because instinctually they could feel what was transpiring, but only a few may have been lucky enough to glimpse, even for a moment, what was occurring on this level of existence. The sunrise meant more to the dead than it did the living. Creatures of pure thought and energy were held to different rules than mortal flesh, and the power of the sun could mean annihilation for some or radiant joy for others.

"Pete! Raven! Hey'ya guys! Over here!" The yell from the big Viking-esque man interrupted Pete's musings, and both he and Raven turned to see their approaching friend. The burly giant's name was Zeus and he came tromping over a small hill in Central Park where Pete and Raven had been relaxing, watching the dawn. Sunlight bathed the well-used grounds in warm spring colors as Zeus neared bearing a small adolescent boy on his shoulders. A big grin spread across Zeus' face when he said, "Hey Raven, Pete. This is my little brother Hank." Raising his bushy eyebrows up in the direction of his passenger he continued, "I don't think I've ever introduced you, have I?"

The little boy laughed from under his Cleveland *Indians* baseball cap as the big man jostled him around in a mock attempt to dislodge him. In a calm voice that was disproportionate to his apparent age Hank said, "I've met Raven before, you big moose, but not Pete. It's nice to meet you, Pete." He waved in Pete's direction.

"Hey, yeah you too, Hank," Pete said waving back at the boy. Then smiling up at the pair of them as they towered over him he asked, "How come you never mentioned you had a brother, Zeus? And why haven't I worked with him yet?"

"Because, Pete," Zeus replied, "Hank doesn't work for Harmony like us. He mostly stays out on the West Coast in California, watching over kids who might be abused or get into trouble, that kind of thing, right?" He asked, looking quizzically over his shoulder at Hank.

"Yes, that's mostly correct. And how are you, Raven?" Hank asked, nodding in her direction.

"I'm doing well, Hank. It's good to see you again," Raven answered.

"Hey wait," Pete interrupted. "Zeus, your brother's an angel? How did that happen?"

Turning back to Pete, brushing a handful of Zeus' auburn hair braids from his face Hank answered for both of them, "Neither of us was ready to move on, Pete, so we stayed here working to our strong suits. If you're a friend of Frank here," he added, tapping his bulging steed on the shoulder for emphasis, "then you know he's a good guy, but a fighter. Me? Well…that wasn't how I lived, so I do what I can to protect others. It's just what felt right to me."

"Frank?" Pete asked. Then as he remembered his first encounter with Zeus so long ago, he said, "Oh yeah, Frank is short for Francis. Ha, I forgot abo-." Pete cut himself off quickly at a glare from Zeus. The big man could not hold the stern look for long. Winking he said, "Hank here came to ask for my help, but I remembered you guys were in town too, and I wondered if you wanted to head to California with us? I know you were supposed to be on your first solo mission, Pete, but things seem quiet around here, and I know Grey wanted you to learn from Raven and me, so you guys up for a little road trip?"

Before either of them could respond Hank started vigorously tapping Zeus on the shoulder. He leaned over to Zeus' ear saying, "Put me down. I want to go play frisbee with that boy over there." He pointed at a small boy of about eight or nine years old, sitting alone under a large maple tree that was just opening up its buds for the season. The boy was spinning a blue frisbee on his right index finger and looking around at the other early season picnickers with a forlorn but hopeful expression. Hank jumped down when Zeus stooped low enough, still a large drop for him, and trotted over to the boy, shrinking down in size until he looked to be about the same age as the hopeful young lad. They were too far away for the others to hear what was said, but within moments Hank was tossing the frisbee back and forth with the boy as they laughed.

Watching them run around back and forth Zeus said, "It's good to see him playing like that. It makes everything we do seem worthwhile."

"Yeah," Raven agreed. "I wish I could see my sister play again. It's good that you have him, Zeus. Little things like that help me to understand why Grey wants to let go and move on to the Source. If not to see them again, then to at least let go of some of the pain…" Raven trailed off, then after looking at Zeus' crestfallen face she quickly added, "I don't mean to make you feel guilty about enjoying it, Zeus. I love to watch kids play; it just makes me sad sometimes, too."

"I didn't have any siblings or children," Pete said looking at both of them in turn. "But when I was a teacher I always enjoyed watching the little ones play. A lot of my students had younger brothers and sisters they'd bring to campus sometimes. Funny, how most Ivy League students are the oldest or only children. I think the parents saw the first semester's bill and said, 'Sorry number two, but you're going to the community college'."

They watched the boys play for a while in silence letting the day pass, keeping additional thoughts and opinions of childhood private. Working toward the same goal of keeping the universe in balance united them, but their backgrounds separated them, living and dying in different decades. *You wouldn't guess it to look at us,* Pete thought, *but we're all a bunch of old farts. Hell, I don't even know how old the two of them really are.* He had learned that the more he started asking questions of his coworkers in the afterlife, the more the questions piled up behind the answers. It was best at times to leave his curiosity alone. Pete's gaze wandered off to the families that had started to arrive as the afternoon wore on, spreading out large blankets, liberally decorated in picnic foods. When he glanced back over in Raven's direction she was watching a group of glowing lights that were spinning around the frisbee being tossed back and forth by Hank and the boy. The lights would cling on when one of the boys caught the disk, giving the appearance that the boy was holding a handful of sparklers, and then go spinning off when it was thrown. It looked like a firework that kept exploding and reforming, again and again, as the boys played.

"Other angels seem drawn to Hank," Raven said. "I don't remember him being so powerful, Zeus. Is he getting stronger?"

"Yep," Zeus replied with more than a touch of pride. "He gets stronger every time I see him. I worry about him though. He's still so young really…at least when it comes to dealing with power and what creatures out there'll do to get it. I wish I could watch out for him all the time."

"That's just what big brothers do," Raven said, standing on her tiptoes to kiss Zeus on one of his big shaggy cheeks. "What did he want your help with?"

"A friend of his, kind of a mentor you'd say, took on a physical body out in Los Angeles and has been dabbling in the media, trying to change things for what he thinks is the better," Zeus said rolling his eyes. "He'll just end up making more work for us in the long run."

"Angel or demon?" Raven asked.

"Whoa!" Pete interrupted, "How could an angel be friends with a demon? I know Grey has friends on both sides, but that's…that's just Grey, right? In his own words, 'He ain't no angel'. But your brother Hank seems pretty wholesome to me."

"Not all demons are bent on universal destruction, Pete," Raven answered. "In fact, most are just tricksters or vandals, doing the same things they did in life, but working for the Balance we mostly run into the apocalyptically evil kind, like Legion."

"Angel," Zeus answered Raven's question. "Goes by the name of Metatron. You know him?"

"Only by reputation," Raven said nodding her head. "He's Old Testament kind of powerful. Been around a long time; I suppose that fits with the arrogance of thinking he knows best and should change things. Let me guess; Hank thinks he shouldn't be interfering and Metatron won't listen to him?"

"That's about the gist of it, yeah," Zeus agreed.

"I want a new name," Pete added and after a few seconds of blank stares from the others he elaborated, "You know? Like you guys and your cool single word afterlife names. I'd take just about anything that sounded interesting. But, I never got into those Japanese cartoons. Why would an angel want to be called a robot lion-like thing, right? I thought you said this guy was old? They wouldn't have even had television when he was alive."

Raven sighed saying, "It's Metatron, Pete, not *Voltron* you numb nuts!"

"Hey!" Pete interjected, "Television was my family's religion. We worshipped at the altar of *Merv Griffin*! I make no apologies for that."

"Anyway," Raven continued, turning to Zeus and completely ignoring Pete, "I assume you haven't cleared this with Harmony or else it would be her contacting us, not you."

Zeus shook his head in response and started chewing on his beard. Hank was walking back toward them, having finished his game. The other little boy had wandered off in the direction of a waiting ice cream truck.

"That reminds me," Raven said, looking in the boy's direction. "If this isn't an issue for the Balance, then Harmony will not be transporting us to California, so we'll have to drive. Don't even think it, Zeus. After last time, I'll get us some wheels."

Raven left them before Hank had made it all the way back. When he was close enough he asked, "Where's Raven going? Oh, is she going to get us a car? Are you two going to come with us, Pete?"

"Uh, yes, and yes," Pete answered, "but… shouldn't somebody clear it with the boss lady first? Shouldn't Harmony give us the okay? What if we're needed elsewhere while we're talking to this Voltron guy?"

Zeus did not respond at all. He just continued to chew on his beard but now he also had taken an intense interest in the grass around his feet. He scuffed and kicked at the turf with his huge black boots. Hank stared, looking back and forth between the two full-grown men with an unspoken question creasing his brow. After a few moments passed and the silence remained, Pete threw his hands up in the air. "Fine! I'll do it! You big baby. Between little Miss, 'I don't talk to Harmony' over there," Pete waved a hand in the direction Raven had gone, "and Hagar the Preschooler here, I guess I'm the only adult she has working for her anyway."

Pete did not have to walk away or perform any odd gestures, movements, or rituals to make contact with Harmony. She was with him and all of the other warriors who worked for the Balance at all times. When each of their physical bodies had perished they had chosen to stay and work for the Balance. Harmony was the caretaker of the Balance (a completely alien entity who had never lived as a mortal human) and she shared a bit of her energy with all of her soldiers, enabling her to communicate or help them in their work for her. In order to allow her agents a measure of privacy or autonomy Harmony would retreat to a small corner of their consciousness when she was not needed. Pete mentally viewed this connection as a lit closet in a dark room, with a door which stayed open to varying degrees when he needed to speak with Harmony or she with him.

He focused on that closet doorway, prepared to knock, but the sultry, smoky, feminine voice of Harmony spoke first, "Yes, Peter, I was listening."

"Oh good," Pete replied, "so no big deal? We can go help Hank and his angel buddy out?"

"Yes," Harmony said opening her connection between them fully. Pete could feel her presence like a lover wrapping her arms around behind him. She continued, "Because it will serve multiple purposes. I believe the situation with Enoch-"

"Who?" Pete interrupted.

Harmony sighed, "The *Voltron* guy, Peter. When he walked the earth as a man his name was Enoch. Metatron is the name he awarded himself when he added his opinions to the human Judeo Christian Mythology. I have watched him a very long time, Peter. He is not an evil creature, not like most of the demons you have faced, but he does suffer from an overabundance of ego. He wants the mortal world to pay attention to his posthumous deeds. His vanity could lead to his demonic conversion and that is something you must prevent. He is too powerful and the shift he would cause would be quite perilous. Peter…Peter, are you even paying attention?" Harmony asked, as Pete stared out at the picnickers watching them go about their revelry.

"Oh…ah yes ma'am," Pete answered after brining his thoughts back to her voice. "The angel is full of himself and that could be what makes him switch teams. Yeah, I got it."

"Good. Now if I need you elsewhere in the meantime I will be in contact to redirect you and the others to wherever that may be. But for now, head west, take in what experiences you can, and enjoy yourself where possible. Even dead, the human psyche requires a certain level of downtime to function properly. I want you to stay in your physical shell as much as you can over this trip. It is important to remember what it was like to live or else you may forget, perhaps start to drift away from humanity and, even unintentionally, move back to the Source. I have lost many warriors that way, Peter."

"Okay, got it. Binge and live it up like a vacation. I think it'll be a stretch, but I'll try to handle it," Pete said laughing. He turned to Zeus and Hank, waving his hand to get their attention. "She said we can go, as long as we know if she needs us she'll just redirect us there instead."

Zeus blew out an over exaggerated sigh, "That's good! I was worried she wouldn't let us after the last time with the alligators."

"The what?" Pete asked.

"Uh…nothing, Pete, it's nothing. Hey look! Raven got us a convertible," Zeus said, pointing in the direction of the fast approaching vehicle. Not one to care overly much about mortal traffic laws, or any laws at all really, Raven pulled the deep blue open-topped car over the curb and onto the grass. She had been driving so fast that when she stopped right next to them chunks of sod were sent showering up, splattering the three men from the waist down. Her sensuous lips curved up into a smile at the disgusted look on Pete's face. As he brushed at the mud on his pants she slid her newly acquired sunglasses down her nose, then leaning over said, "You boys want a ride? Los Angeles is an awful long run, even for us."

"Shotgun!" called Hank jumping over the closed door without opening it, settling into the passenger seat. He immediately started fiddling with the radio. Zeus climbed into the backseat leaving Pete with the smallest amount of space to wedge into. Before attempting the contortions needed to accomplish this he glared at the big man yelling, "Damn it, Zeus! What alligators?"

***

"Check this out, Grey!" The Kid said excitedly as he jumped out from the concealing shadows of the alleyway in downtown Santa Fe. Grey leaned back against the cool concrete wall, crossing his arms around his lean chest. He arched an eyebrow in The Kid's direction, but said nothing when his old acquaintance slapped a passing businesswoman on her expensive pantsuit-clad behind. The woman gasped and turned around quickly, slapping the face of the innocent man whose only crime was following too close to her.

The Kid brayed out a donkey-like laugh, capering about in a little jig of delight upon witnessing the woman's reaction. Grey was the only one nearby who could see it, but that did not seem to lessen the pleasure The Kid derived from the act. He had curled up into a ball on the ground, laughing so hard he was crying. Finally, slapping his leg, wiping away tears, and attempting to catch a breath, that after more than a century of death The Kid's mental conditioning still told him he needed, he said, "God damn,

Grey, but that don't get old no matter how many times I do it. Now, where was we?"

"Malign," Grey said, dislodging himself from his leaning perch. He moved toward the deeper shadows in which The Kid had retreated, in an attempt to regain some of the strength that venturing into the daylight to pull his little prank had cost him. Staring down at the demon, Grey continued, "You were saying she was up to something here, in the States. What?"

"Shit, Grey! I don't know for sure, and I shouldn't really be telling you nothing neither, but we was friends once and that still means something to me," The Kid said, drawing himself up to his full height, placing his bowler-covered head level with the nearest dumpster rim. He placed a dusky-shadowed hand over the area where his heart once beat, in an attempt to emphasize his sincerity.

"Yeah Kid, we were friends once, but you and I know that ain't the reason you're playing snitch. You're scared of her and you don't much like her messin' around in your backyard," Grey finished, glaring down his slightly aquiline nose at The Kid.

"You're Goddamned right I'm scared of that bitch!" The Kid blurted out. "Jesus man, only you and maybe that old Middle Eastern angel you hang with sometimes would have a shot at taking her on. The rest of us either hide like fucking prairie dogs until she passes or lick her boots to stay in her favor. So, no, I don't like her hanging around my backyard."

"Fair enough, Kid, fair enough," Grey agreed, then motioned with his open hand in a cough it up gesture. "So what do you know, what can you tell me?"

The demon, who had once been a man named Billy Bonnie (among a slew of aliases) grinned. His pale and dusky skin, took on a sickly pallor when his dimly lit eyes started to sparkle. He said, "I know plenty, but I can tell you only some without risking my ass. She's up to her manipulative games like always, twisting this person this way and that person that way. I swear the bitch can be in ten different places at once." As if the thought his own words had elicited would make her appear, The Kid looked around, much in a passable imitation of his previously mentioned prairie dog. He leaned in toward Grey, getting as close as he could to whisper one word before vanishing into the shadows.

Grey walked out into the daylight with concern on his features and troubles bubbling around in his mind. He had trod this earth for a good long time, having died before The Kid had in the same fiasco once upon a time in New Mexico. He had dealt with Malign on many occasions before, stopping her and her pets in World War II, but most often she stayed to the less civilized parts of the globe. It was easiest for her to cause unrest in populaces that were not as well cared for and educated. It did not make sense to him why she would start messing around here, now, but then the thought patterns of any demon were beyond Grey's ken. He strode down the hard sunbaked sidewalk for the simple pleasure of the motion. It allowed him a sense of identity or at least a feeling of humanity regained to move about. He felt he did his best contemplating while in motion. Turning his thoughts over Grey said to himself, "What the hell did The Kid mean by, 'vampires'?"

Chapter 2

Grey took me to meet Harmony. I was scared, so scared I thought I might die all over again. Have you ever been that scared? Your stomach aches with it and your legs feel all wobbly. God, I hate being scared. It feels like weakness. I hate that, too.

We walked into a warm sunlit country meadow from the dark dank European night. Little white butterflies danced in the sun among the wildflowers. Grey leaned over and held my hand before saying, "Darlin', we're about to go see the boss lady. She's in that cabin up yonder, and when we get there you'll have to go in to see her on your own. I'll be right outside, but this last step you have to take by yourself. You okay with that, little Raven?"

I told him I was, despite my fear. I was not going to let this hero - my savior - think that I was scared of anything. It's sad how much time has passed and I still find myself doing the same thing when I'm around him. I walked up those cabin steps with my head high, strolling through the open doorway as if I owned the place. They say first impressions are important. Was it my attempt at overconfidence that set Harmony off on her choice in approaching me or was it something else that I could not even comprehend? Whichever the case, the cabin doorway opened into my family's living room, complete with my mother bustling in and out from the kitchen. I wonder sometimes if it was Harmony's desire for empathy that she chose to do that. There are other times where it feels more like an attempt to remind me of my place, to keep me in line. Maybe it was both, and maybe it was neither. It's hard to understand the thoughts of a being that is as old as the world.

In my confusion I asked, "Momma? Is that you?"

"No child, I am what you make of me," Harmony said enigmatically and continued to go about her chores. I was young and confused; I had just died only a short time before. A matured human mind can suffer from disorientation, and I had been anything but mature. "Grey brought you here for a reason, Annabelle," the creature that looked like my mother said. "Do you know why you are here?"

I stared at the woman with my mother's face, as she busied herself in what seemed like my home before the SS had destroyed it. Why was I there? The cowboy had come to my rescue and I thought I had come to his, but had I really? In retrospect I felt it unlikely that he'd needed my help or anybody else's for that matter. It had been the feeling of conquering my fears and enemies that had led me to lash out at my tormentors, and it was that feeling that drove me to want to help others from having to endure the same. I answered her question as simply as I viewed it then; I feel the same way still, to tell the truth. All I said was, "I'm here to fight."……

***

"Okay, one more time. Why aren't we flying?" Pete asked from his squished position in the backseat of the convertible as they drove through the Midwest. He squirmed around in an attempt to gain a measure of comfort as they passed open fields awaiting crops, the occasional farmhouse, or tiny copse of early budded trees as the afternoon wore on.

"Because we don't have wings! Bwaaaha!" Zeus answered laughing. With a glare Pete threw an elbow into the big man's side and said, "It wasn't funny the first two times you said it, Jumbo, and the third time ain't a charm. It's your fault we're so cramped back here anyway. My God man, you're dead. You don't even really have a body. Can't you just 'think thin' or something to give us both some space?"

"Aw, you just love the extra cushion and you want to rest your head on it," Zeus said. He patted and rubbed his stomach that was being pushed up by his cramped knees, and continued in a baby-talk voice, "It's okay wittle Petey wheaty, just snuggle on in with papa."

Pete did not deign to respond, but could no longer ignore Zeus when he started to rub Pete's back with one of his enormous hands cooing, "There, there little one. Hush little Petey don't you–"

Pete interrupted him by slapping his hand. Barely stifling a laugh he said, "Knock it off, asshole. Seriously, why aren't we flying?"

Raven adjusted the rearview mirror so she could look Pete in the eyes and still vaguely concentrate on the road before she answered, "Because, Pete, do you want to be circling the globe, miles high and have some energy spill over onto this plane by accident? You've seen what that can do to objects on the ground traveling at reasonable speeds. Do you want to risk it in an airplane? Some demon, who was only going to let off a foul odor to annoy people in a cramped space, could get spooked at the sight of us and cause a ton of damage. Is that what you want?"

"Well, no," Pete said, "not when you put it that way. I guess a cross country drive for a couple days isn't so bad, even if I'm cramped back here with, Tiny."

As Pete watched the countryside roll past he noticed Hank swimming his right hand out the passenger side window, undulating it up and down, letting the air current do the work. Pete remembered doing the same thing when he was a boy, how free it felt, and his curiosity got the better of him. He turned to Zeus, asking in a whisper, "Why is Hank still a boy?"

When there was no response forthcoming Pete was about to ask again, but stopped when a low growl escaped the giant's chest. Not an angry growl, but a sound filled more with exasperation or exhaustion. Then quietly enough that Pete had to strain to hear him, Zeus said, "None of your business, Pete."

The big man was typically so jovial and garrulous that when he suddenly turned taciturn Pete took notice. He was going to change the subject, in an attempt to lighten the awkward silence that had descended on the car in the wake of his query, when Hank piped in from the front seat, "It's okay Frank, he's your friend. You can tell him."

"I don't care who it is, Hank. I just don't want to talk about it, okay?" Zeus groused, folded his massive arms around himself, and turned his face away to watch the passing fields instead of making eye contact with any of his fellow passengers.

"No, it's okay," Pete said, "no big deal I was just curious."

The car was once again submersed in silence. This time it lasted long enough that Pete felt certain the awkward moment would never pass. He almost went so far as to give Zeus an opening for another one of his silly jokes, the kind that the man was so fond of, but before he uttered a sound a shining fast-moving bright light caught his eye. Pete looked up to see a small winged hummingbird-like creature land on Hank's still air swimming hand. It was bright jade green and climbed up the boy's arm in jerking rapid movements to perch by his ear. The encounter seemed to be a common occurrence to Hank. He did not move or flinch, even when a tiny voice squeaked out, "Bad, bad demon in next town. Good boy and friends not stay? Keep driving, be safe."

With its message imparted the winged angel flew off toward the horizon where the sun was quickly setting like a bullet fired from a gun. Hank turned to look at Raven and taking note of the resolve etched into her features, her tightened grip on the steering wheel, and her dark eyebrows bunched down disappearing into her sunglasses, he said, "We're still going to stop for the night in this town aren't we?"

"Mmm, hmmm," Raven mumbled. Pete could see in the rearview mirror that the woman was spoiling for a fight. *Well*, he thought to himself, *when isn't she?*

***

Eric Metronnie stood with his hands clasped behind his back, watching the sun set over the Pacific Ocean from his office window. Most angels would feel threatened by the oncoming dark. They would be seeking shelter in the places that would afford them sanctuary from the night and its ravenous creatures. He was not most angels. Normally he would go by his appellation of Metatron, but in taking a human body it necessitated that he make certain allowances to match the era. The time and place when he could have gone by his birth name of Enoch, without batting a societal eye in conversation, were long gone. It was always about adapting to change, and Eric Metronnie was quite adaptable.

He ran a well-manicured hand over his sandy brown salon trimmed locks. Eric felt there was no point in taking a physical body again if you could not pamper yourself. The hygiene, the amenities of daily life and the cuisine were all far superior to what he had been afforded in his first lifetime. Sure, he sacrificed some of his power by taking a solid body again, but he had walked this world longer than most and his reserves from his true form allotted him power still in spades. It all but crackled around him when he moved in his tailored Italian suit. The benefits of the human body coupled with his ancient power far outstripped one single form alone. Not that he feared the dark like other lesser angels, but now as long as he kept this body alive, he could wander about at night unmolested or hindered by the dark powers like others of his kind.

His office was located on the topmost floor of a newly constructed building in Santa Monica. He owned the building and the surrounding property, not to mention all the businesses that resided therein. Many others from his metaphysical side of things frowned on his amassing human wealth, but Eric knew that, as sad as it seemed, wealth was still power to wield. And this humble little outpost was his seat of financial power; Re-Vamped Media Incorporated handled books, movies, music, and any other creative cultural expressions he could get his hands on.

"Oh, sorry boss, I didn't know anybody was still here," said a perky voice from behind him. Eric turned to see a young blond woman in her early twenties who had walked in without knocking. She had a small puffy white Bichon Frise squirming around in her arms trying to get loose, but she kept restraining it with her tanned arms and fire engine red nails. It would occasionally let out a piteous whimper when she squeezed it too tight.

"That's alright, Maggie. I was just…meditating on the past I'd guess you'd say. What did you need?" Eric said with a wan smile in his cultured radio announcer's voice, lifting a well-sculpted eyebrow to accompany the question.

"Uh, I just wanted to watch the sunset. Sorry, I sort of come in here sometimes after you leave to do that, if I'm still here. Is that okay? It like kind of helps me meditate too, you know?" she asked in an uncertain tone of voice.

Ah youth, Eric thought, *so eager to emulate those they look up to.* Aloud he said, "Yes, Maggie, that is more than okay. I built this office for that very reason, and I hate that most days I'm so busy that it does not get used for its intended purpose. It warms my heart to know someone is enjoying it, even if that someone is not me."

"Oh good," she said perking up again. "Then you don't mind if Dolphie and I join you? It's kind of our evening ritual." She let the small ball of pale fluff drop to the floor when Eric nodded. It ran over to the floor-to-ceiling window and started to paw viciously at it, to all appearances attempting to dig through the glass and on to freedom. *Who could blame the little bugger?* Eric thought. *If she always dolled me up in bows and the occasional dress or tutu, I'd try to run at every opportunity, too.*

"He likes the water and wants to get to the beach," Maggie excused her dog with a shrug of her thin shoulders. She had been with Eric from the beginning; she had, in fact, been his inspiration for this current enterprise. He had seen her years ago, sitting on a bench at the local shopping mall engrossed in a copy of Bram Stoker's *Dracula*. Eric, or the then Metatron, had been consumed with a desire to thin the herd, as he saw it. More and more people were staying behind after death instead of moving on back to the Source. He viewed it as a polluting of the tranquil waters that were the afterlife. His original claim to fame, his *Book of Enoch*, had worked so well in that regard millennia ago. It had helped to define what was previously undefined. He introduced the world's populous to the angelic choirs and let them know that only he had been allowed to transcend into angelic form. The rest of them would see the angels upon death, yes, but should think of them as guides to the afterlife, not residents. This had really helped with the surfeit of hangers-on, a bit egotistical some would say, but it had worked.

The problem he faced now was that ecumenically, more and more people were giving up on the idea of religion. Where before the right words whispered in the right ears could start a crusade, today one had to be much more subtle in their approach. He had to think in the large scope of years to gain results; it was not like he did not have the time. Perhaps, he had thought, it was time to move things in a different direction. Instead of encouraging souls to move back to the Source, he should encourage - subtly, of course - a shift in morals. If he could convince the populous to want to be monsters while they were still living, then perhaps, when they did pass on they would jump right into the role of demons. The Balance would not be affected, and if it were, Harmony would just send in her troops to clear house. He was doing them all a favor really, when he looked at it from that perspective, just another friendly angel helping keep the peace.

"It sure is perfect," Maggie said, once again interrupting his musings.

"What's that my dear?"

"The ocean I can't think of anything lovelier, can you?" she said, turning to face him, with earnest innocence in her eyes.

"Not off the top of my head, no," he answered with a smile. She mirrored his smile with one of her own, then turned back to watch the last of the color fade from the day, while Dolphie continued in his bid for freedom.

***

"The Beer Bear," Pete said looking up at the hand painted sign depicting a dancing *Yogi*-esque bear holding two frothing mugs in its paws. The ambient light from the parking lot and nearby highway provided enough illumination to see the placard, high above the bar entrance where all four of them stood clustered together. They were watching the raucous crowd through the windows, sending surreptitious glances at the demons that had come out with the night as they capered about in and around the establishment. "That's actually quite a bit cleverer than I expected for the middle of nowhere Iowa," Pete said gesturing toward the sign he had read aloud.

"What were you expecting?" Raven asked turning to face Pete, but keeping the cluster of demonic imps she had been watching scamper about a row of motorcycles in her peripheral vision.

"I don't know," Pete replied, "something along the lines of 'So and So's Roadhouse or Bar'. I just keep thinking back to the last time we were in this area and how the people struck me."

"Pete," Raven said, "that was Illinois. This is Iowa. There's a big difference."

"Ha, not to a New Yorker there isn't," Pete corrected with a smile.

Whatever acidic reply Raven was going to unleash - Pete judged by the look on her face - never made it past her lips, because a body flew at them through the now open barroom doors. Tumbling to the dirt at their feet was a man of average height and weight, donned in a well-cut black leather jacket and jeans. He spoke in a slurry drunken Irish accent, "Gerr off'a me!"

He yelled more nonsensical obscenities, swinging his arms at assailants that were no longer there, lying on his back, pumping his fists into the air like a dying insect, and then suddenly stopped. Raven walked over to within touching distance and toed the now still body with the tip of her boot. He jerked and spun up to a sitting position, eyes still closed, before yelling, "Whose tha-? Inna kitchen I tells you!" and promptly passed back out.

"Shit." Raven said but with little vehemence or invective. "I should have known. Gabe. Gabe, wake up!" she said this time kicking him hard with her boot, no longer delicately testing.

After several more less than gentle kicks he stirred again and slurred, "Whose tha?" When his eyes opened they shined with a fiery green light when he focused on Raven. "Raven love! How are ye?" He stayed lying on the ground, on top of soil soaked in years of spilled beer, blood, phlegm, and oil. His eyes, staring up at her long trim legs towering over him, followed every curve until he stopped, locking gazes with her saying, "Looking lovely as ever you are. How about a fuck for old times' sake, eh?"

"Where there is one…" Raven said ignoring Gabe's solicitations, and keeping her back to the open doors of the bar where a deep masculine voice finished for her, "There is the other. Hello, Raven."

"Hello, Lucifer. How are you?"

"Can't complain I guess," he answered smoothly, "always allowing for the foolish wanton activities of my parole officer here, as it were." He gestured to Gabe, who was now staggering to his feet after a few unsuccessful attempts that brought to mind old *Three Stooges* film shorts had landed him leaning against Zeus, puffing and gasping for breath.

"Bloody hell! Zeus where the fuck did you come from, mate?" Gabe asked drunkenly.

"Wait!" Pete interjected. "Lucifer? As in 'The Lucifer?', 'Pleased to meet you, hope you guessed my name?' Lucifer?"

"Yes," Lucifer responded, "and since you are the only one here I am not acquainted with I can only assume you are Grey's new protégé, yes? Peter, is it?"

"So you're the 'Bad, bad demon' that little cherubim…or whatever it was warned us about," Pete said eyeing the lanky demon. He was immaculately groomed, with gaunt features and a hawkish nose, slicked black hair, attired in much the same wardrobe as his inebriated cohort, only juxtaposed as his jeans were black and he wore a denim jacket. He walked toward Pete with his hand outstretched in greeting but stopped short. Lucifer had a puzzled look of concentration on his face, which Pete misinterpreted as a response to his jerking back a step from the proffered hand. Recognition dawned on Lucifer's chiseled demonic features before he said, "Oh no, I doubt that very much. I believe this is the individual you were warned about."

He pointed over Pete's left shoulder, indicating a presence that Pete had not been aware of until now. Pete turned his head at the heavy panting that was sending sparks tickling down the back of his neck. "Oh, shi-" was as far as Pete uttered before the be-fanged demon landed a solid uppercut to his chin, launching him across the gravel parking lot, to land crashing into the row of motorcycles, sending the lesser demons that had been cavorting there scattering in a chorus of simian shrieks.

The demon stood nearly as tall as Zeus' seven feet but held itself in a stooped over posture, its long limbs trailing on the ground. It bellowed a challenge to the rest of the assembly, maw hanging wide with overtly large and physiologically impractical canines. "What the fuck?!" A voice from the open roadhouse doorway yelled.

Pete was shaking himself back to a level of coherency and he focused up on the angry faces of several agitated bikers who were pouring out of the establishment to see what the crash had been. They started over toward him with evident malicious intent until the demon bellowed again. Pete pointed a finger in the monster's direction and muttered, "He did it." But all of the bikers had already turned at the sound of its shriek, uttering another, now chorus round of, "What the fuck?!"

The demon did not charge, as had been their assumption, because Raven had her Smith and Wesson 500 Magnums out and aimed, Zeus was crackling lightning, and to Pete's surprise Gabe was standing, all signs of inebriation gone, with fists sparkling in a verdant green light. Even Lucifer had drawn a broadsword and was pointing it at the demon. Despite or perhaps in reaction to the arsenal pointed at it, the demon fled in the direction of Zeus. Pete thought the demon to be completely foolish in doing so. *Why try to break the chain at one of the strongest links?* Pete thought. It was not until the creature had lowered its shoulder, knocking Zeus back a step, that Pete realized the target was Hank, not his big brother.

The angelic little boy screamed when the demon scooped him up in its long arms and sprouted a pair of bat-like wings from its back, taking flight without even a flinch as Raven managed to pepper a few purple bullets of energy into its flank. Zeus brought forth a sound of such anguish that Pete had trouble recognizing it as human. The big man tore off on foot in the direction the demon was flying. The rest of them stood around bewildered for a moment until one of the bikers ordered, "I don't care what that fucking thing was, you don't mess with kids! Get the bikes up boys! We're going after that monster!"

***

Vampires? Really? Grey thought to himself. *I know it's cranky and clichéd, but I'm gettin' too old for this shit!* He traced the lead The Kid had given him to a Santa Fe nightclub where the locals went to pretend they were counterculture, Goth, Emo, or whatever term the kids were calling themselves these days to break away from their parents and say, "Look at us, we're different than you. Look at us." *Yep, Grey, cranky and old,* he continued to mentally berate himself. *That's about the long and short of it anymore, ain't it?*

Grey felt even older when he passed through the club's front doors, tinted in a reflective mirror-like substance to keep passersby from casually glancing in, and was assaulted by a bass beat that resembled a primitive warrior rite more than music. Young bodies full of piercings, brightly decorated in tattoos, scantily clad with hair dyed all shades of the rainbow gyrated to that bass beat in what looked to Grey's ancient eyes to be mock intercourse. There were a few succubae and incubi (souls that had been so obsessed with the physical pleasures of the flesh in life that they could not move on from it in death) shifting and groping among the copulating crowd. *What we used to call "dry humping" once upon a time. Jesus! I knew men who paid good money for less than that! Alright, old man, stop talkin' to yourself and just focus on why you're here, maybe…oh good lord, I see a nipple!* Grey thought, then shaking his head to clear it. *Just look for the most "vampire-like" kids, and go talk to them.*

    Out of a sense of tradition Grey moseyed on up to the bar, at least he thought it was the bar. With all the neon tube lights reflecting on ink black surfaces it was only the bottles of booze along the back wall that resembled anything like the bars he had frequented when he was living. He turned around leaning his back against the rail to survey the room, just as he had in those roadhouses of yore. Out of the corner of his eye Grey could see the bartender approach. He was a young man just barely able to legally imbibe a drink himself, with floppy hair that fell over his eyes, and a waxed torso bared to his waistline. When he was close enough for Grey to smell his generic cologne he asked, "What can I get you mister?"

"Just a beer, son."

"What kind? Imported, domestic, or we also carry a number of local microbrews?"

Grey turned around to face the young man, placing his back to the throng of bodies, an action that may have been the death of him in another place and time. Grey was not the type to be short on patience. It was actually one of his hallmarks, what he was known for, but the idea of having to go vampire hunting, after a long career of keeping demons in line, had left his fuse a tad shorter than it would normally have been. He leaned his arms on the polished black surface and said, "I know you're just doin' your job son, but I ain't in the best of moods. So just reach into that there cooler behind you, pull out something made from barley that don't got any fruit in it, and I'll be just fine."

The bartender was either unaccustomed to being spoken to by someone so direct, or he did not know that beer was made from barley, because he stared blankly at Grey. Grey sighed, reached into his back pocket, pulled forth a ten dollar bill, slapped it down on the bar and said, "Just surprise me kid."

That at least the bartender seemed to understand. He pocketed the ten, then strolled over to the cooler and grabbed the cheapest bottle of beer, popping the cap off before placing it front of Grey. Then he went over to see if there was anything he could do for a couple of giggling girls who did not look old enough to Grey to be able to drink legally. "Huh, the little shit didn't even ask if I wanted my change," Grey groused aloud.

"Kids these days," said a sultry female voice, close enough to his ear to make him jump. Grey, never being one to let his guard down, was immediately set on edge. He turned quickly to see who had overheard him, with a bit of energy crackling from his fingertips twitching at his side. She was a stunning figure in a slinky black dress that showed enough curve to be intriguing, yet covered enough skin to be elegant. Her blond hair was pinned up to reveal a cream colored expanse of neck, and by her features Grey would place her along in his apparent age group of late thirties, older than most in the club by a good decade or more.

"Sorry," she said, "I didn't mean to startle you. I'm Kendra."

Seated on a stool next to him she held her right hand out for Grey to shake but did not fully turn her body to face him, leaving her left elbow resting on the bar, propping her chin up. Ever the consummate ladies' man, Grey turned to his left to grasp hands. "Pleasure to meet'cha darlin'. The name's Jasper."

He had found it easiest when interacting with the living to use his birth name. People always seemed to balk when he told them his name was Grey, so he went by his original name to cut down on the questioning looks of derision and contempt. *I bet Cher never had to deal with that shit,* Grey always thought.

"Well now, if we don't have ourselves an honest to goodness cowboy," Kendra said smirking at Grey. "Even here, out west, I thought you boys were a dying breed. No wonder you stick out like a sore thumb in this club. You're from a whole different age, aren't you?"

"Ha," Grey chuckled, "you have no idea darlin'. You well and truly don't. But I thought I blended better than that. I guess age slows us down in more ways than one. You'll find that out someday, but not soon I'd imagine."

Kendra smiled seductively and in a throaty purr said, "I like men who take things slow, Jasper. It makes *things* last longer." She had turned to face him completely when she said this and Grey could make out two little puncture marks on the left side of her neck, lightly pink from recently scabbing over. *Well, well*, Grey thought to himself, *I guess I'm not as slow as I might have thought. Bingo.*

Chapter 3

I don't think that Harmony liked my response, but she didn't stress the point, only frowned at me which was very disconcerting to see that look again from my mother's face. I thought those looks of disapproval were gone with her. Some ghosts just don't die do they?

"Fighting is really only part of what you will be doing for me, Annabelle," Harmony said. "There are many levels and reasons behind what we do. Violence is only necessary because humanity, whether alive or deceased, seems to know no different. But if fighting is what you want to do child, then there will be plenty of that, do not worry. Please, if this is what you want, then come here and take my hand."

She wiped her hands on an old paisley apron - the same one my mother had worn so often - before walking over to me. It seemed an odd gesture even to my young mind. If we were dead, and this...well this thing that was pretending to be my mother never had a body, then why would she or it feel the need to wipe her hands off? Was it for my benefit? Had this being become so used to interacting with humans on our level that it had picked up our ticks and gestures subconsciously? Did it even have a subconscious? I won't try to convince you that I'd had all these thoughts when I was a recently deceased seventeen year old girl. I had some then and others have come to me over the years as I have thought on this being, on Harmony.

Back then I wanted to fight. I still do, of course, but I needed to prove myself, so I took her proffered grip. When our hands met there was a flash of light that seemed to climb up my arm, but, when I look back, it traveled so fast it may have been my mind filling in the blanks. The flash consumed me, for all I know it consumed her as well. Have you ever stood up too fast; all the blood rushes from your head, leaving crackling lights dancing behind and in front of your eyes, sometimes you even lose control of your body? It was like that but on a scale a thousand times worse because I knew that I was still there; I existed. I just couldn't find myself. Strange I know, but it was how it felt, aware but not.

When I came back to myself my mother's face was looking down on me. In my swoon she had, I assumed, moved me to the threadbare chaise lounge we had in our living room. I hated the color pattern on it when I was a little girl, too many odd combinations; it looked like a rainbow had thrown up. It still looked that way when I leaned against it to help me stagger to my feet. I shook my head to clear it, mental conditioning or not, some things transcend physical boundaries. Once I had my wits about me again I noticed that Harmony was no longer in the room with me. Her voice echoed in my head, "Annabelle, I have no task for you at the moment. I do not know if you would be ready if I did. Please, go back outside, send Grey in, and wait for him to return."

Oh great, so even in the afterlife I'm relegated to the children's table, I thought, but I still went out and did as she asked. Some old habits are hard to break I guess. Opening the door provided me with a different view than the one that had been there when I entered. The prairie meadow was replaced with a pine-laden forest, filled with chirping birds, and other wildlife frolicking among the trees. I looked around in wonder as I walked out of the cabin. It was just like the forests in my Grimm's Fairy Tales book, and it was beautiful. "You okay there, darlin'?" Grey's voice asked from behind my right shoulder.

I just nodded my head at his question and stood there watching with my mouth gaping wide. All I did say was a whispered, "I wish my little sister could have seen this."……..

***

The even dozen motorcycles roared into the night. Twenty-four wheels all but flying down the highway in pursuit of the winged demon that had taken Zeus' little brother Hank. Pete was surprised at how easy the monster was to track, given the black on black of the monster's skin to the starless sky, and the fact that they were keeping to the physical world to interact with their new chauffeurs. It should have been difficult, but it also helped that Zeus was sprinting along underneath it - occasionally leaping from rooftop to rooftop - firing off orange lightning bolts, transforming him into a giant hairy mobile rescue flare. The Lone Riders, as the gang of bike enthusiasts called themselves, were more accommodating than Pete would have expected. *Granted, I based those assumptions on a lifetime of television and not actual experience,* he thought to himself as he held tightly onto the back of the bike belonging to his new friend Dante.

      All four of those who were from the other side of life had jumped onto the back of a motorcycle at the encouragement of Bulldog, the gang's leader. Lucifer came as well, more by dint of Gabe wanting to go than of his own volition. It was not until they were speeding down the road that Pete started to wonder how it was that these humans were able to see Zeus as he gave chase. To move at the speeds he was traveling the Viking-esque man had to let go of the physical *shell* body he had created to interact with the living world, as soon as the demon had nabbed his brother.

      Pete was about to ask his driver how he knew where to go, when he realized he could not expect to have an audible answer come from Dante with the wind whipping so frantically about them. When he glanced over at Raven he noticed that she was pointing, directing Bulldog from the back of the lead chopper as to where to go, or where to turn. *So they can't see Zeus or the demon from this plane of existence, Raven's showing*

Bulldog where to go, and the rest are just following his lead, Pete thought.

"No Peter, they cannot." Harmony's voice intruded from within Pete's mind, startling him enough that he almost let go of Dante's back. *Jesus Christ woman! Now is not a good time to pop in and out of my head!*

"I do not believe there is ever a good time for that, Peter," her sensuous voice responded.

Oh, sarcasm from the immortal creature of balance. You have been hanging around us humans way too long, ma'am.

"There are times, Peter, when I wonder if that is not entirely too true."

Yeah, we're a bad influence alright. Only humans could invent deep-fried cookies and candy bars; if that isn't corruption enough for you I don't know what is. So, if these guys can't see what's going on, why are they being so accommodating? Don't get me wrong, it's great to meet some modern-day biker gang Good Samaritans, but why?

"Peter, there are moments when I believe you forget that I am not some omniscient god," Harmony's voice continued to echo through Pete's mind, with an added hint of concern in her tone. "Truth to tell, my purpose would be entirely easier to manage if I were. I can only inform you of things that pertain to the Balance. These men are living beings, with their own story to tell.

Perhaps they will share it with you if you succeed in this task and perhaps they will not. I wanted to let you know that that demon's actions have taken it into your jurisdiction to destroy it. Raven still will not listen to me, Zeus is beyond the ability to focus at the moment, and Gabe just asked me if I wanted to shag, so I am telling you to instruct the rest of them to use extreme prejudice in recovering Hank."

Kill the demon; okay got it.

Pete leaned in close to Dante's ear, after he felt Harmony retreat back to the closet in his mind. He shouted to make sure he was heard, "Get us closer to Bulldog! I need to tell the lady something!"

Dante nodded, suiting action to action, and revved the engine on his motorcycle even harder. He twisted in and out among his fellow riders, either through practice or skill they all moved enough to allow him to edge up parallel with Bulldog and Raven. *Synchronized biking*, Pete thought, *now there's a badass new Olympic sport for you.* Noticing movement in her peripheral vision Raven turned to make eye contact with Pete. He yelled, "Harmony says kill the demon!"

She shook her head, looking quizzically at him, obviously unable to hear what he had said over the roaring army of engines. *Damn it woman! I hate charades!* Pete thought, but he pointed up at the soaring demon, then at Raven.

She nodded that she comprehended him so far, then he slid his index finger under his throat and tilted his head at an exaggerated angle, sticking his tongue out. She nodded again with a gleam of blue light flashing from her eye in an electrified wink.

Dante allowed his bike to fall back apace from Bulldog's once their message had been conveyed. Pete could see Raven lean in close to her driver's ear, once again giving him instructions. She punctuated whatever she had said by pointing at an overpass barely visible on the horizon. Bulldog turned his head back quickly to look at his passenger with wide questioning eyes, but then shrugged when she nodded, pushing his motorcycle to its maximum acceleration, closing the distance between them and the demon. As the bike tore away from the pack Raven stood up, balancing herself precariously on the small sliver of seat. They sped down the highway flashing between the pools of illumination cast by the streetlights, to all appearances looking like a combination of *Hell's Angels* and *Cirque du Soleil*.

The timing was exact, and so unlikely that had Pete not seen her preform such feats in the past he would have said it was impossible. But, the second before Bulldog raced under the overpass, Raven launched herself from the back of his motorcycle. Like a bullet shot from one of her guns she soared up toward the safety rail on the overpass. Pete and Dante passed under the structure just as she redirected her momentum toward the demon as it flew overhead, leaping from a streetlight, looking like a diving board plummet in reverse, soaring up instead of down.

Turning around so he could see the outcome, Pete watched as Raven wrapped her left arm tightly around the monster's neck as it struggled to maintain flight. It bucked and kicked attempting to dislodge its unwanted passenger and still hold onto the angel grasped tightly in its talons. Flashes of light, riddling holes in the demon's skull and lighting it up like a lavender jack-o-lantern, told Pete that Raven had produced one of her guns and was firing point blank into the back of the monster's head.

Bulldog led the Lone Riders down the nearest graveled service connection, completely ignoring a large *No U-Turn* sign. One of the Riders even reached up and smacked it in passing. As the gang raced back toward the fray Pete could see all three of them - Hank, Raven, and the demon hurtling toward the ground like a meteorite. The impact from their fall spilled enough energy over into the physical world to crater the east bound two lanes of the highway, sending chunks of flaming asphalt scattering all around. Zeus had caught up to them on foot - at the same time the gang had brought their bikes to a stop - and scooped Hank out of Raven's arms as he passed in a blur of tears and hair. Raven let the boy be carried away from her and turned to what was left of the demon as it dissolved into unbound negative matter.

It was unnecessary, because the monster was quite obviously finished, but that did not stop her from casually shooting the black pulpy mass that had been its head one more time in passing. She walked away with a fashion model's sway of hips and slid onto the back of Bulldog's chopper. With the simplest of nonverbal instructions Bulldog raised his right fist into the air and motioned it forward. Zeus had piled onto the back of the gang's smallest and only female Rider's bike, with Hank tightly sandwiched between her back and his chest. As the biker gang pulled slowly around to both sides of the crater, dodging the gaping hole and kicking the larger hunks of road out of their way to pass, Pete realized he was thinking much along the same lines as Gabe, when he overheard the Irishman mutter to the biker he was riding with, "Bloody hell, that is one crazy ass woman, eh? She's fuckin' hot though!"

***

"Thanks for taking me with you, boss," Maggie said over the wind noise that the convertible's downed top no longer blocked. Eric turned to face her and smiled before saying, "Of course, Maggie, you know I'm hopeless without you. If Re-Vamped Studios is out filming night scenes on the new movie and the director wants me there, then I need you there too, right? Who else would be able to handle my idiosyncrasies, hmm?"

Most dogs seem to enjoy riding with their head out the window, but Dolphie was doing his best to throw his entire little fluffy white body, head and all, from the moving vehicle. Maggie kept an iron tight grip on the dog's scruff, restraining him after his first failed attempt to hurdle from the convertible into oncoming traffic. Eric quirked his face into an odd frown before saying, "Little fellow has a death wish, huh?"

"Oh, Mr. M., he had a very hard life before I started taking care of him. Didn't you? My itty-bitty-Dolphie-kins." She said the last while bringing the diminutive dog up to her face, kissing it on the nose even though the dog whimpered like it was in pain.

Eric never had the chance to respond to her, before a huge bat-like demon landed with a thud, on the hood of his Bentley Azure, crumpling it. The force was not enough to cripple the expensive convertible and it continued to speed along with the demon riding on the hood like an enormous rear facing gargoyle. Eric froze, staring at the demon. He had witnessed plenty of creatures that spilled over into the mortal world over the millennia, but oddly none had ever been directed at him. The evil creatures had always given him a wide berth. He had assumed it was either a result of keeping a low profile when it came to the common confrontations between angels and demons in their constant vying for power, or they were simply afraid of facing him. He had always excelled in subtlety and manipulation as opposed to brute force, but power was power, no matter how quietly that power was held. Maggie's scream of terror pulled him from his reverie and his instincts had him slamming on the breaks before he could think clearly.

The convertible started to tip. At the speeds they had been traveling Eric was not surprised that he had lost control of the vehicle. He reached out with some of the energy he had held in reserve and steadied the car, keeping them from tumbling end over end in a spectacular Hollywood style crash. With his added metaphysical manipulation the Bentley stopped quickly enough at the side of the road, sending the demon catapulting and somersaulting from the hood. It grasped at the road's shoulder as it tumbled, digging deep furrows in the soft scree, and landed in a heap several dozen yards ahead of them. Eric bounded from the driver's side as soon as he started to see the monster stir in hopes of subduing it. Maggie continued to scream as she sat frozen in the passenger's seat clinging to Dolphie. The demon was on its feet before Eric could reach it. Not having much practice as a warrior, Eric missed the creature in his awkward attempt at a tackle. It bounded over top of him, pushing off his back, and sending him stumbling into the loose dirt of the roadside as he fell, and took wing back in the direction of the car.

It landed back on its previous perch, crumpling the Bentley even more this time. Metal and plastic shrieked in protest of the monster's crushing weight. It snarled at Maggie in its menacing demonic language that Eric had never been able to comprehend. The words were barely audible over the blood rushing in his ears and the crunching sound of the gravel under his feet as he ran back toward the car. He supposed that the language was something they learned through absorbing the energy of other demons, a way to ensure that the speech would always be secret, a Darwin-ish approach to knowledge. *It sounds like someone taught a lion to speak French,* Eric thought as he grabbed hold of the demon from behind. It thrashed about in his arms as he moved it away from Maggie and his now crumpled luxury car. He knew the universal rules he was subject to as well as anyone. As an angel (a being of positive energy) he could not lash out in anger, he could only defend others or risk becoming what he would fight. He could, on the other hand, create a *Faraday* cage out of positive energy to trap a demon and keep it from harming others.

He did so now and the azure light folded around the demon in a cube preventing the creature from harming him as it swiped its ink black claws at his abdomen. When it realized the cage was impenetrable to its strikes the demon froze and gazed at Eric with hate-filled glowing red eyes. The cage would dissipate well before sunrise, allowing the monster to leave and carry on its existence. It was one of the few loopholes a being like Eric could capitalize on; he had caused it no harm, and it would be free long before the sun could take it. The demon hissed, spitting its language at him like a curse, when Eric set the cage down by the roadside like an owner abandoning a particularly vicious pet. One word of English slipped through the snarls and by now laughter as he turned his back, walking away from the creature. He did not understand the context, but that single word was quite clearly directed at him, "Puppet."

***

Kendra had convinced Grey to leave the nightclub and accompany her to a more private gathering of what she called, "Friends with similar *tastes*," accentuating the last word with a throaty purr. She had even less trouble convincing him when she suggested that she drive, since they were her friends at a place she knew. What she did not know was that Grey hated cars; he hated driving them, hated just about everything to do with them. He was a man from the time of horses, wagons, and foot traffic. *Give me one horse darlin'; that's all the power a man needs. I can tell what ails it by its gait and I know if it's going to throw a shoe or not. Do you know by feel alone when you're about to get a flat tire?* He kept these thoughts to himself as Kendra drove down streets that had built up over the dirt roads and throughways Grey had known in his youth. *Progress progresses, that's for sure; don't rightly know if I'd call it advancement, but it sure does keep on movin'.*

They were heading out into the suburbs where prefabricated adobe houses lined the streets, each one looking just like the next to his cynical eyes. They did not say much to each other during the trip. He kept his own thoughts and judged by the way Kendra was squirming in her seat that she was keeping hers. *Another junkie of one type or other, itching for her fix,* Grey thought and as the homes became increasingly more and more identical, he wondered, *how the devil do people tell which house is theirs?* Kendra seemed to know by count or maybe she was looking at the addresses as they passed because she pulled into the drive of an adobe bungalow that looked indistinguishable from all the others, and placed her car in park.

It has a few extra cars parked in the driveway; mayhap that was how she recognized it. Hell, Grey, for all you know it could be her house; maybe she thinks she is a vampire bringing you back for a snack. A woman's voice with a strong Italian accent interrupted Grey's train of thought as she hustled down the front walk toward their car. "Kendra, you look lovely, Oh and you brought a friend. He looks…delicious."

She paused, oh good lord, she actually paused for effect. Harmony, darlin' are you hearin' this?

"Yes Jasper, I am," her voice echoed in his mind.

I know I don't exactly have my finger on the pulse of the people anymore, if I ever did, but is this for real, or am I just yankin' my crank, chasing this shit down?

"Whether it is for real or not, Jasper," Harmony said, "you are on the right track with this. Something is amiss, and Malign is behind it. This stinks of her brand of manipulation and you know it. She loves to turn a populace in on itself, make one group dislike another for whatever reason she fancies."

Aye, that she does. I know I don't need to say this, but you let me know the second you have a better direction for me to go in. This shit is starting to wear on my patience, and fast. I don't mind protectin' people that need it, but I ain't in the mood to play these "I need to belong to something" games.

Kendra and her Italian friend were still laughing over her little bon mot when Grey stopped conversing with Harmony and approached the women. He held out his hand, "Pleased to meet you ma'am. The name's Jasper."

"Oh my, oh my, a real cowboy, Kendra, however do you get so lucky? Antonio is just going to die when he sees him. I am Angelica by the way, you gorgeous man you." She lightly touched Grey's hand letting him know she wanted him to play the charming old world card and kiss the back of it. Grey had his moments when charm was the deadliest weapon in his arsenal. *It could be any one of a thousand factors, but I'm not in the mood for this right now,* and for the first time in a very long time Jasper Reynolds, now known as Grey, did not do what came naturally. He let Angelica's hand drop out of his without bending over to kiss it.

Kendra stopped the moment from becoming awkward by linking her arm through Grey's and saying, in an overly protective voice to show she was teasing, "He's my find, Ange, get your own."

The women shared another round of giggles - dissolving the slight tension Grey's lack of playing along with their game had engendered - before steering Grey into the open front door. The living room was done in a Navajo motif, with native patterned rugs spread about the open floor spaces, and faux art work adorning the walls. A group of men and women all of an age with Kendra and Angelica sat around a coffee table designed to look weathered and old, but was manufactured only the previous year halfway around the world. Coasters liberally strewn about it kept any real weathering from happening. They were dressed like Kendra in variants on the elegant black evening wear theme. One man turned his head at their approach saying, "Oh look, Kendra came, and she brought a friend."

All heads turned giving Grey the once-over, Botoxed lips pursed, and salon groomed eyebrows arched. He stood there for a moment feeling like a bull on display at a cattle show. Kendra pulled on the arm she was still looped through saying, "Come on over, Jasper, and meet the rest of them."

Grey allowed himself to be led over and introductions were made around the table. Each name drifted right in and right back out of Grey's consciousness; these were not the people he was looking for. There was no need to remember their names. It was cold, but to him they were nonentities. If they did not have a bearing on his work at this point he did not need to know who they were. Sure, they had stories, lives filled with hopes and dreams, but Grey, typically a people watcher and student of human behavior, could not invest himself as he normally would. Detachment was required for his job at times, but at others it was just the easiest course to take. After the last name had passed by him and the last hand had been shaken, Kendra asked, "Where's Antonio? I brought Jasper just for him. I knew he'd just *die* to meet him." She emphasized the word *die* to the point where it became its own sentence and placed her fingers gently over her heart, as if saying so might cause her to pass away also.

"I'm in the kitchen, Kendra, love!" yelled a voice that must have been Antonio from a direction that Grey could only assume was the kitchen. The voice was also heavily accented toward Italian like Angelica's, but to Grey's discerning ear it was obviously a ruse and farce. *Antonio, whoever you are, you sure as shit ain't*

Italian, Grey thought as the man shouted again from the kitchen, "I'll be right out with *Bloody Marys* and snacks!"

"Oh, Grey, you'll love Antonio. He's from the 'Old School' too, all charm and class like you," Kendra said patting the top of Grey's thigh, leaving her hand there after she finished her reassuring gesture.

Antonio bounded into the room back first to keep the swinging door from slamming into the tray of food and beverages he was transporting. "Okay, where is this cowboy I could hear you all cackling about from out here?"

He turned around with a huge open smile on his tanned Mediterranean face, tray outstretched to start offering refreshment. His hazel eyes locked onto Grey's, where he sat between Kendra and Angelica. The tray of appetizers and aperitifs fumbled from Antonio's hands, pouring down on the heads and backs of the party goers sitting across from Grey, as Antonio yelled in recognition, "Oh fuck! It's you!" All traces of his previous accent were gone from his voice. He took off running for the back of the house at a dead sprint, swinging kitchen door flapping in his wake, while the rest of the guests - except for Grey - stared in confusion after him.

Chapter 4

I worked alongside Grey for many years, shadowing his every move, observing how he manipulated energy, both positive and negative, and then tailoring those abilities to my own strong suits. I learned how to right wrongs, to help those who couldn't help themselves. In short, all the things I had found wanting in my physical life I was able to redress and change in this existence. So, I fought.

I fought whenever the opportunity arose. I fought when I should have run. I fought when I should have talked, coming close to tipping the Balance myself with my overzealous actions. Every time it was Grey, my hero, who saved me. He would pull me back at the last moment or come riding to my rescue without hesitation. I had my doubts, like any woman does from time to time; would this time be the one that I pushed him too far? Overextending what he was capable of? Or even allowed to do? Where was his line for love? To what ends would he go for me? Where would he stop and simply give me up for a lost cause? The breaking point had to be there somewhere; everyone has that line they won't cross. What was his?

All those years, all those battles, boil them down to their core and you'd find my entire existence had been based on two things: Passion and Love. Passion drove me to fight, to help, to protect, and to simply just be. Love turned me into an addict, pushing myself to impress, overstepping boundaries to see if love was strong enough to pull me back. I realize that my addiction is why I am so afraid of Grey moving on to the Source and leaving me. What would you do? Hmm? Do I let a red fern grow, and follow him to the next phase of life like a good little lovesick puppy dog? Do I stay here without him, falling back into my routines until I push too far or too hard, and there is no longer a cowboy there to ride to my rescue?

What would you do? Don't you dare brush me off with an, "It's your choice to make," canned response! You know the rules now; there is even a chance you could be faced with my exact choice one day. What would you do?

I think too often people rush to judge others without taking into account love. What love can convince a person to do - it can cloud your perceptions of right and wrong. Love can make a person capable of actions they would have otherwise deemed atrocious. Love can even lead a good person to evil, but I've also seen it bring an evil person to good. Can hate do that? No, can lust, sorrow, or envy? No, there is no other human emotional condition that can pull on the Balance like Love…….

***

"Look, I know he isn't really a kid I get that…I do. But, there is just something so wrong about that," Pete said to Raven gesturing across the room at Hank who was dancing on the bar of the Beer Bear. It had started out with *The Macarena* and had kept going through the jukebox's repertoire to *I Will Survive*, and he was now shaking his pelvic region, in a very un-ten year old fashion, to *I'm Too Sexy*. Leaning across the booth they were sharing, Pete continued, "Just wrong. Why is he like that anyway? If Zeus won't tell me I want to know. Come on, spill the goods sister. I know, you know."

Zeus was currently playing a drinking game with Gabe, standing along the bar that his younger brother was cavorting around on. The object seemed to be simple, whoever could drink the most, and still stand, won. Gabe said the only rule was that you had to stay in your physical shell without altering that body's chemistry; simply stay human while the game was on. They were matching each other, pint for pint, when Raven said to Pete, "I can't tell you much. Zeus talks to me about it, but that is a confidence that I just won't break, Pete. I won't violate his trust and love just to satisfy your curiosity, and if you ask Hank, he'll say Zeus is his big brother, so what he says goes. No surprise that Grey won't say much either. The most you'll get from him will be that they died young and tragically, Hank so much so that he has always retained his childlike innocence, although you'd never guess that by watching him 'ride the train' up there." She finished by nodding her head in the direction of the bar.

Zeus yelled a hearty, "Bwaaaa Ha!" as the last round was imbibed. He was laughing because Gabe had had to steady himself on a worn barstool after setting down his last tankard. The Lone Riders were clustered in a semicircle around the two men, with the boy dancing atop the bar at the opening to their human horseshoe. Only Lucifer stayed aloof in a dark corner of the barroom all alone, his hands cupped around a mug of coffee.

They had all returned to the Beer Bear after their chase of the demon and subsequent rescue of Hank. What Pete and Raven had been able to piece together of the Riders' story over the raucous shouts, cheers, and drunken toasts was very interesting to them.

Upon pulling into the parking lot Pete had asked Dante, "Why did you guys help us? After seeing that demon most folks would have run right back inside."

The tall, spare man shrugged and responded by gesturing his hands about his dusky face and torso. *Oh shit*, Pete thought, *well it's a good thing I didn't ask him any questions while driving I guess*. Opening their connection wider Harmony said, "It is alright, Peter, I will translate for you. He obviously understands what you are saying, so just allow him to believe you know American Sign Language, too."

Alright…wait, there are different types of sign language?

"Yes, Peter."

That must be a pain in the ass. That's the perfect chance to form a universal language, and still people got to mess it up. I wonder-

"Peter, not now."

Ah…right.

"He said, 'We live for the road, and the road has shown us many strange things. We killed a vampire like that one a few weeks ago'."

"Vampire?" Pete asked Dante. "You think that was a vampire?"

Harmony translated for Dante once again, "What else would it be? We cornered it and dragged it into the sunlight where it melted. That's what vampires do, right?"

Shit, what do I do boss lady? If these guys took out a demon like that one there's obviously more to them than we know. Do I correct him? Tell him about demons, angels, and the rest of us dead people, or do I just let him think he's the star of his own Wes Craven movie?

"For now let him go on believing that," Harmony said. A hint of trepidation crept into her voice as she continued, "I do not know to what extent their part is in this. Peter, there are powers at work here that I cannot divulge to you at the moment. I apologize, but even you will have to operate on a need-to-know basis with things here. For now, I see no need to correct his assumption until *they* need to know the truth."

Alright fine, play your cards close like Grey does. You know I hate that, right?

Harmony sighed, "I know, Peter. Believe me, it cannot be helped."

Their connection allowed them to converse at the speed of thought, making it possible for there to be little lag time in the conversation with the mute Rider. Turning his attention back to Dante, Pete said, "Well, Dante, I guess that's as good a logic as any for it being a vampire."

Dante nodded his head once in agreement, but the gruff voice of Bulldog cut off their conversation. "You know ASL, Pete? Fucking fantastic! We've been trying, as a group, for years to learn how to converse with Dante there, but most of us dogs are too old to learn new tricks, so he just types things out on his cell phone and texts us to join in on a conversation."

Dante rolled his eyes and shrugged at Pete as the gang's captain approached. Bulldog plowed into them both, snagging an arm around either of their shoulders. The barrel-chested leader was shorter than both Pete and Dante. His hairless pate shone in the sodium glow from the streetlights and his long belly length beard swayed about as he led them up the steps to the bar saying, "Come on boys, that was some crazy shit we just pulled and I'm overdue for a drink."

Everyone else had already gone into the roadhouse and they were the last to join in the revelry. Pete grabbed a tankard from the bartender and headed over to join Raven in a booth where he filled her in on what information he had garnered. She did the same for him. Bulldog had told her The Riders had been together for a long time and had worked alongside each other for years on the same assembly line in an automotive factory in Fairfax. Learning after a while that they all loved to ride and would much rather be riding than working, they started pooling their resources for a weekly lottery entry. Each week for years they played two hundred tickets with the same numbers. One time they lucked into a minor sum that had covered the amount they had invested over the years. "That would have been enough to stop most people," Bulldog had told her slyly, "but we ain't most people. We, foolishly some said, doubled our entries to four hundred a week, but guess who the fools were? Not us; we struck a major jackpot that next month. Me and this merry band have been riding and doing what good we can ever since."

Pete and Raven watched the crowd cheer as Gabe slammed down another tankard and sang a passing rendition of *Oops, I Did It Again* in his lilting Irish accent as an accompaniment to

Hank's eerily Spears-like dance moves. Pete gestured to the group as a whole saying, "Let me see if I have this right. Zeus and Hank died young and tragically and that's all I'm going to get. We have the philanthropic Lone Riders off battling injustice via Harley Davidsons, and the drunken Irish warrior for the Balance who is the Prince of Darkness' parole officer. Oh, and we're still off to convince the Voltron guy to not be human anymore, right? Christ, and here I thought that shit with Legion was weird."

Raven chuckled a bit, finished the sip of beer she had been swallowing, wiped her chin and said with a smile, "Yeah, oddity goes with the job, but that's why I like it."

"What about Lucifer? I mean, I obviously have no freaking clue on him," Pete said looking a bit bug-eyed. "Is that just his 'Name' like yours or Zeus' or Grey's? Or is that really the dude people think of as 'The Devil'?"

She did not have the chance to answer his question, because Lucifer's voice issued from directly behind Pete, "Oh…some of those stories are indeed me, but most are Malign's doing. I just end up taking the rap."

Pete jumped, splashing his beer down the front of him and choked on the sip he had been taking, earning a glare from Raven as a portion of his swallow ended up showering her. Wiping at his mouth with his sleeve he turned around quickly with the intention of yelling at Lucifer for sneaking up on him, but when he looked, no one was there. Raven smirked as she dabbed at her face with a napkin, then nodded her head in the direction of the table in the corner where Lucifer sat sipping his coffee. Pete watched him for a minute. Lucifer was still there, sitting in the same spot, shadows dancing around him, nursing his mug as if in deep contemplation of far and fancy thoughts. He lifted the mug to his pale lips, closing his eyes as in appreciation for the blend. While the mug was still to his mouth his voice issued from behind Pete again, "I could even make your lips move as I spoke if I wanted to, Pete. A gift some would call it, but nothing more than a paltry party favor really."

"You know," Pete said to Raven, "there are times when I think most of the people who stay behind aren't afraid of moving on to the Source. It's that the Source just doesn't want these assholes."

Lucifer's chuckle poured over their table like a warm wave of living Jell-O. Pete shook his head and took another drink, but Raven arched a black eyebrow in Lucifer's direction, raising her beer in salute. He reciprocated the gesture with his coffee mug, nodding his head once, slowly down, up and back to center. A thundering crash followed by resounding cheers from the crowd drew their attention back to the bar where Zeus had just toppled over onto the nearest table, upending it along with the stack of empty glasses they had been accumulating on it. Gabe was thrusting his hands in the air with his victory and shouting inarticulate Gaelic phrases. He turned, swiping a bottle of whiskey from the bartender, walked over to the female Lone Rider, spun her around like Fred Astaire ending in a deep dip, and gave her a long lascivious kiss. *Ah…eww… with tongue too,* Pete mentally noted.

Setting his latest acquisition aside to catch her breath, Gabe headed over toward Pete and Raven. He pulled a chair up to their booth, spinning it around so he could straddle it backward. With a resounding thud he planted the bottle of Redbreast onto the table saying, "You two are as thick as thieves over here. What'cha goin' on about?"

He produced three tumblers out of what appeared, to Pete, to be thin air. Lining them up in a cluster he poured each glass nearly full then deftly passed the shots across the table to both of them, keeping one for himself. Raven sighed, but took her drink and downed it in a pull. Gabe grinned like a shark. "Aye, atta girl."

When he motioned to refill her glass she shook her head, placing her hand over the tumbler's top and with a smirk said, "Once is quite enough, Gabe. I believe I've told you that before?"

"Oh! She wounds me, mate!" he yelled dramatically, holding a hand to his chest as he elbowed Pete with the other. "All I do is giver' me heart and all she wants is me body. What's a bloke to do, eh?"

Pete looked at Gabe with a bewildered expression of inquiry. "What's with all the booze and sex, man? You're one of us, right? So, why bother?"

"Why bother!? Why bother, he asks! Sweet Jesus...is he for real?" Gabe asked Raven. She only nodded her response. Another loud crash from the bar interrupted whatever Gabe had planned on saying next. All three of them turned to see Zeus staggering to his feet on what must have been his second attempt at rising. Hank was slowly coaxing him toward a barstool. Gabe shouted, "The fuckin' game's over, mate! You can purge it from your system now!"

"And you," he said turning back to Pete. "If you're hanging about with the *Wookie* and the Girl Wonder here then you've got to be one of Grey's through and through. That old cowboy likes to eat don't he? That's one o'the fringe benefits of the job, right? Me, I like fightin', drinkin', and fuckin'. Since fightin' comes with the job, the fuckin' and drinkin' are up to me, mate. Shite! What's the point in clinging to this ball o'mud hurtling through space if a bloke can't get a little female companionship now and again, eh?"

"Typical Mick," Lucifer's melodious voice wafted over the table again.

"Shut up you! I wasn't fuckin' talkin' to you," Gabe yelled without looking in Lucifer's direction.

Another round of liquid laughter blanketed the table, even Raven joined in his merriment this time with a chuckle of her own. Gabe looked around the booth before saying, "Fine, that's the way you want it? Hey there, Pete, I hear tell you want a 'Name' like the rest o'these fools. Don't look surprised, mate; word travels fast in the afterlife. Now, take me for example, Gabriel Daniel O'Connor at your service. That's who I was and am. I don't want to go forgetting the past like the rest o'them. Isn't that right, Annabelle?" He quirked an eyebrow at Raven and turned around this time to say in Lucifer's direction, "Or how about you over there, oh mighty Alexander? Not so fuckin' funny now, eh Alex?"

When neither one of them responded to Gabe's needling he turned back to Pete saying, "See what I mean, mate? There ain't no runnin' from your past; be who ye are. Me? I'm a drunkard and a libidinous fool, aye, but I'm honest with meself about it."

He poured another copious shot of Redbreast whiskey into his empty tumbler and passed it down to Raven without being told to. Then taking a long pull off the bottle he said, "That's the trouble with most o'the world, from my perspective mind you. They never want to take the responsibility, only the credit. I'm stuck babysittin' that piece o'work behind me, because my jurisdiction is the calmest on the planet, metaphysically speaking o'course. Hell, even the British demons know to comport themselves in a reasonable manner, not like the rest o'you savages. A British demon is like a fuckin' Yankee angel, mate, believe you me," Gabe punctuated this last statement by finishing off the bottle.

"So now," he continued, "if we've all gotten that out o'our systems, what were the two o'you going on about? If we dressed you in drag, Pete, we'd have our own miniature version of 'The View' the way you was going on."

"Just going over what info we've been able to glean on our new friends over there." Pete said, gesturing toward the Lone Riders who were clustered around Hank, trying to convince him to start dancing again. Zeus had managed to remain upright on a stool, laying his big shaggy head on the bar, occasionally groaning, or responding to a question with a grunt.

"Ah," Gabe said in mock sagacity, "the great vampire hunters you mean?"

"Hey," Pete said, "so, you knew them before the demon chase?"

"Knew them? Who the fuck do ya think tossed me out'a the bloody door at your feet, mate?"

Raven smiled, leaving thoughts of her past behind, and returned to the conversation with, "Oh, however did they resist your charms, Gabe?"

Not bothering to rise to the bait with ire he chose to treat her sarcasm as an honest inquiry.

"I know, love, it shocks me at times how little taste some people have." Turning to Pete he continued, "Aye, Lucy and me been hanging around these parts for a bit now."

Lucifer's calm detached voice said, "I hate it when you call me that."

"Well, no shit peckerhead! Why do ya think I do it," Gabe responded to the interruption. "Now where was I? Oh, right. You ever want to go someplace where they know how to hold their liquor, mate? Then head out to the middle o'nowhere. It's all they got. These blokes here have been bragging about takin' out a vampire for a bit now. Lucy." He paused and smiled before continuing, "Lucy and me just laugh at 'em a spell. It's an old European demon shtick, mate. Pretend you're one o'those creatures what goes bump in the night and mess with the locals some. Demons out here are just as bored as the fuckin' living people are."

Lucifer's voice joined them, yet his body still remained at his corner table. "And on occasion this backfires on the demon, as it did with the Lone Riders. The creature was stupid enough to be caught in a solid body come daylight and these philanthropic troglodytes destroyed it."

Harmony's voice intruded on Pete thoughts, "Peter, I need to speak with you."

"Ah I'm getting a call guys. I'm going to take it outside, okay?" Pete said already extracting himself from the table. The others nodded and

Gabe said, "She calls and we answer, mate, understood."

When the front door settled back into place from Pete's passing, Gabe turned to Raven and said, "So he's going to replace the cowboy, is he? He doesn't exactly look like much."

Raven laughed and then said, "That's how I felt at first too, but Pete's got power, Gabe. He just doesn't realize it most times, or if he does he pretends not to. Besides, Grey isn't leaving yet; he's sticking around, 'For the moment,' as he puts it."

"Sure, love," the Irishman said, sounding less than convinced. "Who am I to disagree with a lady?"

"He's staying, Gabe," Raven said, with anger creeping into her tone.

"I believe you, love," Gabe said raising his hands in a placatory fashion.

Lucifer's laugh crept back over in their direction as Raven downed her second tumbler of whiskey.

***

Pete stepped out into the cool spring night of rural Iowa. It was a novel experience for him, a city boy from birth and still at heart. Grey always said breathing and doing typical things that the mind remembered the body doing helped to calm him and give him a sense of self. Pete drew in a deep breath filled with the dew heavy air, the smells of newly tilled earth and the oily pitch of the highway filled his senses. Harmony spoke up after a moment, "Peter, I am starting to feel how this is going to play out. Grey has come across a demon pretending to be a vampire and is pursuing it at the moment. As is so often the case, I do not believe these to be isolated incidents. They are connected."

"A job's a job boss lady," Pete said with indifference. "What do you want me to do? Should I tell Hank we're on hold with his Voltron friend for the time being?"

"No, interestingly enough I still want you to head west. You should meet up with Grey out there somewhere. I will direct you if need be. But, what is of concern to me is that I need you to convince Lucifer he should go along, so I can send Gabe with you, too."

"We'll need a bigger car; it's already cramped with Zeus' big ass…oh, you want me to have the Lone Riders take us cross country too, don't you?"

"See, Peter, you are learning. Yes, that is exactly what I want from you. The motorcycle gang has me concerned. Please do not be insulted, but I am unsure if you will understand why. But I do owe it to you to attempt some rationale. The universe is all encompassing, Peter, even in my capacity I play a finite role, albeit an integral one. I am the Balance, but there is always the element of chaos; by the Source's design or just the laws of reality, there must always be wild cards. These entities are beings on different planes of existence that can tip things for good or ill, beyond what would be typical for their station. It is not often that there are such creatures on the physical plane, but I believe that the Lone Riders may be acting in that regard here."

"And you thought I wouldn't understand that? Wow, boss, thanks for the vote of confidence. Way to make a man feel all warm and fuzzy inside, you know?"

"Sorry, Peter, even I forget at times that you play the fool only as a defense mechanism, to keep others from expecting too much from you."

"Hey…who's playing?" Pete said with mock indignation. "Just kidding, boss. Consider it done. I'll round up the troops to go battle us some vampires. Man, that sounds stupid even for me; I hope Grey's having a better time than I am."

Chapter 5

Hope is an odd state of mind. Every woman feels hope, more poignantly than men I think. I don't mean that to sound sexist, we just worry more. And with worry comes hope. They aren't opposites, more along the lines of an interrelation. We hope for the future, hope for others, or just…hope. If you wanted to you could simply swap out hope and replace it with worry and the meaning would be almost the same, only hope gives you that feeling of the positive, where worry borders on the negative. It's only a small step from worry to anxiety.

I have held on to many hopes in my afterlife. Hope is the last thread we can grip before we fall into despair isn't it? I almost lost everything because of a hope. I was never very good with the Eastern Philosophies. Many of the great Buddhas would say something ambiguous like, "What is, is." Or maybe, "This is the thusness of something. It has Buddha nature." They would tell you not to waste energy on hope because you can't change what will be, not to cause yourself needless pain and suffering over what you cannot control.

Do you know what I say to that? Just you fucking watch me! I'll tear myself apart to try and change whatever I think needs changing.

I had hoped to live a full life, raise a family of my own, see my children, hold them, grow old with the father of those now imaginary children, and hold our grandchildren. All of those hopes were denied me in my physical life. Why? Fate or coincidence? Neither? It doesn't matter now, because they were taken from me. What would you do if most of your hopes were taken from you, leaving you with nothing but anger? You would either fight like I do, trying to change things for others and keep the tiniest of hopes alive, or you could fold like a house of cards, just give up, letting "What is" be.

Maybe that is the essential difference between hope and worry. With a hope you will fight for it, to the death if need be. With a worry you may fight to not have something come about, but if it does, it crushes you entirely. These are all just maybes mind you. I don't claim to know, but I prefer to err on the side of caution, don't you? I'd rather cling to a hope than be crushed by a worry………

***

Running full speed, Grey chased after the demon that was calling itself Antonio. He had left Kendra and the other vampire groupies in a whirlwind of confusion as he darted across the faux Navajo living room. Spilling excessive energy over into their reality as he sprang from his seat, Grey knocked the couch over backward, with the pair who had so recently had the tray of appetizers dumped upon them tumbling along for the ride. Abandoning his physical shell before he had passed into the kitchen, it appeared to the house guests as if their new acquaintance Jasper merely disappeared into thin air. Moving at speeds the human eye would have trouble comprehending, even if they could see him, Grey sped up and over fences, leaped cars, hurdled dumpsters and any other urban detritus that was in his way, as he chased after the demon.

In moments both men, moving as only energy, were free of the encumbering city, churning up the miles north of town, heading straight for the Tesuque Indian Reservation. *Fuckin' demons*, Grey thought, *always runnin' some angle, tryin' to get energy and power. How hard is it to just stop and say 'Sorry, Grey, you caught me…Hey I'll knock it off. Did you have any questions for me?' They never make it easy for anybody.*

The demon Antonio all but flew along in the desert night, passing over rock and brush as if they had no substance. He was just another shadow among many. Hoping to have left Grey far enough behind he risked looking back over his shoulder and screamed in terror when he saw the feared warrior barreling down on him closer than he had anticipated. Terror tripping him, Antonio sprawled out on the hard packed soil, sending up a cloud of dust and dirt as Grey used his strength to keep the demon from sinking into the ground seeking sanctuary. Had it been another demon chasing him Antonio would have worried that the end was upon him. On his side of the afterlife, once prey was run to ground that was that: done, gone, ingested, and incorporated. Antonio held on to a sliver of hope that he had not given Grey enough of a reason to destroy him, so he lay still, cooperative and compliant.

Heavy footsteps approached the downed demon as it lay on its back looking up at the night sky. When the scuff and shuffle of Grey's feet stopped, the cowboy's weathered face hovered into place, obscuring the demon's view. With an arched eyebrow of disdain he said, "Antonio the Vampire, huh?" Grey motioned with the first two fingers of both hands, placing visible quotation marks around vampire.

"Come on, Grey," the demon wheedled, "do you honestly think I'd get any women if I called myself 'Mitch the Vampire?' The ladies want an old world persona to go with the fangs and flash, not some insurance salesman from Wichita."

"Yeah, Mitch," Grey said correcting him, "but you were an insurance salesman from Wichita."

"Hey you caught me, you don't gotta rub it in, man," Mitch said sitting up, brushing dust from his torso. "So, what do you want? The usual, leave the poor humans alone, stick to playing with the other ghosts, naughty demon naughty. Can I go now?"

"No," Grey commanded, keeping his tone level in hopes that his laughter would stay internal. He had trouble separating, at times, his personal feelings from his job. *I suppose all cops do at some point,* Grey thought. *It's hard to keep your opinions from shading things, but damn it I always liked Mitch. He's the kind of guy I would've been more than happy to play cards or share a beer with back when we were alive.* Aloud he continued, "I hear tell Malign is in the States, specifically here, out West, and she has something to do with this vampire bullshit spreading near and far. I don't much feel like wanderin' around another Goth nightclub so, Mitch, I need some information."

"They call themselves 'Emo' now, Grey. Well…at least I think they do. My tastes run to the older crowd, the women from my generation are so much more- " A glare accompanied by flared nostrils from Grey interrupted Mitch's train of thought, and he continued, "Never mind that, but Christ, Grey! Do you think I'm dumb enough to cross Malign? I like you man, but you can't exactly protect me from that bitch if she finds out I've been talking to you."

Grey crouched down next to the demon, looking him directly in the eyes, "Why yes, in fact I do think you're dumb enough, 'Antonio'."

"Knock it off man. That's not cool," Mitch whined. "You think I enjoy that shit? I get what I need and that Euro-trash racket works, man! I'm a lover, not a fighter."

"You're a user," Grey said in a growl, not having to hold back his feelings on that subject.

"I'm sorry, isn't that what I just said? Look, Grey, I don't know why all this is happening now. Is Malign behind it? Jesus, what isn't she behind, huh? The kids and housewives are into it, so I go with the flow. If I gotta wear parachute pants to get laid, then I'll say, 'It's Hammer Time!' and I'll do that, too."

Grey did not say anything. He stared past the demon, as it justified its existence, thinking, *We all do this don't we? Sad, even I feel the need to justify my actions at times. There'd be no need for therapy if people'd just content themselves with who they are, but carryin' this shit over into the afterlife, too? What a waste.*

The demon either took Grey's silent ruminations as a sign he was in trouble further than he feared, or that it might be more prudent to just appease the badass in front of him and risk the enmity of another badass, who was elsewhere, but only if she found out. "Alright, alright! Christ, Grey, stop looking at me with that flintlock stare of yours. It's fucking creepy. I'm not privy to her ultimate plans mind you, but word came down the pipeline a few months back that she'd look favorably on any of us hanging our hats in the States who would start up the vampire scam. I figured it was better to err on the side of caution I mean, I'd worked that angle before; it was no skin off my teeth to start it up again, right? Most of the news I hear lately comes out of Vegas. There's a community of demons pulling the same scam I work here, but they are way, and I mean *way* more violent, than what I'm comfortable with."

Mitch stood up, looking askance at Grey as the lean cowboy mimicked his rise. "Look man, that's really all I got. If I head back now I can probably work this whole story into an incubus' wet dream, with those yuppies back there in Santa Fe. And man, you know better than most, that's saying something."

"Yeah," Grey agreed, "fair enough, Mitch. You ain't tippin' the Balance doing it, so go back, but mind you watch how far you push it."

"You're a prince. I promise to keep things controlled. You won't have to come back looking for me," he said emphatically, nodding his head.

Grey sighed and said, "A man's promise ain't nothing but a well-shaped puff of air. Now, a man's deeds? Well, those can echo through eternity."

"You know," Mitch said, "you could have just said 'Actions speak louder than words'. I would've gotten the point."

"Mitch?" Grey asked calmly, but his eyes started to glow with a cold blue light.

"Yeah."

"You want to start runnin' again?"

"Right!" Mitch exclaimed with wide eyes, "point taken. I'll be going now." The demon turned, heading back south in the direction of town and his awaiting groupies with undulating oil-like grace. Grey watched him go until he was out of sight, kicking over a large rock before sitting down to check for snakes or spiders, a habit from his life that never seemed to leave him when he was back in his homeland. "You can take the cowboy out of the West, but you can't take the West out of the cowboy. What? Is a rattler going to bite me now? The things we take with us when we cross over, huh?" he said aloud, knowing Harmony was there with him, as she always was, but now concentrating the bulk of her focus directly upon him.

"I often wonder what it would be like to have lived a physical life," Harmony said appearing beside Grey. She did not normally take a solid body when she interacted with her soldiers, but every now and then she wanted to be a part of what she was protecting, to be a part of things, walk among the living as she had instructed Pete to do. "This seems like a paltry taste, to me, but it is all I have," she said gesturing to the form she had created.

She sat down next to Grey, smoothing her sundress across her legs, and shoving him over on the small patch of rock he had commandeered as a chair. He grunted in mock discomfort. "Easy darlin', I'm an old man."

"By your standards yes, but not by others' young man. You know better than to insinuate that a lady is *old* even if it was unintentional." She giggled, poking him in the ribs. Harmony tossed her honey brown hair about her shoulders, letting the desert's night breeze flow through it. The moon cast her features in an icy silhouette, causing the freckles across the bridge of her nose to stand out in stark contrast.

"I suppose you're one of the few who can say that and rightly mean it," Grey agreed. "I don't know Harmony, maybe I should have let go and moseyed on before. I just keep findin' excuses to stay. It seems like a rationalization, but I don't have the same drive to do this kind of thing any longer." He gestured out to the displaced soil and rocks where Mitch had fallen down, to emphasize what he meant.

"You say that so often," Harmony said waspishly. "I wonder sometimes if you really mean it, or if you just like telling us all how tired you are?"

"Ouch darlin'. I think Pete may be a bad influence on you," Grey said, chuckling to acknowledge he was not upset, and she smiled to let him know that neither was she.

They sat in silence looking around at the nightlife going about their hunts and escapes. Demons slunk at the edges of their vision, keeping to the horizon in misguided hopes of not drawing the attention of either of the powerful creatures that had invaded their territory. Grey looked down at his side where a large brown scorpion scuttled over toward a cricket, grasping it in its pinchers, and striking hard with its tail. It tossed its tiny prey aside and scurried off after a second meal it could sense close by. Grey placed a hand on the ground, interposing a solid barrier between the scorpion and another cricket. "Slow down there little killer. Just one for you tonight."

He scooped the scorpion up in his left hand. After a pair of futile strikes with its tail, the arachnid settled on his palm. The tiny creature seemed to stare at Grey when he raised it to eye level; it stayed frozen at this sudden juxtaposition of prey and predator. After a moment's study Grey allowed the scorpion to scuttle from his hand down by its first kill. When it saw that there were no longer any other possible meals moving about, the scorpion tore into the cricket with ravenous zeal.

"See, Jasper, you still do the job, even when you propose that you no longer want to," Harmony said like a schoolmarm, using the scorpion to illustrate her point. They fell back into a companionable silence for a time, enjoying the sounds and feels of the desert night through their makeshift bodies. As a creature created for a single destiny Harmony was the first to break the reverie, to place them back on topic. The drive of duty was something she could never escape and it always impeded her ability to relate to Grey and her other soldiers. It was a pressure on her mind, a weight that could only be shifted for ease but never dropped. She said, "I am sending Peter and the others out your way. They have come across similar demons masquerading as vampires; also they appear to have encountered a group of *wild cards*."

Grey raised an eyebrow at this. "Living?"

"As far as all my abilities were able to ascertain?" Harmony said. "Yes."

"Hmph," was Grey's response. "Well, I do suppose it has to happen from time to time. Do you think any of them might end up in our camp when their deadline comes?"

"Anything is possible, Jasper. One of them in particular is something very special, but for now I have asked Peter to enlist their aid in bringing him and the others west. It will allow us to keep an eye on these wild cards and be prepared, as much as we can be, for the ripples their actions may cause." Harmony paused before saying, "Gabe and Alexander are with them."

"Oh, goodie," Grey said, turning to look her directly in the eyes. He met her gaze, watching her irises dance about the colors naturally given to mankind: blue to brown to green to hazel to gray to burgundy and back. It was as close to a warning as he was likely to receive from her not to push this. Grey did not care; he continued, "I know you don't rightly want me retiring just yet, but you bring those two in on a job with me, and you know damn well I may just up and walk. You have any more swell news for me, darlin'? Has Legion shown back up yet?"

"Do not be so melodramatic," she said, dismissing his sarcasm with a shooing flap of her hand. "You like both of them, just in small doses, but you refuse to admit it. No one said you had to get each other heart shaped pendants with *BFF*s engraved on them."

Arching an eyebrow at her last comment, reaffirming his previous observation, he said, "Yeah, definitely too much Pete. So, Vegas huh?" letting her know he would go along with things for now by way of changing the subject. "How many times have I told you to just permanently station someone there? It would cut down on my workload if you did." He stood, swiping the dust and grit from the back of his faded denim jeans. "You going to stay here for a spell, darlin'?"

"Yes, I think I will," Harmony declared, looking up at the moon. "We take what pieces of solace where we can find them. Right, Jasper?"

"Yeah darlin', that we do, that we do," he said, walking off to the north, not bothering to ask Harmony if she would transport him to Las Vegas. She knew him better than to ask. Some men think, feel, and decide how best to move forward in life by doing just that, moving forward.

***

"Oh my God!" Maggie all but screamed, "What was that thing?"

They were riding in the back of one of the company cars that Eric had purchased to shuttle celebrities, writers, or the varying types of movers and shakers about town when they were in the process of negotiating contracts. He usually preferred to drive himself, but calling in one of his chauffeurs seemed the proper thing to do, allowing him this opportunity to calm Maggie down, or come up with a suitable lie at the very least.

Eric was posed with a problem he had not considered. What would he do if something from his side of things spilled over into the world, becoming noticed by one of his human employees? It was not something he had anticipated when he was concocting this venture. In the past when he interacted with the living it had always been in a time or place when the ideas of monsters and demons were commonly accepted as fact. As little as a century or two ago he could have said to her, straight faced, "That, Maggie, was a demon." And she would have solemnly made the sign of the cross, believing his explanation as the God's honest truth.

Now things were different. He could wipe her memory of the incident, but that bordered too close to the actions of a demon for his tastes. Dolphie's constant yapping was starting to edge on his nerves, too. *Blood of Christ, child*! he thought to himself. *If the damn dog wants to get away so bad, let the annoying little ball of fluff go.* "Mr. M.? Eric? What was that, and like, what did you do to stop it from hurting me?"

Aw, the hell with it. In for a penny in for a pound. "Maggie," Eric said, "that was a vampire." *Okay son, the money is down, all bets are placed. Will she buy it? Most people believe what they want anyway. You are a gambler at heart like any artist, and people just haven't changed all that much over the millennia.*

"I knew it!" Maggie exclaimed, staring at him with glassy wide-set eyes. "I knew they were real, like, all these years; it was just a matter of time before I….I knew it."

She turned away from Eric looking out into the passing night. He could see her eyes reflected in the window, with their resolute belief and honesty shining through, and for the first time he started to have doubts over this enterprise. Here was a girl whose devotion to a fad was only a poorly veiled desire to belong to something. Yet it had inspired him to influence mankind, and she was so confident in her belief that she would convince herself that anything fit her fantasy. He leaned over, touching a hand to her shoulder, thinking, *the price of zealotry*. Aloud, Eric said, "Yes, Maggie, informing humanity was the driving force that led me to create Re-Vamped Media." *A partial lie is always easier to swallow that an entire one. Tell her what she wants to hear just so you do not feel like a monster yourself.* "I want people to know how to defend themselves. Those who embrace the darkness become one with it, or the honest few can be a light for others. What I did, and am doing, Maggie, is…God's work."

Oh sure! Lay it on thick there salesman, Eric thought as he watched her red rimmed eyes in the glass. Maggie did not respond at first; she kept her face turned away from his, looking out the window at the passing housing developments. She had insisted they continue on to the production set even after Eric offered to have the driver drop her off at her apartment. When she turned back toward him her features held a seriousness and solemnity that were incongruous with her blond Kewpie doll looks. She said, "I guess that makes sense. If there are dark things like vampires, then there must be good things like God too, huh?"

Eric breathed a sigh of relief saying, "Exactly, my dear. You are quite astute for one so young, did you know that?"

Maggie giggled. "I'm not that young, Mr. M., but thanks."

"Now, I need to ask you a favor, Maggie. Will you do me a favor?"

"Um…sure?" she said with a measure of dubiety.

"I need you to keep this just between us, okay? If you went off talking to everyone about how vampires are real, the press would simply claim it was a publicity stunt, purported by me, to up the ticket sales come opening weekend. That would ruin the entire point of this little quest of mine. Can you do that for me, Maggie?" he asked, staring at her, pleading with her via looks alone to say yes. He did not want to cross that line of manipulating her memory, but at this point, for the greater good, he would do it. She saved him the trouble when she answered, "Sure thing, Mr. M., anything. The secret is safe with me. Well…and Dolphie here of course."

She picked the dog up and squeezed it tight to accentuate her point. "And he can't tell anybody anything….can you my sweetie little Dolphie-kins….No, he can't," she cooed, rubbing the dog's nose with her own as it whined, sounding like a condemned man begging for mercy to Eric.

He smiled, nodding indulgently at the young woman and her pet, all the while thinking, *It's annoying, but it's probably for the best. Can you imagine how she would treat a child if she acts like this with her dog?* In one of those quirky twists of fate she seemed to read his thoughts. Producing a pair of pink dog bone shaped barrettes; she snapped them into the fluffy white fur above the dog's ears.

Chapter 6

I missed my family something awful those first years tagging along behind Grey. Sure he had become a surrogate father, Freudian though that may sound, it was true. He would be there when I needed him: when I cried over seeing a teddy bear just like my little sister's, or when holidays came around bringing with them all those held-over emotions from my mortal life. Zeus took on the role of eccentric uncle, the kind that you love no matter what he says because he doesn't know any better. He would never hurt someone's feelings on purpose, but his innocent perspective can lead him to say things others would think twice before blurting out.

That was my family, for many a long year, with a distant and disapproving maternal figure in Harmony, an iconic hero, and a lovable goof. I have seen people with far less, so I enjoyed the family I had found, but it still hurt to think of the one I had lost. I suppose that's what it means to grow up and grow old. You learn to love, and then you learn to lose the things you love. You can either keep moving, or lose yourself, too.

My sister Elizabeth used to have this set of colored beads that she loved to string in different patterns. She would spend hours playing with them, then when she had the pattern to what she felt, at least to her critical child's eye, was just right, she'd hold it out to me, beaming with pride and say, "Look! Look! Anna! I make a rainbow." God, it still hurts now...

The wounds to the psyche that form when someone we love is taken from us scab over, sure, but they never really heal. Especially when that someone is taken so tragically, so cruelly, so...

Have you ever wanted revenge so badly that even after justice has been served it does not seem like it was punishment enough? That if you could, you would bring the offender back to life, only to take it from them again and again, just so that they may know a measure, just the tiniest hint of what they had stolen from you? Eye for an eye is bullshit! How is that fair? You never wanted your eye taken in the first place, but it was taken anyway. I say blindness for an eye. Of course, it doesn't have the same Biblical ring to it, but it makes more sense to me. I think the Wiccan's rule of three has more merit. If you don't know it, it means that any harm you bring to others will be visited back upon you threefold. It's supposed to work the other way around too if you give to others, you'll be gifted back thrice. I haven't seen that happen all that much mind you. No, most often people - or the demons they become - would rather harm than help, and angels get too wrapped up in questions of should or should not that they lose sight of what it means to be human.

That impotent rage and desire for vengeance that goes unsatiated is, I imagine, how many people feel when a child goes off to war never to return, or the mother who finds her child cold in his crib due to some faceless monster called SIDS. You want to lash out at those that would harm you and yours, for no discernable reason, other than that they can.

Strange how I can start talking about love and family, the two strongest connections for me; then through the actions of other's, that love can be twisted into having me talk about hate, the emotional polar opposite. I know little Elizabeth is somewhere out there. Besides my memories, somewhere she is waiting for me, and she wants to show me another rainbow, but I just can't let go of my hate enough to be with her……yet…….

***

"Okay people listen up!" Raven yelled at the milling throng of bikers and Balance warriors, plus one angel and one demon. "We need to organize who is going to be riding with whom. Plus, despite Bulldog's assurances to the contrary, you all need to rest before we head out. The bartender here at the Beer Bear said there is a cheap motel a couple of miles down the highway. The rooms are on me people, but I need you all to rest up."

She neglected to mention that if they wanted Lucifer to accompany them (Harmony did, according to Pete at least, but the rest of them were not so sure) then they needed to stay in one place during the daylight, keeping his exposure to the sun at a minimum. He was powerful enough he could withstand quite the solar beating, but he would not do so willingly to aid them. "Please, I am a demon after all I do have my limits," he had said when Pete asked him to come along and ride during the day.

Lucifer and Gabe could always wait around while the others traveled west and catch up to them when darkness fell. They would have to move exceptionally fast to do so since Harmony would be able to transport Gabe, but not Lucifer. She hardly wanted to leave the fallen angel unattended, and relying on the two to be motivated enough to follow on their own was not a likely prospect.

"We don't need no sleep lady!" Bulldog shouted at Raven to a chorus of agreeing grunts from the other Lone Riders. Raven looked at him, smiled, and said, "Fine big fella, I believe you, but we do, especially the boy."

"Oh…yeah, sorry, Hank, I kind'a forgot about you, little one," Bulldog said leaning over to ruffle Hank's shaggy brown hair.

Playing the part of tired little boy, Hank had curled up in Zeus' massive arms and was rolling his head droopily about, but smiled sleepily at the biker. Raven continued addressing the group at large while they congregated around their motorcycles in the Beer Bear's parking lot. "We'll stop for the day, get some sleep, and travel by night. That way we can spot any other vampires that may be on the loose out there, too."

Only those who knew her well heard the hesitation and hitch in her voice when she said *vampires*. Lucifer made a sniffing noise of disdain muttering, "Amateurs," under his breath. Whether he was referring to the demons who were play acting or the Lone Riders was not quite clear. The Riders were arguing, trying to work out who would ride with "luggage" and who would be free. Zeus piped in loudly, "For God's sake! Let's just ride with who we did earlier. How fucking hard is that?"

Hank stirred a bit to mutter, "Language, Frank."

"Sorry, but it ain't that hard, is it?"

"Easy, *Chewie*," Gabe said. "This is a big deal to these folks. The road is their home, mate. You wouldn't just break in the front door and make yourself at home would you? Well maybe you would, but a normal person would think twice and have some bloody manners."

While the others were quarreling over the riding assignments and Gabe was instructing Zeus on road etiquette, Pete turned to Raven and out of the side of his mouth said, "Hey if Zeus is *Chewie* can I be *Lando*? Do you think that would catch on?"

Raven did not deign to give Pete a response. She glared at him for a moment, blew an errant bang out of her face, then looking up directed her response to the star laden sky saying, "This is like corralling a bunch of children…"

Lucifer's voice interrupted her, "Albeit, hairy tattooed children, but the simile is sound." He had moved away from the cluster of people, standing on the other side of the group, yards away hiding among the shadows. He smirked when she jumped, startled, and turned to glare in his direction.

***

After the extensive quibbling had been resolved, *for this night's travel at least*, Raven thought, looking around and taking stock of her austere yet clean motel room. *Always ugly prints for the comforter, carpet, and curtains. Ugh, plaid-tricide.* She sighed. *You're putting off the inevitable girl. You have to do it, so just do it like removing a Band-Aid, quickly or you'll only cause yourself more pain.* After looking once more in disgust at the bedspread, she sat down on the edge of the bed, back straight, as if she were attempting to meditate. She spoke in a tone of resignation to the empty room, "I need to talk to you."

Where Pete mentally viewed his connection to Harmony as a lit and closed closet door in a dark room, Raven felt her connection as a fire in a cold stone hearth, raging or burning to different degrees depending on the activity of their bond. The dim ashes in Raven's mental fireplace stirred to life in a flickering flame, accompanied by Harmony's voice. "Yes, Annabelle?"

"I'm mature enough to realize I cannot function fully on this case if I continue to receive my information second-hand through Pete," Raven said aloud, sounding like a woman resigned to committing a distasteful act.

"I can understand that," Harmony's voice said over the crackling flames.

"But no ham-handed attempts at therapy or mothering; that is not our relationship. It never was. You're my boss, that is all," Raven said, drawing lines of distinction in the air with her fingers, even though the gestures were completely unconscious and unnecessary.

"Again, I can understand that," the warming fire agreed.

"Good," Raven said, "as long as we have that clear. Now, what is all this vampire business?"

"It is what it always is, Annabelle. Sentient beings with their lust and greed for power, doing whatever it takes to gain that power," Harmony said. "But this is a more slippery slope toward power than is typical for demonic kind. It is a fast track to power, but one not easily noticed by the rest of us in the afterlife.

They can take from the living what they need to survive but without the overt actions that may lead them to our attention, or the attention of more powerful demons that would take their gained energy for their own."

"Then why start now? Why haven't I encountered this before?" Raven asked, stretching her legs out and flopping back onto the bed with a sigh. "If they aren't tipping the Balance by pretending to be *Count Dracula* then why should we be involved at all?"

"Normally I would agree with you on that, but Malign is involved in this somehow. I do not know how she is connected with Metatron yet. But I do know she was the one that suggested the increase in demons masquerading as vampires here in the United States. Jasper is trying to run her to ground as we speak, but you of all people know very well what she is capable of and how secretive she can be. So I would rather have all of you ready to strike when the moment is right than run around scrambling at the last second in hopes of avoiding a catastrophe."

Even alluding to World War II, however obscurely, was dangerous ground for Harmony to tread on when speaking with Raven. Harmony, for all her power and knowledge, never knew why the physical deaths of her soldiers affected them so strongly. They could look back on it as just a continuation of existence, one phase to another, but not many of them did. Perhaps it was her immortality that kept her from comprehending or empathizing. It is hard for any creature to understand something it will not be faced with; humans cannot know the mind of birds, insects, or fish. Though Harmony loved all of her warriors - as much as a creature like her could know that emotion - she still could never be like them. Raven's death was more violent than others, but Harmony would have felt wonder at continuing life, when humans, despite their religious theories did not have any assurances of a continuing life after death. It would be a joyous moment for her; perhaps that was one of the many factors contributing to the gulf between them.

A knock on the door interrupted them from following that conversational thread further and possibly widening that emotional chasm Raven had so recently tossed a rope across. Raven reluctantly rose from the bed, heading toward the door just as the knocker delved into another refrain of *Shave and a Haircut*. She threw open the safety latch and yanked the door ajar. A grinning Gabe stood outside with a bottle of Champagne in one hand and a pair of crystal flutes in the other. "I was just wonderin' to myself, love," he said in his lilting Irish vernacular. "Why waste a perfectly good motel room, right? Eh? I even brought a bag'o quarters with me for the vibrating bed." He lifted a small bag and jingled it about in time with his bouncing eyebrows to stress his sincerity.

He grinned lasciviously at her. Raven inhaled a deep breath, closed her eyes, mentally counted to three, and then slammed the door so hard in Gabe's face that the frame rattled. As she walked back toward the bed she heard him call from the other side, "Some other time then, eh?" She flung herself back onto the plaid mattress in a swimmer's belly flop with a resounding thump.

To Harmony's relief Raven continued their discussion without becoming sullen or despondent. "Is Grey having much success pinning her down?"

"At the moment no, but he is following a chain of leads. It is bound to end at her."

"If he gets too close before we meet up with him will you take me to him? If she has exerted herself enough this time maybe between the two of us we can take her," Raven said, rolling onto her side, and drawing her knees up to her chest.

"Perhaps child, perhaps," was all Harmony said before her fire inside Raven's mind dwindled down to ashes once more, allowing Raven a measure of peace and quiet.

***

The sun was dropping low in the western sky as Zeus and Pete watched Hank playing with the motel owner's Labrador puppy. A cloud of small glowing lights were dancing around them, much like with the lonely boy in Central Park and his frisbee. The lights congregated around the masticated, now swamp sludge green tennis ball that the puppy was playing with. The lights would bathe Hank for a moment, swirling around him in a cyclone, and then go zipping away with the ball as the puppy chased it. The tiny angels beat the dog to its objective, spinning in a whirlwind of color over top the tennis ball until slobbery jaws clamped down and oversized paws galloped back to Hank with enthusiasm.

The little black Lab dropped the ball before it reached Hank. The boy crouched down to grab it, but the puppy continued its charge toward Hank's arms bowling him over, knocking the baseball cap from his head in a torrent of sloppy dog kisses. The puppy started to yap as Hank laughed, roughing the dog's fur up, wrestling in a tangle of arms and paws.

Sitting on the raised concrete curb in front of their motel room doors Pete turned to Zeus saying, "He makes me want to go play, too."

The big man grinned around his beard, "Yeah, the little fella has that effect on people. Even when I was too old to play he'd grin at me and I'd stop whatever chore I was doing to play with him. I just couldn't help myself."

They both laughed when the thrown ball rebounded off a dumpster on the other side of the parking lot from where they were sitting and the puppy stopped its chase short, causing its awkward backend to go tumbling over its front in a somersault. Right back up on its paws the puppy started sniffing out where its toy had gone to. The angel lights were hovering over an area of high grass and weeds, showing those that could see them where the ball had come to rest. With night fast approaching, shadows from a nearby copse of trees were falling long over the area where the lights danced. The first pair of demonic eyes watched them greedily from an overhead branch, hiding deep in the conifer's shadows.

An old, poorly dressed vagabond of a man stepped out from behind the dumpster, shambling over to scoop up the tennis ball. The lights shot away from their marking duty to hide behind or cling to Hank as he walked over to help the puppy retrieve its toy. With serpentine reflexes the old man snatched the puppy off the ground by the ruff of its neck. The dog yelped and wiggled as the old man brought it up to eye level. It was clear the puppy was terrified as its bladder let go, soaking the old man's already filthy pants. Snarling in disgust the old man slapped the puppy across its snout with his free hand, causing the pup to whine all the louder. Hank screamed, "Stop that!"

The old vagabond darted his eyes in Hank's direction for the first time, and from the overwhelming distance of the motel's parking lot Pete could see a deep maroon glow blaze out from the empty pits that were the old man's eye sockets. Pete yelled, "Shit! Shit!" as he leaped to his feet and sprinted toward Hank, but even with their enhanced speed Pete could tell there was no way he and Zeus would reach the boy before the demon did.

The demon glared at Hank, snarling out, "Slime and snails and puppy dog's tails…..Hmmmm? That's what little boys are made of, right?" To punctuate this he grabbed the puppy's tail in his other hand and ripped it from the dog's body, causing it to yelp from an all new level of pain. The demonic old man lifted the tail up to his lips, licking the dripping blood from his fingers and the stump of fur-wrapped bone they clutched. When the limp tail was clean of fresh blood he flung it at Hank, cackling madly.

Without regard to the danger he was in, Hank moved toward the demon to help ease the puppy's cries. At the boy's forward momentum Zeus screamed, "Hank stop! We'll take care of this, just wait!"

The warning came too late; the demonic old man reached a bony hand out grasping Hank's shoulder with his free hand and tossing the puppy into the tall grass with the other. The demon purred in Hank's face, "Now little boy….let's see what you're really made of."

Hank closed his eyes and raised his arms up as blobs of blood-tinged spittle splashed out in his direction from the demon's maw. He tried to shield himself from the old man's invasive touch with a warm pulsing light. Zeus screamed, "Hank!"

A dark form in a denim jacket stepped out from behind the dumpster that had so recently concealed the demonic old vagabond. In one hand it held a flaming sword; orange and red fire danced along the naked blade as it swooped in without warning or challenge taking the demon's head from its shoulders. A following vertical swipe carved what was left of the creature in two equal portions that folded to the pavement in a puddle of smoking goop. Still remaining silent, Lucifer reached into the tall grass, pulling the puppy out from where it had landed. He pressed the flaming side of his sword to the dog's bloody wound cauterizing it. The animal was in shock; it barely responded to the demon's ministrations. Lucifer turned and started walking back toward the motel. In passing, he handed Hank the injured dog, saying only, "Be more careful young one."

To Pete and Zeus, who had stopped in their tracks when they realized that the boy was safe, Lucifer said, "It is close enough to dark and the night calls to its children. It is time that we moved on. I will go fetch the others."

Zeus rushed over to Hank, finding the boy using his energy to fully heal the puppy's wound. It would go through life sans a tail to wag, but at least it would have a life to go through. Pete stood watching "The Prince of Darkness" walk away to gather an army of vampire-hunting motorcycle vigilantes after having just saved the existence of an angelic boy and a Labrador puppy. Pete muttered to himself, "Man! This job gets weirder and weirder; the devil saves kids and puppy dogs?

What the hell kind of sense does that make? Okay fine, what's next, Jeffrey Dahmer feeding the homeless?"

Chapter 7

You can call it a wish or a prayer, but it all comes down to the same sentiment: wanting something stronger than you are to intercede on your behalf. I have issues with weakness if you hadn't noticed. Wishing or praying just smacks of weakness to me. Some of my earliest memories are now tainted by weakness, going to worship as a little girl dressed in my paltry finest, holding the gnarled and palsied hand of my grandmother. She died a few years before the war destroyed everything we loved. Contrary to my previous statement, I take that as a blessing.

Not much can compare with the weakness of childhood, where every experience is something new and often times confusing. I never saw worshiping God as a weakness as a child. How could you? You are told, "This is how things are little one," by trusted adults, so that is how they are, right? These are the people who love you and want to keep you safe, so they must be right.

I never doubted my Bubbeh when she told me, "Yahweh wants us to go see him." She would then pat the top of my head, leading me into the Synagogue, slipping me these awful anise candy drops that she thought were a treat, but I hated. I never had the heart to tell her how disgusting I thought they were. She liked them and so I liked them because I loved her. Isn't it funny how often we swallow something that tastes bitter for the people we love, just because we don't want to speak up and risk hurting their feelings by telling them what they like makes us want to gag? Mostly that would be a metaphor, but I guess in my case it was literal, too. I find when someone is gone I even miss the things that I couldn't stand about them. It's silly, but true.

I remember the Synagogue as a dark, dank, and quiet place. It scared me more to go than I wanted to admit, even as a young girl. So many grownups looking dour and depressed, why would a child want to go be around that? It was even harder for me to sit still on Sabbat, especially in my adolescence. It's Saturday people! Come on, let's do something!

I can barely see their faces now, just smoky impressions in my mind: Mother, Father, Elizabeth, and Bubbeh. I would give almost anything to sit still in our living room again, and let them prattle on about our faith, or even meaningless chit-chat. You never do realize what you have until it's gone; even now I will pick up a stick of Blackjack gum when I see a pack, which is admittedly rare. It still tastes like shit, but that's the point. The past is bitter because we don't appreciate it while it is the present, and we are too stubborn to let it go once it's gone.

We all have moments where we want to go back and do things all over again, even to make the same painful decisions, just to see the old faces we left behind so they can come back into focus instead of falling into hazy memory. Is it more painful to lose someone, or lose them from your memory? Are they even the same person? What you remember and who they were?

Ah...there are times when I just want to see them. I just wish………

***

Vegas…I hate this town, Grey thought as he walked down the sidewalk lining the Strip. *They finally put that stupid neon cowboy to rest, only to drag him back out as a shopping mall decoration. People are people, and vices are vices. We all have them. It just ain't right to profane such a quiet desert valley like this. This place was created for a few folks to enjoy at a time, unspoiled, a little "Desert Solitaire".* He had arrived via foot from the south and was slowly headed up Las Vegas Boulevard, past the giant onyx pyramid, lingering in front of the castle that looked, to Grey, to be made from monstrous children's stacking blocks. The sun was starting to drop behind Red Rock Canyon to the west, and the lengthening shadows around the casinos were all but boiling over with lesser demons waiting for the sun to set fully. They reached out with clawed fingers to touch passersby or growl out suggestions, trying to influence the weaker-willed tourists. They did none of these things when Grey came near; they simply drew back as far into the shadows as they could and watched him with hooded eyes whispering to each other until he passed.

Not knowing where to start, Grey sat down on a bench next to a handful of Hispanic men handing out flyers for female companionship. Las Vegas was a large place to be directed to search for something, especially when that something was over-the-top demonic activity. *Like a needle in one God damned big haystack*, Grey thought as he watched a succubus guide a passing couple into the path of the prostitution hawkers. Vegas was one of the few cities he had visited that actually came alive more when the sun went down than when it was up. Demons cavorted about among the living, without anyone batting an eye, colored lights bathed them all, mortal and demon-kind alike as they paraded in front of him on his bench. He toned the power levels emanating from him down in hopes of blending in more with the surroundings, just another gray shadow among many, as the darkness was held at bay by flashing billboards the size of movie screens. He was well-known the world over; the bogey man that other bogey men were afraid of. Grey would need to disappear to both mortals and the dead if he were to find what he was looking for.

Like any hunter he sat as motionless as possible in an attempt to lull his prey in. Hour after hour passed and Grey sat statue-like, legs crossed in front, arms stretched out along the bench's backrest, a picture of relaxed silence. The night moved forward without any hint of the crowds thinning, when Harmony's voice spoke within Grey's mind. The stoic man showed no outward sign that he had heard her say, "Are you simply going to sit there all night, Jasper?"

If I have to darlin', he responded mentally, never uttering a syllable or shifting an eye.

"The others are on their way," Harmony continued.

Good, Grey thought in response, still not moving the tiniest bit of his countenance for risk of alerting any demons that may be obliviously wandering close by.

"Raven spoke to me."

Grey's reserve all but cracked, causing him to lift an eyebrow, *No shit?*

"Perhaps she is healing, growing, and moving past her anger," Harmony said warmly. "Any of those would be a welcome change."

Always her that needs to change, huh, darlin'?

"Oh shut up, Jasper! I do not need your condescension," she snapped. After a short pause where the nocturnal fauna of Vegas continued to pass Grey by, her tone still held an unaccustomed level of petulance when she said, "They should be here the morning after tomorrow. Just sit there and do whatever it is you are doing for the next two days for all I care." The huff in her voice followed her as she retreated from Grey's consciousness.

Oh, I don't reckon it'll take that long, Grey thought, looking over at a group of diminutive rodent-like demons that were congregating around a fan that blew a mist of water on passersby, to offer a bit of respite from the desert heat. Even at night the city could still bake a person. The demons were chatting in a loose circle, taking the occasional break to glance up the skirts of the more attractive female tourists who stopped for the cooling mist, gesticulating wildly if one of them happened to not be wearing undergarments.

Grey left his bench and moved casually in their direction, just another tourist out among the throng, hoping to win big, recoup some loses, find a little company, or some form of small release from their daily grind. Grey was within a few steps of the demons when he started to overhear the one whose back was turned in his direction telling a story. "So, Eduardo says to this blond, 'Look baby if you want a *Zhu Zhu Pet*, Eduardo can squeak when you rub his tummy, too'!"

The other two looked up at Grey as he towered over their companion. The smiles vanished from their diminutive features as the innumerable city lights made it so he barely cast a shadow across their little gathering. "What?" asked the demon whose back was turned. His companions simultaneously pointed tiny fingers at

Grey and then shot off into the night in opposite directions, leaving the speaker on his own. He turned around slowly, eyes casually following up all of Grey's ropey six feet glaring down at his barely one foot of stature.

The typical reaction was that of the demon's compatriots, so Grey was surprised when the rodent-esque creature blurted out in a no nonsense voice, "Well? What the hell do you want?"

The demon punctuated this with gestures of raised eyebrows, paws cocked on hips, and toe tapping in impatience. "Come on now tall, dim, and ugly. Eduardo ain't got all night? Spit it out, what you want?"

Grey started to laugh; he could not help it. The humor of the moment overwhelmed his natural inclination to intimidate the demon. "Ha! Ha hahaha."

"And what's so fucking funny, string bean?" the demon demanded stomping a foot no larger than a rabbit's.

"You, littl'un," Grey said when he caught his breath, "standing there, barely a foot tall with the neon lights makin' you look like a giant blue hamster. Do you know who I am?"

"Sure do 'Officer Badass', but guess what, amigo?" Eduardo said, pointing a finger in Grey's direction. "Eduardo knows the score. He ain't doing anything outside of his nature, or threatening to tip the Balance. You can't do shit to him. So, either spit out what you want or keep moseying on cowboy. This is Eduardo's spot!" He stomped his foot again for emphasis.

Grey stopped laughing completely, and sized the tiny demon up. After a moments consideration he said, "My apologies… Eduardo, was it? You're right, I ain't here for you. So I'm asking your assistance in findin' a group of demons pretending to be vampires. Can you help direct me?"

"What's in it for Eduardo?" he said with a sniff of his snout.

"Pardon me?"

"Look, Eduardo ain't got to help you," the demon said pointing another claw at Grey. "If Eduardo does, he should get a little sumpin sumpin out of the deal, you know? Why should Eduardo stick his neck out for you?"

Grey mulled this over momentarily. "Fair enough. What would you like?"

It was Eduardo's turn to fall silent, thinking of viable requests. His fevered mind spun at the possibilities before he stammered out, "Uh…from you? Guess an I.O.U. would be enough…..within reason of course." He added quickly at the look of disapproval on Grey's face. As an afterthought, to sweeten the deal, he squeaked, "Eduardo does know where they are."

"Done," Grey said nodding his head once in a gesture of approval.

"Really? Cool! Um….They're north of the city, hiding out in some caves by day and prowling through the old downtown at night. They ain't doing that sexy European vamp act neither, officer. These mother fuckers are just tearing into people, angels, and demons alike; it don't matter to 'em. When they get their claws on ya, it's over. If it's living people, they dump the bodies out for the sun and desert scavengers to take. So many people from all over the world come through here; these dipshit meat puppets don't even realize what's going on," Eduardo said sweeping a hand out at the passing throng.

"Where north of town?" Grey asked. "Do you know specifically?"

"Not for sure no, but Eduardo overheard someone say something about 'Valley of Fire'. Maybe they're hanging out up there in those rocks? Dunno for sure."

A very buxom brunette, sheathed in a tight black dress, slinked past them, pausing at the cooling mist fans, oblivious of Grey and Eduardo. Her presence completely stopped their conversation as she tilted her head back to let the spray land seductively on her neck. Quietly groaning, she traced her index finger along the moist places the fan left on her skin as a group of Asian businessmen eyed her from a nearby café table. Eduardo stammered, tongue lolling from his stubbed rodent features, "Uh, is that enough cowboy? Because Eduardo needs to go take a look at this, okay?"

He was already edging off in the woman's direction when Grey said, "Yep, thanks littl'un. I do owe you one."

Grey started to head north along the strip, walking toward old Vegas in hopes of catching a glimpse of his prey while they fancied themselves the predators. Eduardo laid down on his back, squirming around between the brunette's tanned legs to get a better vantage point, as Grey left the demon to his pleasures. Passing the herds of vacationers out for a night on the town, Grey was almost beyond ear shot when he heard Eduardo yell, "God damn Vegas! That was a dude!"

***

Pete decided that riding a motorcycle, traveling at insanely fast speeds down a highway at night, was not the experience of terror he had always assumed it would be. Of course, since he was dead and no longer had to worry about his skin becoming ground hamburger if he crashed, this admittedly changed his outlook a bit. The question of who would ride with whom on the motorcycles became moot after the incident with the pedophile demon. Zeus would not allow Hank out of his sight. He had trudged back to the Beer

Bear, with Hank on his shoulders, to retrieve the convertible while the Riders were rousing and fortifying themselves for the trip west.

The convertible raced into the motel's parking lot as the Riders were mounting their chrome steeds. If anyone was surprised to see Hank's small baseball-capped head peering out from behind the steering wheel they kept their opinions to themselves. Gabe and Lucifer piled into the backseat of the convertible, leaving only Pete and Raven to ride piggyback. This seemed to appease the Riders. Pete did not ask who it was that they did not want to chauffer. He was content that it was not him, but the surreptitious glances they continued to send Lucifer's way were answer enough. Being able to converse with Dante, via Harmony's translation, had engendered some camaraderie between Pete and the tall mute. That, and Dante had smiled and winked instead of asking questions when he overheard Pete tell Raven, "Hey since we're dead, could this make me the *Ghost Rider*? That would work for a nickname, right?"

Raven simply ignored him as per an agreement she and Grey had made months ago to stop acknowledging it when Pete suggested a new name for himself. Dante's reaction had surprised Pete and worried him until Harmony had spoken up, "They suspect there is something more to you all than they know. Dante there is simply the most perceptive of them. He can see more than most, but not all. Do not worry overmuch about it, Peter."

Glowing eyes glaring, upside down bat-like from the underside of an approaching overpass brought Pete out of his ruminations. He tapped Dante on the shoulder and pointed in the watching demon's direction. Dante shook his head, cocked his neck as far back over his shoulder as he safely could, and raised a questioning eyebrow at Pete.

"Never mind!" Pete yelled to be heard over the engine; Dante shrugged an acknowledgement and went back to watching the road.

Not letting themselves be seen by the living, huh? Pete mentally asked of Harmony.

"No, Peter," she said. "They are keeping a low profile, observing. I am not sure if it is a result of what transpired last night or if they are taking orders from someone else."

Someone else, huh? Like Malign or do I need to start worrying about some new badass demon? Adolph Hitler still hanging around somewhere? Is he going to start destroying all the Jewish and Black ghosts?

"Not yet."

"Not yet." Not yet? Great, wonderful, let's give old Pete some ambiguous answer. That way later when something is chewing on his ass she can say, "Now is the time to worry." Well no shit? Gee thanks, I never would have figured that

out on my own...You and Grey are just two peas in a tightlipped pod, lady.

"Oddly, Peter, he says that you are rubbing off on me," Harmony's voice held more than a trace of mirth as it echoed through Pete's mind.

Pete was quiet for a time, both externally and internally as the distant Midwestern plains soared past them, under the cover of night. Occasionally lights from a small town, more likely a village or municipality, would shine out like an island of illumination in the dark, only to be swallowed by the night's ravenous appetite once again. This was one of the aspects of his relationship to Harmony that Pete had come to enjoy. He could stop in the middle of a conversation to collect his thoughts - even though she knew what he was thinking before he said it - and pick up the conversational thread without the social hitch this would cause among living people. When he finally responded he said, *This is another one of those perspective things isn't it? We interact with you however we perceive you. It must be hard for you, never really being yourself. Is there really a 'you', Harmony? I don't mean that to sound rude ma'am, but I wonder at times.*

"Yes, Peter," she said with an edge of sadness coloring her tone, "to all of them."

Her presence retreated in Pete's mind after she spoke. It was the farthest she had placed herself from him, without completely closing the door, as she had done only once before when Pete had first started to work for the Balance. *Great, Pete,* he thought to himself now. *You never were good with the ladies, even while you were alive. No wonder Raven ignored you when you suggested "Lando" for a nickname. Billy Dee would be ashamed of you man.*

Another demon, this one perched atop a highway light post, stared down at him as they passed by, going well over the speed limit. It looked just like the one from the night before and it was identical to the one that had glared down at him from the overpass; possibly it was the same one. Pete had not been paying attention when they had passed before to see if it had taken wing, following them. Different version on the same design, he guessed. Large bats with fangs, vampires, each demon was an entity unto itself. Some were strong enough to become shape shifters on this side of life, and others, as Grey had taught him, were subject only to their nature. What a person looked like on the inside for their mortal life was what they turned into in the next one. Grey called it poetic, but Pete sided with Raven's more direct opinion; she called it justice.

Pete had once asked Grey during a lull in missions why the less powerful demons they came across always had the appearance of animals or beast-like creatures. Grey responded in his typical cowboy drawl, "Well, Pete, you ever hear of reincarnation? Yep, I thought as much. Most people now-a-days have. Somewhere along the line some holy man or swami or whatever it is they call themselves could see enough of our side to notice all the animal-like demons, and they made the assumption that those demons were just people being reborn into a lesser creature than man because of their actions in life. Well, like so much of the world's religions, they got close, but mixed up the details a bit. Got to give'em credit for trying though."

As Pete watched, the vampire bat demon took flight from its post and followed their motorcycle cavalcade down the highway. He spoke aloud, even though he knew nobody would hear him, "I wonder, *Count Chocula*, do you really look like that, or are you just wearing a mask? Maybe you're just somebody's pet, and your master made you look that way. Yeah…I wonder."

The demon flew ahead of them going far beyond where Pete could see even with his augmented sight; all he could make out was that the creature was also heading west.

***

Three vampire demons slunk in and out of oblivious passersby as they prowled down the sidewalk. Grey watched them from a discreet distance. He had been tailing them for the last half hour after he had spotted them from the roof of The Fremont Street Experience where he had set up his stakeout. When he first saw them among the crowd, the vampires had grabbed a small passing demon that was spending his time much as little Eduardo had and tore it to pieces, laughing at its feeble protests. The vampires had not devoured the lesser demon, taking its energy for their own. This in and of itself was cause for concern. Grey had seen many things over his long years, but it was a very rare sight to see a demon pass up the opportunity to gain power of any kind, even a tiny morsel such as that. *Like a politician telling the truth*, Grey thought as he watched the vampires, *that just ain't done. Something's up*.

Even if he had not been looking for these particular demons, he would have trailed them to see what was going on. He had dropped down from the pedestrian mall's roof, looking back to see "Vegas Vic" giving him a wink. Grey sighed and rolled his eyes at the Las Vegas cowboy icon, thinking to himself, *You'd have been shot dead on sight back in the real West. Nice hat and scarf, asshole. It would only be justice if a hundred years from now they put up a neon yuppie in cabana wear instead.*

The demons had already passed by, giving Grey enough distance that he could follow them inconspicuously. He observed them from behind the crowd, walling off his power as much as he could in an attempt to lessen his presence, much as he had earlier in the night. Only doing so was harder on the move and he had trouble achieving the state of equilibrium he needed to disappear completely while in motion. From behind a corner kiosk selling timeshares, Grey watched the demons bully their way through the throng. They did not take physical bodies but were purposely pushing energy over into the land of the living: bumping into people, groping women, and upending coin buckets to the owner's dismay. *Harmony*, he spoke internally, *you seeing this darlin'?*

Her response was instantaneous and succinct, "Yes."

Well, earlier they tore apart a sub-demon without absorbing its energy. You see that, too?

"No, no I did not."

You know better'n I do how rare that is. Look at these fools, strutting around like a bunch of thugs. I don't know what your take on it is, but even if this ain't what I'm lookin' for this needs to be checked into.

"Yes, Jasper, I fully agree. Follow them, though I suspect that was already your intention."

Damn right, Grey thought as he watched the vampire demons pick up another lesser demon that was too slow to avoid them. It screamed like a man stepping barefoot on a child's ill-placed Lego while going for a midnight pee as they tossed it around like a football. They had progressively moved south so that they were now on the uppermost reaches of the Strip. None of the tourists were reacting to them; Grey had not expected them to, but he had dealt with many demons who flouted the rules before, showing themselves to the living whenever it pleased them. One of the vampires darted across the heavy traffic as if going out to receive a pass. The vampire holding the squirming sub-demon cocked its arm back, and then threw the small creature like an All-Pro quarterback. The massive amount of energy being literally tossed about spilled over into the physical world as a tour bus hurtling past, well over the speed limit, crashed into the small demon. The little demon screamed even louder as it soared through the air, but fell silent when it splattered against the windshield of the bus. Safety glass caved in causing the bus driver to jerk the wheel in surprise. Never regaining control the driver futilely spun the wheel as the bus crashed into oncoming traffic and tipped over onto a milling throng that was standing along the curb waiting for the light to change so they could cross.

      Screams and shrieks filled the air, and to Grey's hearing, laughter as well. The vampire demons were sitting in a grassy area next to the Strip laughing hysterically at the mayhem they had wrought. *Like a bunch of God damned teenagers*, Grey thought. Turning his attention back to the wreckage he could see the slow transformation of the tourists. Minutes ago they had been simply out for a night in a city that never slept, staring wide-eyed at all the goings on. Then the next they were being forced out of their scintillating idyllic setting into a nightmare of chaos, blood, and death. The vacation was over now for many of them and their minds did not want to process that information.

People were running about half terrified and half drunk. Some were checking on the passengers of the overturned bus, others were attempting to drag a woman out from under the bus whose legs were trapped under the roof. The pandemonium was compounded by the fact that Las Vegas had changed over the years in regards to what nationalities the tourists were. The devaluing of the American dollar had caused an increase in foreign travelers who could make an average wage in their country and come to Vegas for vacation, only to go to a currency exchange and double their spending money. *I remember a time when it was just fat white folks in Hawaiian shirts, now look at this. Fifty people screaming at each other in five different languages. Christ people! That woman under the bus is screamin', "Don't move me!" in Portuguese, but those Japanese men yanking on her arms don't understand her. What a cluster fuck!*

Grey stood back, shaking his head, taking it all in. He had seen much worse in his tenure, but it always bothered him when people compounded their misery, doing the demon's work for them. As if the universe wished to recognize Grey's observation, there was an overweight man in a Hawaiian shirt running about in a stooped posture. Grey focused on him after having so recently thought of how the man's type was a dying breed in Las Vegas. *What are you doing there, partner?* Grey thought, as the man continued to crouch and scoop, *Oh for the love of…you're stealing all the dropped winnings, aren't you, tubby? Yes sir, I've seen enough.*

He was so busy musing on the scene that he did not notice a sleek black limousine pull up alongside the vampire demons until one of them stop laughing and walked over to the rolled down window. It leaned in speaking to a figure Grey could not see, placing a clawed hand on its cocked hip as it conversed. While the EMTs raced onto the scene of the crash the demon chatted to the occupant of the limo like a neighbor across a picket fence, just gossiping away. Grey stared more intently at the limo as another of the vampires bundled a startled tourist into the backseat when the door sprung open. All three of the vampires then hurried into the luxury vehicle. In all the commotion with the overturned bus, not a single soul looked in the direction of the limousine as it left with its victim.

It eased into the slowly moving traffic that was being directed around the accident. The vampire demons had piled out of the sunroof and taken positions on top of the luxury car sitting Indian style, soaking in the last drops from the chaos they had wrought. When the limo was close to passing Grey's vantage point an elegant blond woman in a blood red dress stood up in the open skylight. She had her back to him, but Grey could make out a graceful curving neck exposed by hair held up by jade chopsticks. She turned in his direction just as the car passed him; her features were beyond beauty. Wars had been fought for women of lesser grace than she.

The woman winked a shadowed blue eye in Grey's direction, sending him a kiss with her right hand, and waving a tiny *prom queen on her float* bye-bye wave with her left. The vehicle turned a corner and disappeared into the night. Grey stood motionless, watching after the limo, and breathed in a deep lungful of the desert air to calm his nerves before growling, "Malign."

Chapter 8

In my early years of service for the Balance I spent a good deal of time with a "babysitter" when Harmony needed Grey for a mission she deemed too dangerous for someone so new to the trade. That was when Wandjina would look after me. She had been an Aboriginal Australian in her physical life. She taught me about her people's beliefs, and how the Dreamtime, as she called it, her people's religion and mythology, was so close to the world she inhabited now that her people did not have the fears and issues so many other cultures do when they die.

Not many of my fellow soldiers can understand Wandjina. She flits in and out of this world and the Source; some think she comes back after moving on, but she still leaves a certain portion of herself here to come back to. She is in two places at once, like she was in life, awake and asleep. Some even have trouble seeing her because she may or may not be wholly with them. It is a beautiful way to exist, but one that I could never duplicate. To do so would necessitate a level of letting go of this world that I just can't seem to do.

Dreams are important; they act as a sort of pressure relief valve for the physical body's psyche. I never gave them much thought when I had a body that required sleep...at least not until the end. In Auschwitz, dreams were an escape, a needed deviation from reality that could keep your sanity intact for another round of brutalization the next day. Before then though, a dream was just a dream; some good, some bad, but, for me, they never held the power Wandjina claimed they did.

"The spirits dreamed us into existence; the Source had a dream my child, a dream of wonder. Harsh truths, soft falsehoods, all intertwined to create this world," she told me. "It is beautiful and awful at the same time that is why we stay and do what we can to help. Yes?"

I agreed with her without knowing what she was talking about. How could I not. Maybe she was right. She seemed to exist as a shade among ghosts. If she wasn't correct, then at least she believed it strongly enough for it to work for her. I think that is all anybody can take from their faith or religion; if the dream is real enough for them, then that is all that matters. To the rest of us it is just confusing images jumbled together, and told as a story or dream...or nightmare I guess, depending on your perspective..........

***

Eric Metronnie - the being who had once been an angel, but a very long time before that he had been a man first, a man named Enoch - had forgotten what it was like to have nightmares. It was one of the drawbacks to a physical body he had not had to deal with in so long, that it surprised him when he realized he needed to sleep again. Let alone, that the human psyche was such an odd, almost foreign, construct that it would insist on showing him images of his fears or failures all through what was supposed to be a period of rest. He had not been a very sound or comfortable sleeper before the incident with the demon and his now trashed Bentley. That occurrence had gifted his subconscious mind with a whole new parade of images to torture him through the night when he attempted to sleep.

Each time he dozed off the resulting dream was the same. The vampire demon landed on the hood of his car, Maggie screamed, and her annoying little dog barked. Each time in the dream he could not move, could not react as he had in real life, stopping the demon from harming her. In the dream his foot was frozen in place on the accelerator. He was unable to shut his eyes as the demon tore Maggie's throat out and lapped at the gushing blood, all while they sped out of control down the deserted ink-black highway. Admittedly the dream was not all bad for Eric, the part where the demon snapped the yapping dog's neck was quite satisfying, but still he kept waking up yelling in a tangled heap of sheets and sweat, Egyptian cotton soaked and reeking of terror, failure, and rose petal fabric softener.

Three times in the same night were enough to prove to Eric that he should let go of his futile attempts at rest and just stay up until the sun rose. He brewed a pot of coffee and loaded a tray with fine baked goods to accompany his full carafe, carrying them up to the roof of his house where he had a pool, spa, and lounge area that he liked to frequent during his regular bouts of insomnia. It was a comfort to him, to watch the slowly lightening sky creep toward dawn, reminding him what it was that he was trying to preserve - the beauty and splendor of an untainted world, given a fresh start every morning.

He sat back in a poolside Adirondack lounge chair, putting his feet up on a weather-treated ottoman and sipped at his coffee. When he tilted his head to the side he could see several vampire demons perched on his nearest neighbor's Spanish tiled roof. Eric could make out their silhouettes and glowing eyes from where he sat. Not sure if they knew he was aware of their presence, he kept still and thought, *Have they been there all night? And if they have, how many nights have they been watching me? Is this the first, or have I been stalked longer than they've let on?* As if they could hear his thoughts the demons took wing and flew toward his deck. In one fluid motion all four of them landed. They were all identical in shape and size. He could not tell if one of them was the same demon from two nights previous or if they were all new.

In his surprise the coffee mug fell from his fingertips shattering, sending fragments of porcelain into the pool, as the group's obvious leader prowled forward, snarling and hissing in that not quite language of theirs. The brown beverage that had trickled into the illuminated water with the ceramic shards gave the impression of blood diffusing. Eric could not be sure with their identical outward appearances, but some instinct told him the demon moving in his direction was the same one he had left by the highway in a cage of light.

It stopped out of reach snarling, this time in English, "You are getting weak old one. We can feel it, taste it, smell it, but she warned us not to take you….yet. It is enough for now that you know that we could, if she let us."

The demon took wing, hovering over the pool causing the surface to ripple and slosh, before it flew into the bruised colored sky. The first rays of the sun were brightening the horizon, seeming to chase the monster away. Its followers leapt to join it, cackling madly as they flew off. Eric was sure of the demon's identity when he heard it call back to him before disappearing completely into the shadows, "Sweet dreams….puppet."

***

The rising sun set the eastern rock faces ablaze in a riot of colors: oranges, reds, yellows, and ochers. Grey topped a rise and descended into the valley without a doubt as to the origins of its name. After miles and miles of brown characterless desert the Valley of Fire burned up from the ground. Weary from his travels Grey took a moment to soak in the energy of the landscape as it poured from the rocks, illuminated by the sun and bathed by the sky. Many places on the earth were natural fonts of power; humanity is drawn to them instinctually, yet as a species man cannot enjoy the beauty and energy of what exists naturally. It may have drawn them there, but it is not enough to keep them there for a vacation. Very few spots exist that have not yet been tainted by mankind's desire for extra activities and diversions. *Thank goodness*, Grey thought, *this place is just far enough and yet close enough to Vegas to keep them from slapping up an amusement park or go-cart track.*

The valley was remote enough that the tour groups would not be heading to it in throngs until after they had had their buffet breakfasts. He had time to explore the lay of the land without dodging the day trippers who wanted a break from the electric glitter and felt the draw to natural settings. Grey climbed to the top of a columnar spire and sat down to survey the desert landscape Eduardo had said the vampires were hiding in. The power bubbling up around him led him to believe it was a probable location for their daytime hideout. Normally the absence of an angelic presence in such a tableau of natural splendor would have been enough to signify heavy demonic activity, but out here, where there was very little human life to accompany them, it was not the give-away it would typically be. Angels were social creatures; often they stayed behind out of love, most times for their fellow man.

Upon reflection Grey found it sad that most times he could bully if he had to, or at least barter, information out of demons. They seemed to be more inclined to understand threats than angels. Demons would look at a situation from many angles, searching to find the best possible outcome for themselves, so handing over information to the bogeyman typically seemed like a good way to go on existing. But angels, with a few exceptions, gave him as wide of a berth as they could. Had there been an angel out and about in the state park, he doubted it would have been willing to help him. *I wonder*, Grey thought, *just who is that a reflection on? Them or me?*

He jumped down from the rock spire, sending a cloud of reddish grit up into the morning air as he landed, pushing some energy back into the solid world. He decided to follow the road that ran through the park, if only for a trail to meander along, because Grey doubted even the blatant demons he had seen in Vegas would have the audacity to set up shop along the blacktopped throughway. No matter how brash the vampires had been in the city last night, in the day they would want to be left alone, not be subject to an endless parade of Bermuda shorted legs tromping in and about their lair and then rushing back to their air-conditioned cars or buses all day long. No, their den would be somewhere far off the road, in a cave, hiding within the rocks or under the loose soil until dusk swept across the landscape once again.

    The road twisted and turned in among the red plinths of rock, never providing much of a view from ground level beyond the next curve. A jackrabbit hopped out in front of Grey as he rounded a bend, its huge ears sticking up almost comically from its head. It stopped in the middle of the road staring directly at Grey. He had not bothered creating a physical shell since the yuppie faux vampire party in Santa Fe, so it surprised him some that the rabbit seemed to notice him. Animals could, at times, see past the physical world and into the realms of the spirit, but those were typically the creatures who shared more time with humanity: dogs, cats, and horses - not the wild ones like this desert hare. "You see me, friend?" Grey asked the jackrabbit.

    The rabbit cocked its head when Grey spoke, wiggling its hindquarters in preparation of bolting. "Go on! Shoo! I don't want to be responsible for some car runnin' you down." He took a few steps in the rabbit's direction, but the hare did not flee as instructed. Grey kept walking slowly toward it. The jackrabbit looked up at him when he stood over it. He crouched down, slowly reached out and started stroking the rabbit gently behind its massive ears. It bristled as Grey's energy mingled with it, but leaned into the touch when light blue sparks started to cascade down its coat gathering around its paws on the red sand soil. Grey chuckled, saying, "I'm going to be mighty pissed off if a tiny maroon eye starts blinking out at me from between those big old ears of yours, friend."

A slight growling sound punctuated by the small skittering of gravel rolling down a hillside interrupted them, startling the hare, and breaking the connection it was sharing with Grey. It looked quickly in one direction and then took off bounding in the other.

Grey stood up from his crouch, looking off in the direction of the sounds. He started walking toward where the noises were coming from out of no definitive logic other than needing a place to begin his search. Only a few yards from the road, just out of the line of sight for a passing car, Grey found the source of the commotion in this quiet panorama. A coyote was gnawing on the lower portion of what Grey assumed was the tourist he had seen bundled into Malign's limo the night before. The wild canine was so busy worrying on the exposed calf muscle that it did not sense Grey's approach. *It can't be this easy*, Grey thought to himself.

Leaving the scavenger to its meal he started to follow the drag marks the coyote had left - deeper into the park - as it had pulled the large hunk of traveler. Along the way he found an arm and what was left of the poor soul's scalp. *Well I don't suppose I can call a toupee a scalp*, he thought as he kicked it over, *but out of respect for the recently deceased, partner, I suppose I can let the rug slide as a scalp this time.*

After a long hike he discovered a large area of disturbed soil that told him the coyote had defended its meal against another of its kin and torn bits of cloth, and fur scattered about the surrounding creosote bushes proved it to have been quite the tussle. Looking around, Grey realized that he had followed the trail deep into the park, possibly now off park property. *Borders don't mean much out here and Malign ain't exactly averse to trespassing in any event*, he thought. Inspecting the disturbed patch of ground where he now stood left him no doubts that this was where the vampires had dumped the body. There were no tracks leading off in any direction other than from where he had come. "Well shit, I suppose I should've given the bitch more credit than that. She'd have devoured any demon too stupid to cover its tracks, just like a post-nookie praying mantis."

The surrounding rocks did not respond to Grey's monologue. The sun had risen high enough now that the rattlesnakes and other coldblooded critters were starting to venture out to soak up the heat. Grey walked over to the nearest mound of boulders to climb up and hopefully gain a better vantage point of his location. When he neared the rocks he noticed primitive art adorning their surface. In many places the indecipherable blobs and whorls were high off the ground leading him to wonder how primitive humans had reached those heights. "Shit, more importantly, why would they?" Grey asked the empty desert.

"Why would they what?" A cultured female voice called out from just behind Grey. He spun around faster than a mortal man could blink, coming face to face with Malign. She had changed out of her elegant party attire from the previous night into a well-tailored sun dress that, to Grey's eye, was far more pleasing in its simplicity. She arched an eyebrow at him and asked again, "Why would they what? I notice that you're still randomly shifting between thinking and saying things aloud. I shouldn't be surprised really. Everyone says, 'Grey never changes'. "

Grey did not bother to respond to her. He stared without emotion, and held as much energy as he could at the ready. She smiled at his bland expression saying, "Oh, we're going to play it that way are we? Fine, I suppose I should not have expected anything as civil as a conversation out of you."

She turned, nodding her pert chin in the direction of the indigenous art, "They call them *petroglyphs* now. I assume that's what you were inspecting, yes? Historians love to label things don't they? Silly old men sitting behind silly old desks. Of course, they are so far removed from the men and women who etched those that it is all guess work, but they'll tell their contemporaries and the common peons that it is established fact. That one there." She pointed to a red blur that looked oddly similar to a roulette wheel, lending the ancient artwork a hint of profane prophecy given what city would spring up a short distance south from there a couple of millennia later. "That is *enyette*, a word forgotten in time, by most. It signifies the power that radiates all through the valley, the natural energy that has drawn so many here. I'm sure you feel it, Jasper, running deep and strong." She leaned forward, tracing a long red-nailed index finger along the carving.

"Don't you call me that," Grey ground out from his clenched jaw.

"Oh good, so you are going to speak to me. Here I thought I'd just go on prattling to the desert like you so often do. And I'll call you by whatever name I like, Jasper. It is yours after all or was I wrong all those nights long ago when you had me calling it out to the stars as I lay on my back? Hmm?"

"That don't mean a damn thing and you know it!" Grey snarled at her, breaking his calm, "I had no idea who or what you were at the time. I didn't even know creatures like you existed back then. I was a man; there was no way for me to know better. I do now, so don't you dare address me so personally again, you disgusting monster."

Malign placed her hand to her breast as if wounded. "Disgusting monster? Come now, sweetie, I know so many who would say the same of you. Besides, we're a little old for name calling, aren't we?" She started to walk away from him, hips swaying suggestively and unhindered by the sunlight as a lesser demon would have been. She tilted her head up toward it as if taunting the enormous ball of hydrogen to do its worst. Grey did not know how old she was, neither did Harmony on the numerous occasions he had asked her. Malign was possibly the oldest thing on the planet next to Harmony herself and Harmony was a part of the world. She could not exist without it and vice versa, but Malign was an independent entity with a mind all her own. *You sure as shit ain't of this world bitch, but you're definitely in it,* Grey thought. *Who you were don't mean a damn thing in the face of what you are now.*

She turned to look over her shoulder at Grey and casually asked, "Aren't you coming? Or are you just going to go on standing there thinking to yourself all day?"

Chapter 9

I think everyone makes connections in this world differently. It does not matter if it is men and women, girls and boys, friends, lovers, acquaintances, or professionals. Social bonds either form or break depending on how strongly they were forged to begin with. Plus, we also can't discount how hard they are pulled on, of course. The strongest bond can still be broken.

Sex. Looking back it seems like sex used to form a stronger bond than it does now. I suppose in some cases that still holds true: in some distant countries without an overabundance of media exposure where sex isn't used to influence people's choice in purchases, or when the couple forms a strong enough spiritual connection that sex is only a physical representation of that bond. To my jaded perspective it doesn't seem like those cases happen very often. I was still a virgin when I died – I know, you Americans are laughing, saying, "At seventeen, really? Annabelle, you must have been a real uggo." Times were different. It was not like I didn't have the opportunity. It was my heart that held me back. I lived in a world of disapproval and gossipy small town busybodies. I don't imagine that has changed all that much, but my family would have been heartbroken if word started to go about our town rumor mill that I was a tramp or whore. Girls don't seem to care what their family thinks of them anymore; that makes me sad. I would give a thousand hot, young, wax-chested men's desire for me to stay respectable to my family. So, it was out of respect for them that I didn't sleep around during my hormone-driven youth.

Now, sex is still a connector, but not in the spiritual sense, oh no. It is used as a drug to hook people in, to get them off, to sell them things and ideas that they don't need or would never have viewed from that perspective had they not seen some sex symbol act a certain way on the magic box. We had a radio in my home growing up. I don't remember if there were any programs that were suggestive in nature, but no matter how lewd or proper the programming might have been, it is kind of hard to airbrush a voice.

Sure, people had little kinks to their sexual psyches back when I lived. As long as there has been human life I'm sure there has been someone out there who was turned on by something outside of the norm. It seems kind of gross to me to think of a caveman with a foot fetish, but I guess it could have happened. But now things have escalated.

Why, you ask? I say with too much free time in this world full of modern conveniences humanity has become a bunch of monkeys sitting around in suburban cages. You ever watch bored monkeys at the zoo? What do they do? Play with themselves, right? Well, either that or they fling poop around. Though there may be some people who are into that particular kink, most of the apes who lost their hair stick to masturbation instead of the excrement tossing. That's what Grey told me when I asked him about this cultural shift. He said humanity has started to see procreation and sex as two separate things. One is for the continuation of the species and the other is for recreation. Well, what he said verbatim was, "Darlin' once that interweb thing starts coming in interactive 3D, stocks in baby oil will skyrocket and the value of diamond wedding rings will plummet," but with Grey it's the meaning that's important, not how he says it.

Having not experienced the connection of sex in a physical body caused me some...I guess you could call them "mental hiccups" in the afterlife. I wasn't sure how much of my attraction to Grey was leftover mental conditioning from my highly hormonal teenage years cut short and how much of it was honest love. I find it funny now when I hear people refer to an orgasm as "The Little Death". I guess I experienced "The Big Death" first, huh? Talk about giving a girl high expectations; if I'd already had the big one, then how good could the little one be?

Those hiccups and expectations led me to a one night stand with Gabe. I felt if I took a mortal shell and had sex then maybe I would know the difference between that and my feelings for Grey. I think women still - no matter the current cultural views on sex - feel a closer emotional attachment to sex than men do. That's not an accusation boys, don't take offense, but perhaps an inclination toward being more receptive, or in crude terminology, since women take it, we have more of a desire to hold on to it. Men just want to give it away, and get off. Men can still be emotionally connected, don't misconstrue my meaning. It is that they have to fight their natural instincts more, whereas women embrace theirs.

Gabe - now if you ever meet him do not be put off or suckered in by that Irish Sir Humps-a-Lot veneer he shows the world. He is one of the few men I know who still tries to hide what he is…even in death. He is a very passionate and caring man. He hides this because…well his reasons are his. If he wants to share them with you fine, but that isn't my place. Trust me when I tell you the man has fire running through him: spiritual, metaphysical, and metaphorical fire. Don't get me wrong ladies. If you say "yes" he'll do anything you want and most likely a few things you don't want and will be sore from later, but at the time he'll sweep you away so far you won't mind at all.

Did I form a bond with Gabe? Yes. Did I realize what my feelings for Grey really were? No. I suppose that is as close to love as a person can get. You have no idea why it is you want to be around someone; you can't disconnect it from your body, emotions, heart, or soul. It's all tied into one big knot that settles in the center of your chest and connects you to them……….

***

"Raven, I need you to come with me now," Harmony said hurriedly, just as Raven was lying down on a different, yet similarly decorated, motel bed. They had stopped for the day just outside of Denver, and were planning on making it to Las Vegas by sunrise the next morning. Reluctantly sitting back up and scooting to the edge of the bed Raven asked, "Why, what's wrong?"

"It is Grey," Harmony clarified. "He found Malign in the deserts north of Las Vegas. They are conversing for the moment, but I do not trust her with him."

"What?! When…I thought he was just going to scope things out and wait for us?" Raven asked taking a keener interest with the possibility of action looming. "That was the plan, but she made contact with him," Harmony explained.

"She risked daylight?" Raven asked, "Just to talk to Grey?"

"Such concerns are beyond her now, Raven," Harmony said. "She is so very dark that I believe the light only sets her to contrast instead of actually harming her. I do not know what she is planning. She tried to take Jasper from me once, before he passed on. She could not corrupt him then and now I would say such a thing would be as close to an impossible feat as there is in the universe, but still. I would rest easier with you there to back him up and keep him focused."

"Okay, I'm on it. What about Pete and the others?" Raven asked.

"I will notify Peter and he can inform the rest of them. Please, come quickly now." The motel room vanished in a warm light and Raven found herself no longer sitting on the edge of a worn and sagging mattress, but on a rustic log bench. Harmony stood a few paces in front of her, still in the guise of her mother, one arm folded across her waist, and she was nervously chewing on the nails of her other hand. Raven tentatively walked toward her. It was obvious to Harmony that she wanted to say something. "There is no time for us to say anything face to face child. I need you to go to him, now," Harmony said by way of personal greeting and dodging whatever Raven had to say.

She gestured to an area off to Raven's left, and the fairy tale pine woods blurred into a warm orange tinted light. Raven nodded her head, swallowing whatever she had meant to say and moved toward the glowing place. Never turning around, she stepped into the light. Cool damp coniferous forest gave way to oppressive desert heat. Raven took a moment to look around, huge red rocks that looked like insect mounds stuck up from the ground in forms that bordered on artistic. *Where am I?* she asked Harmony.

"You are in a place known as Valley of Fire State Park in Nevada, on the northern tip of Lake Mead," Harmony's voice answered within Raven's mind. "Grey and Malign are just on the other side of that rise where the rocks and buttes are particularly thick."

Harmony guided Raven's vision in the direction she had indicated. Without waiting for further instruction Raven set off on foot at a speed that most race car drivers would envy. She had not bothered to form a physical body when she passed back into the material world via Harmony, so her footsteps made no sound, not even a dab of energy spilled over as she made her way toward the silhouettes on the horizon. Grey was always recognizable to her, from any distance, a functional moving icon, but Malign had so many different forms she favored that identification was only certain if she wanted you to know. Raven had only met her twice before, so she had to take Harmony's information as fact.

Not waiting until she was close enough to overhear the conversation, Raven shouted out, "Get the fuck away from him you bitch!" Raven angled her approach so Grey was not in the line of fire as she materialized twin handguns to shoot with. She started firing at Malign. Violet tinted bullets tore through the dry desert air, all aimed directly at the she-demon's head. Raven was considered by most to be quite the marksman. If she shot at something, she hit it. That, of course, did not take into account when an object, or as in this case demon, disappeared into the ground faster than the eye could track.

Grey finally acknowledged her presence. Turning to her he yelled, "Damn it girl! Now how the hell am I supposed to find out what she's up to?"

Raven kept moving closer to him; she spoke as she closed the distance, "But I thought…Harmony said you were in danger, that I should back you up…"

"Did she or is that how you interpreted it?" Grey asked caustically and started to carry on a conversation internally that Raven was not granted access to. He had his head tilted at an odd angle with his eyes holding that far off dreamy quality that he so rarely allowed others to see. Raven watched him in silence, starting to fume and simmer in her own perspective over this miscommunication. *God damn it!* she thought. *This is the kind of bullshit that keeps me from talking to her. She jumps the gun and Grey blames me! God damn it!*

They stood there, two figures out in the bright desert sun, not saying a word to each other, but carrying on separate arguments. The only audible interruption was the cry of an eagle farther off bemoaning its lost prey, as a ground squirrel or mouse lived to see another day. Into the silence Grey finally shouted, "Enough! Ladies! All of you: human, demon, and…other. I can handle myself just fine. I believe I've rightly proven that time and time again. If I need help, God damn it, then I'll ask for it, mark my words. But, until then, let me handle things my way."

After speaking Grey nodded his head and raised his eyebrows in an acknowledgement that this was the final time he was going to say so, and there should be no more arguments on the subject. He turned his back on Raven and started walking toward the little wisp of Lake Mead that was sticking out on the horizon, his boots crunching over the crumbled red sand. He had only gone a few paces when Malign shot back out from the ground like a sped up time lapse film of a plant growing. She wrapped her body sensuously around Grey's waist hauling all but his upper arms and chest under the ground with her before Raven could shout a warning. Pushing hard on the desert soil, Grey was keeping Malign from dragging him under completely. He managed to turn his head back, rolling his eyes in Raven's direction, and yelled between grunts, "Alright, fine. Help!"

***

"Maggie, I need a favor," Eric asked first thing when the elevator doors opened to his office suite. Maggie was sitting behind the reception desk chomping away on some chewing gum as a counterpoint to her typing. She turned her face away from her computer monitor at the sound of his voice and said, "Sure, Mr. M., anything. What do you need?"

"I need you to…" Eric trailed off as he walked around the office. Looking down at the floor next to Maggie's desk he saw Dolphie was lying perfectly still, fuzzy face buried in his water bowl. The dog had been squeezed into a Halloween costume of a hotdog that proclaimed in embroidery designed to look like ketchup and mustard "I'm a real big wiener". No bubbles escaped the dog's muzzle and its eyes stared glassy and unblinking at nothing. "Uh, Maggie, I think Dolphie…it looks like he had an accident?" Eric asked pointing a finger in the dog's direction, trying to politely tell the girl her dog had drowned in its water bowl.

"Oh, don't worry about him, Mr. M.," Maggie said waving her hands in a shooing gesture. "He's just playing."

She kicked the dog, none too gently by Eric's estimation, and the fluffy white face pulled out of the water bowl, turning, water dripping from its muzzle, to glare up at its master. Maggie said, "See he's fine. What can I do for you, boss?"

"Ah, well…um, yes," Eric said shaking his head to clear it. "I need you to hold down the fort here for a few days, Maggie. It's not like you need me really. I just get in your way most of the time anyhow. You could run all of Re-Vamped Media on your own."

"Well boss," Maggie said with a grin, "when you're right, you're right."

"Ha, thank you Maggie," Eric said, his tone still distracted. "It's always nice to feel needed."

"You know you're irreplaceable, Mr. M.," Maggie said grinning again. "You just like to hear people tell you that. What's up that you need me to hold the fort? Oh! Wait!" she said excitedly waving her hands in front of her face, rapidly fluttering them as if trying to dry nail polish or take flight. "Is this about the…the you know what's? Did God give you like a sign or something? Oh, this is so cool! I bet-"

Eric interrupted the young woman, "Maggie, yes it is about the vampires. I need to find out what that one who attacked us is up to. I cannot do that and run a multimillion dollar company at the same time. Can you handle things while I do that?"

"Absolutely boss," she said, "you can count on me and Dolphie to take care of business." She punctuated the last by giving the small dog another jab with the toe of her pump. The dog whimpered, then submersed its head back in its water dish.

Eric started to leave, absently chewing on his fingernails as he walked. When he reached out to press the down button an idea dawned on him, giving him pause and concern. Turning back to face his aide, he said, "Maggie, one more thing."

"Sure boss, what's up?"

Eric thought for a minute before saying, "If you see any other vampires, please, run for the nearest sanctuary of light: sun, ultraviolet, gosh I suppose even a tanning bed would work. Will you do that for me? Do not, at any instance, try to kill one yourself. Please, promise me. These are very dangerous creatures, Maggie. They may try to harm you to get to me."

"Aw, boss," the young blond woman said looking a bit crestfallen at his request.

"Please, Maggie, I won't feel safe leaving you here alone if you don't promise me," Eric said resolutely.

"Fine, you win," Maggie answered. "Sure thing boss, I promise."

Chapter 10

When I left the bed I'd shared with Gabe – do not think that I snuck away like some precursor to your modern "booty call"; he knew I was leaving and neither of us had needed to sleep once our deed was done, so I left – I, of course, had to pass by his charge, or some might say keeper, Lucifer. Because though Gabe is the current babysitter of that tragic man, it can be hard at times to differentiate who is taking care of whom. He stood, leaning against the same wall as the door I was exiting, arms folded across his thin chest. He turned his head slowly to look at me. I had no shame over having sex with Gabe. It was something I needed to do, but still I felt myself becoming embarrassed at Lucifer's single arched eyebrow. I stammered out, "Hello, Alex."

"Please, Raven," he drawled pushing off from his perch to face me, "there is no need to use our old names. They hardly have even the slightest connection to what we are now. Alexander is simply a title echoing down the ages. I am no longer that man...if I ever was."

My family, and then respectively my community and the religion of my birth, did not have much to say on the existence of the Devil. Many Jewish scholars will argue - they'll call it politely discussing, but they're arguing - over the existence of Hell and the Devil in their scriptures. It doesn't matter to me; I was still familiar as a child with the name Lucifer and what it meant to many other peoples and cultures, so I had trouble calling this handsome, charming rouge by that name. He has always been particularly apt at reading people's thoughts. It was what made him a great leader in his lifetime and it has made him an even greater individual in the afterlife. Only...I think that reading other people's thoughts led to his downfall, too. How could a person cope with all those voices, all that babble and nonsense people think?

"I deal with them one at a time," Lucifer said, "just like any other problem or task. If I did not, they would surely drown me with their shouts."

I cast my eyes away from his. I never have been able to deal with other people who are stronger than I am and flaunt it with such disregard. He reached a hand out to my chin, lifting it up so I would look at him once again, saying, "No, Raven, I hold you in the highest regard. That is why I take an interest in you and your affairs." He said the last with a nod of his head toward the door where Gabe still lay in the warmth of our bed. He continued, "Tell me, did you get what you wanted from him? Did you get what you needed, or neither?"

I thought for a moment before responding. Looking deep into his ice blue eyes I saw honest interest, not something to pass the time for a creature that had walked the earth for millennia. He truly wanted to know what I thought and felt. I said, "I think I got what I needed, but it wasn't what I wanted. Does that make any kind of sense?"

"Perfect sense," he said letting his fingers fall from my chin. He looked away, as if caught up in another place and time. I had thought he was finished speaking, but when I turned to go he spoke again in a dry raspy voice. "When I was a young man, very close to the age you were when you died, there was a story told by some Eastern monks. There was once a traveler who had been wandering the desert in search of answers or salvation or enlightenment; what it was he was searching for is not important though. What does matter is that he was searching, endlessly looking, never finding what he sought, and after a long time he came upon a monastery deep in the sun baked hills. He had had very little to drink or eat on his quest and he was all but perishing due to dehydration and malnourishment. The young man stumbled into the monastery's open doorway, falling to the cool dirt floor bathed in the shadows."

"An old monk came running to his aid. The monk was all wiry gnarled limbs and wrinkles, a lifetime inhabitant of the harsh dry world. He helped the young man to a chair where the boy croaked out, 'Water, please, cold water'."

"The old monk shook his head saying, 'No water. Tea. I have some on the stove. I will be right back with a cup'."

"The young man was nearly delirious, but he had enough cogency to yell after the monk, 'Bring me water you fool! I'm overheating already! Tea will surely be the death of me'."

"But the monk returned with only the promised tea and placed it down next to the boy. The boy was thirsty enough to sip the scalding tea. It was a fluid and his body was demanding that he drink, so he did. When the cup was empty the boy sat watching the monk go about his chores; after a few minutes the monk returned with a slightly cooler cup of tea, saying, 'Drink'."

"The boy drank and the monk subsequently brought him cooler and cooler tea until he finally fetched the young man a cup of water. The shadows had fallen on the sands with the approaching night before the monk said, 'I am sorry to have only brought you tea at first, but your body would have cramped painfully if I had fetched you cold water when you demanded it'."

I smiled and interrupted him, "What he needed, not what he wanted, right?"

"Exactly," Lucifer said waving a hand at the closed door I had so recently shut. *"But that does not mean you have to like it. What they do not tell you in that story is the true ending. How I was so pissed at the monk for proving me wrong that I slit his throat and walked out of that desert monastery into the cold open night."*

He smiled at me, then turned and walked away, without looking back to see my face. I suppose he didn't need to………

***

"God damned she-devil!" Grey yelled while he struggled against Malign's grasping talons as they tried to drag him underground. He could feel her fingers digging claw-like and cold at any of his being that had been submersed under the soil, as if she had a thousand grasping appendages and not the typical ten. Energy was spilling over into the physical world in torrents as the two powerful entities clashed. The ground was cracking open in places, loose dirt and stones were tumbling away on invisible currents of energy. A small ground squirrel whose burrow was too near to ground zero went tumbling end over end into the wind with the debris.

Raven sprinted across the distance separating her and Grey. She hurdled over the tumbling desert detritus and fought her way against the push of energy coming from the fast forming crater where Grey was struggling against Malign. A large dust devil had formed, swirling high about the pair. The evicted ground squirrel had been caught in the hot air draft and squealed as it spun in circuits past Raven. Taking inspiration from the imperiled rodent she let the wind carry her up, rotating around the crater, so she could see down into the pit. She opened fire with her twin Smith and Wessons – mental constructs of the actual weapons used as a focus for her energy – as the dust devil spun her, pouring radiant energy down around Grey's waist where Malign's hold was strongest.

The scream of the demon echoed up and around the canyon land as Raven's violet bullets struck her. Grey pressed his escape as the demon bellowed in pain and anger. Once he had scrambled up the slope of the now large hole that had been dug into the earth, the ragging energy storm dissipated and Raven landed in a graceful spin as the whirlwind vanished. Running over to Grey she could see that from his hips down he had massive black wounds oozing a tar-like substance. He noticed her staring and waved her concern away with the flap of a hand, smoothing out his injuries as he drew energy from the font around them.

Grey flopped to a sitting position, bracing his back against a large boulder, giving his mind the illusion of cover. Raven joined him, crouching down, but still training one gun at the crater's lip she asked, "Are you alright, Grey?"

"Oh, I'm just peachy darlin'," Grey said sounding winded. A rustling noise from the crater had them both staring intently at the hole as Malign hovered into view. She sat cross-legged like a queen on a throne, an invisible throne made of air and darkness, but a throne nonetheless. She was attired once more in an elegant evening gown, delicate feet cradled in high heels, slim and shapely legs begging the eye to follow them up to where the slinky black dress covered skin, but not curve. She tilted her ski sloped nose up toward the sky in recognition of Grey and Raven as they sat at her feet. She cooed, "Well that was rather unpleasant, wasn't it?"

"Unpleasant?" Raven shouted. "Unpleasant? Bitch I'll show you unpleasant." She started firing rounds of energy from her guns up at the hovering demon. Malign glared disdainfully down at her and waved a shadowed hand, deflecting the energy into the surrounding hillside.

"That is quite enough child," Malign spat. Shadows swirled from her fingertips morphing into a pair of black manacles as they shot out at Raven, each enveloped her wrists, pinning them back above her head into the rock wall. "Let the adults play, or you'll be banished to the kid's table until you're big enough to back your threats up properly, hmm?"

Raven glared at the demon while she was held against her will, anger pouring off her in almost visible waves. Red sparks started to fall from her wrists as she strained against her captor and her eyes vanished to smoldering hot pinpoints of similarly colored light. Grey stood up and shouted, "Enough!" With a wave of his hand Malign's control over Raven vanished. A push in the other direction sent Malign somersaulting over the back of her throne. He checked Raven's wrists to make sure she was uninjured and it was her turn to wave off his concern. He turned to the demon as she struggled to regain her dignity, sitting back upright. He growled, "What do you want, Malign?"

"What do I want?" She mimicked, rolling her eyes in disdain. "Jasper, what do I always want, hmm? To cause mischief, mayhem, chaos, and destruction. Honestly, it's like you don't know me at all, you silly man." She chuckled, shaking her head. "I have other more far-reaching designs, but why on earth would I tell you? So you could try to stop me or talk me out of them? Don't be such a clichéd fool. Next you'll tell me this is my last chance, that I should surrender and come quietly."

Malign continued to laugh at them as she turned around, stepping down from her invisible throne onto an equally invisible dais and walked away, slinking and swaying her hips suggestively. She passed through the red rocks of the nearest abutment in the direction she was headed, disappearing from sight, leaving only the echo of her derisive laughter bouncing around the hills.

Under the echoing laughter Grey could hear Raven crying. He looked down to where she had stayed sitting, now with knees drawn up to her chin and her arms wrapped tightly around herself. He took a deep breath of the aromatic desert air, burned stone and carbon from his struggle still lingering heavily about. He kneeled down, placing a hand on her shoulder. He half expected her to shrug it off, but she sat shaking with her sobs as if she had yet to notice the solace he was trying to offer her.

He did not say anything. Never a man to waste words under normal circumstances, he was not about to start now. Grey knew Raven well enough that coaching her out of her sadness would come with action and listening on his part, not platitudes or encouragement. After a time of Grey sitting, sending her soothing energy pulled from the world around him through his hand - the afterlife equivalent of a backrub - Raven spoke, "I hate feeling so weak like that. There was nothing I could do against her, Grey. The bitch could have destroyed me, right then and there. I don't think even you could have stopped her in time. How am I supposed to deal with that, with any limitation? And why am I asking you? It's not like you have limitations. Christ! You didn't really need my help just now, or ever. I bet she jumped you just because of your challenge. I doubt she could have taken you anyway. She was just pushing more buttons."

Grey gestured to the damage he and Malign had caused the formerly pristine landscape saying, "Does that look like the work of a man without limitations to you, darlin'?" As if his question was the cue for some twisted cosmic punch line, the second he stopped speaking the ground squirrel that had been caught up in the whirlwind fell from whatever high spired perch it had landed on, thudding a few feet from Grey's outstretched hand.

Raven snorted over the laugh she tried to hold in. "Sorry, that's cruel, but isn't that how life works, funny and tragic at the same time? We aren't rats trapped in a maze. We're rats trapped in a damn tornado."

Grey nodded, watching the broken rodent twitch its last. A small spark of energy - no larger than a firefly - swirled up from the dead squirrel. It flew a few laps around the corpse, as if looking for a place to land, or a way to get back in, then in a small explosion of light it dispersed and vanished.

After the small animal's spirit had finished moving on Raven turned to Grey and said, "Why can't things ever, just once, work out the way I want them to?"

Still looking out at the desert where the squirrel had died, he said, "By *things* do you mean, universal all-encompassing *things*, or do you mean you and me type *things*?"

Raven shrugged her shoulder and said, "Both, I guess."

"That's what I figured," Grey answered. Shifting so he could face her, Grey said, "Look, darlin', I love you. You know that. I'd do just about anything for you, even lose what's left of myself, but there are times where I wonder if I wasn't wrong in bringin' you over to our side. I think mayhap you'd have been better off like that there critter, passing on tragically then movin' on like your folks and kin did."

Grey gestured again toward the deceased squirrel and looked up at the deep blue sky, checking to see if any more rodents would fall to earth at his motions. When none did he continued, "Darlin', life and afterlife just ain't going to work out for us. That's part of the job; we're the ones who life screwed over, so now we want to do the screwin'. That's my crude way of segueing around to your topic, because I'm past those drives. I left them on a dirt alleyway back in the later part of the nineteenth century. I think you dying so young twisted some of your mental baggage up a bit."

"I love you, but attraction don't have the same meanin' to me no more. Hell, I don't even see the world like that anymore, darlin'. It ain't men and women; things ain't black and white for me!" Pausing to calm himself down, Grey whispered, "All I see are shades of gray."

When he finished Grey turned to look at Raven. She had been facing him through his entire speech and now she was crying again, not body-racking sobs, but leaky faucet tears streaming down from the corners of her eyes. Grey grimaced, "Aw, damn it. I didn't mean to hurt your feelings kid. I just needed to say that is all. Come on don't cry. I - Hey!" he shouted when she reached over and smacked him on the back of the head, sending red and blue sparks tumbling down at her touch. When he turned a questioning expression her way, rubbing the back of his head, she stood up and started walking away.

She called over her shoulder, "I wasn't crying *because* of you jackass! I was crying *for* you!"

Grey watched her walk away in the direction of Las Vegas, still rubbing the back of his head. He looked around in hopes of finding some support in his confusion, but the desert was void of sympathy on all human topics, cares, or concerns. Mentally speaking in his Pete voice, Grey thought, *Crazy ass white woman.*

***

"You did what?" Pete yelled at Harmony when she told him that she had sent Raven to help Grey. "And you didn't think that maybe I could lend him a hand, too? He's my friend, lady! I wouldn't even be here right now if it weren't for him."

"I am well aware of that, Peter," Harmony said. "Apparently it is my night for making mistakes with my soldiers. I apologize; it is nothing personal. I know how you all feel about each other. I only direct you where, in my opinion, you may best be utilized; thoughts of personal choice or preference do not always make it into my calculations. If it makes you feel any better, both Raven and Grey are angry with me as well, though for very different reasons."

"Actually, it kind of does," Pete said around his gas station coffee cup. While the Lone Riders had gone to sleep for the day, Zeus had taken Hank over to a fast food restaurant to play with the other children on the indoor playground, Gabe had headed for the nearest store dispensing alcohol, and Lucifer had suggested coffee instead. Pete had thrown his support behind the demon and Gabe had grudgingly conceded. They had gone to the closest gas station convenience store to buy a few cups of coffee and maybe a snack or two.

Gabe took a sip of the brew before they headed to the counter to pay and grimacing with disgust said, "Seattle's fucking finest my arse!" He then purchased a bottle of Bailey's to liberally garnish his cup with. After a second sip of his now spiked libation he said, "Aye, that's the stuff. Now its Ireland's finest, boys! And how much finer she is." He raised his paper cup in a mock toast to all around him. The young girl at the register giggled when he winked at her with raised cup. "And what's your name, love?" Glancing down at her name tag he continued, "Sasha, now that's a beautiful name for a – hey, knock it off, Lucy!" But his protests were useless as Lucifer drug him out the front doors by the scruff of his neck.

Once the bickering had settled down they set up their own café out behind the station where Lucifer could safely stick to the shadows. That was when Harmony had contacted Pete to tell him she had sent Raven to help Grey. Gabe and Lucifer were staring at Pete as he argued with – to their point of view – himself. Once Pete had filled them in on what had happened Gabe said he would go get Zeus and Hank, while Lucifer said he would awaken the Riders. Both men wandered off to perform their tasks, leaving Pete alone with Harmony. He headed over to the parking lot where the Riders had left their bikes.

"I am not sure that is necessary, Peter," Harmony said to him as he walked. "Things are under control. Besides, even if you leave this very instant, you still will not arrive in Las Vegas until the sun has set."

"Yeah, well at least we'll be there," Pete countered. "If the Riders are too tired, some of us can drive through the day for them."

"And what about Lucifer?" Harmony asked. "Is he supposed to lose power by exposing himself to the light of day, all so you can get to your friends soonest, especially when their need is not the least bit dire?"

"Does the Devil need to know that?" Pete asked her, his voice harder than she had ever heard it before. Reminding her once again that Pete would one day take Grey's place as her strongest knight. Pete's tone and manner were emphasizing why Grey had picked him.

"You are going to lie to him, Peter? Do you think you can bear false witness to a creature as old as Lucifer is? He can read people's minds. He will know you are lying to him before you utter a word."

"Are you going to tell him otherwise? Or Gabe?" he asked.

She was quiet for a span of several breathes, then she cautiously said, "No, I will not. It is your choice. You can deal with the consequences of trying to lie to Lucifer."

Pete nodded his head saying, "Good, then you just watch me."

Chapter 11

We all get so wrapped up in our own stories where we are the main character, the hero, the heroine, the villain, or whatever, so much so that other people around us cease to be real and only count for how they affect our lives, a bit part or a cameo, but they never really exist. Not to us. They don't have stories of their own, lives they live and share with others, where their actions matter beyond our front doors. I have noticed this lack of empathy, this phenomenon - for want of a better term - increasing as the world becomes more technologically advanced and addicted. Everybody is snug inside his or her sanitized little Ziploc bag lives and nothing else exists beyond it, unless it pops up on their phone, computer, or television screen. Yet, even the most sociopathic among us, when they dig way down inside, realizes that every face that passes by them has a story to tell.

When that pizza delivery boy hands you your change and pulls out of your driveway he doesn't disappear or cease to be. He goes back to work, dreaming his dreams as he puts in his hours. Maybe he wants to be a rap music star, sitting in his mother's basement recording videos to stick on the internet in hopes of becoming famous. Or, maybe after he passes out of sight, dreaming those dreams, he isn't paying enough attention and runs over a woman jogging after work - the only time she has to herself between her nine to five workday and the responsibilities of family life. She looks forward to that run every day. It is her "me" time and that poor pizza boy who wants to be a star cuts her run permanently short. Her children won't have mommy kiss them goodnight tonight or ever again. That woman's son goes on to dabble in politics, in the hopes of passing stricter safety laws, so some other little boy does not go through a motherless childhood.

Of course, none of this has affected you yet. It's all hypothetical anyway. I'm simply illustrating a point. You go back inside, turn on the television, and ignore the sirens, because honestly how often do you hear them? They can't always be a real emergency, right? It's probably just some old person falling in the shower. So, you eat your pizza; maybe complain about the cold toppings, or how they can never cut the damn thing even or properly. One slice is always stunted and tiny compared to the rest, right?

Meanwhile a dream ends, a life ends, and a boy cries himself to sleep. It's not callous. I'm not saying you are a bad person. No, there are seven billion other souls running around doing the same thing; it's life.

Then a few decades go by and the motherless son does run for office. He does win, by a landslide. He enacts those stricter safety laws that had driven him so long and so hard. But after a while he realizes that he has spent the better part of his life devoted to putting up a fucking blinking light on a corner. All because some pizza delivery boy, who wanted to be a rap star, happened to drop off a deep dish extra-large deluxe pizza at your house on that particular night? He doesn't know his own children or wife, because don't you believe for a second that politicians still have time for the day to day. When they are elected they no longer live like the rest of you. Sorry Bobby, Daddy has to run, maybe I'll make it to the next big game, slugger. But, he never does; his children hate him and his wife is sleeping with...oh yeah, you guessed it, a pizza delivery boy. So the motherless son jumps off a high building, a pariah to his family, the champion of a cause, but at what price?

So, you see every single face you pass has a story behind it. It is not just you out there. Remember that the tiniest action can affect so much. Maybe all those lives could have been changed if you'd just held the pizza boy up for a second or two longer by giving him a fucking tip. Or maybe a little extra cash distracts him enough that that is what causes the accident. How the story goes doesn't matter, as long as you remember that it is going………….

***

"Raven, darlin' wait," Grey said chasing after her. "Look, I just assumed you were upset over what I'd said about us. It didn't even cross my mind that it'd be otherwise."

Raven was walking south along the desert highway. Cars were passing at high speeds in both directions, their drivers completely ignorant of the two spirits tromping through the rocky median. Raven turned, shouting over her shoulder, "Forget about it, Grey. It's no big deal. If you don't understand me well enough by now it's fine. I don't blame you and I do love you, but you're right. I have to face things as they are not how I want them to be."

Grey had run up alongside her. Once he matched her pace he said, "That's not what I meant, darlin'. I just wanted you to see what the world looks like to me. I wasn't trying to tell you what to do."

She sighed again, blowing another stray bang out of her eyes, "Jesus! I thought you were better with women than this, Grey. Don't you get it? *How* you see things makes me sad. I was wallowing in self-pity over my weaknesses and there you are the great badass cowboy, Grey, who has things worse than I do." She stopped and faced him, as traffic whooshed past, either flocking to Las Vegas or fleeing it. She placed the palm of her hand on his stubble-covered cheek. Looking right into his gunmetal gray irises she said, "The truly sad part is that you don't even see it that way. Do you?"

Staring back into her indigo blue eyes Grey said, "No darlin', I surely don't." Taking that as his cue to walk away first, Grey started moving south toward the city as the sun slowly dipped toward the mountains. Without looking back, as she had, Grey shouted, "We have work to do darlin', let's go."

"Work?" Raven asked running to catch up. "What work, Grey? Shouldn't we wait for Pete and the others? I assume you plan to clear these vampire want-to-be demons out, right?"

"Yes, I do. But I don't need Pete for it. There's only a handful here in the desert. When the sun sets and they come out, you and I will take care of it, Pete or no Pete."

Raven spoke softly, "You just wanted me to change the subject, didn't you?"

"Yep."

"Okay," she said, "I can live with that. So, why don't we gang up and take Malign down? She's been due for ages. With all of us together: you, me, Pete, Zeus, and we have Gabe too - for what that's worth - we could do it. We -"

"No," Grey cut her off, "we can't ever *take her down*, darlin'. That's what always gets my dander up when I got to deal with that bitch."

"What do you mean? If she upsets the Balance, then we end her! Case closed," Raven said confusion blossoming on her normally confident features.

"Wrong, she's too powerful. All we get to do is clean up her messes as they come. Stop her from destroying things with her actions, but as for destroying her? That would cause a power-vacuum without her on top of her demonic pyramid, and who would fill the hole? Lucifer? He ain't nowhere near strong enough; I'd had hopes he would be at some point because Alexander is a more rational, pragmatic creature than Malign. There ain't anybody else I know of who is strong enough. So if we take her out we would end things just as surely as she would with her little wars and games."

They walked in silence for a while as the heat from the sun continued to bake anything not encased in plastic and steel with built in air-conditioning. Despite Grey's prodding neither of them was in any real rush to move things along and go hunting vampires. After mulling it over for a while Raven finally said, "Well…well that sucks. I'd been hoping for years to kill that bitch myself. Why didn't you ever tell me that? How many times have you heard me say those exact words, 'I want to destroy that bitch'? Why didn't you correct me?"

"Sorry, darlin', I didn't want to take that from you," Grey said not looking at her. "Like so many other things, it's just better if we hold on to our versions of how we think things are or should be. It gives us hope, you know?"

***

The chamber was small and cramped, without a single source of illumination either natural or artificial. Malign sat in an amorphous state, hovering around, and only marginally aware of her direct surroundings. She had many such caves, rooms, chambers, and hideaways scattered around the globe that only she knew of. Some were natural fonts of energy, such as the one she had recently been using in the Nevada desert, and others where only she knew of them, secret from prying supernatural eyes, places where she could leave the bulk of her consciousness, safe and ensconced in power, while pieces of her mind where free to travel to other places doing her bidding. From this repository she reached out to a demon who was working for her in Los Angeles, keeping watch on the angel Metatron and how far he was pushing his enterprise. She shrieked the demon's name into the dark, "Gregor!"

Thousands of miles away deep in the City of Angels' sewer system the demon Gregor stirred at his mistress' call. His gaze fell out of focus and his fellow demons stopped what they were doing and stared, knowing only "She" could be calling if Gregor was willing to pay such rapt attention. For the benefit of the others in his cabal Gregor spoke aloud, "Yes, mistress?"

It is time, Malign's voice echoed through his mind. *Gather your group and lead the fool to the others. I will contact the rest of my children and when you arrive we will have...oh, we will have such fun.*

"Of course, mistress," Gregor said, nodding vigorously. "The puppet will follow our trail just as you planned. We will not fail."

Malign's voice rang out clearly in the minds of the other demons, not only in Gregor's cabal, but in the mind of every vampire demon in the United States. She forced extra power through herself, channeling it into the minds of all her servants. *Children of the night!*

Thousands more minds stirred besides Gregor's and focused in her direction: some were rooting through filth, rutting among bodies, causing pain and suffering, or hibernating the daylight away. No matter what they had been doing, they now all devoted every ounce of their attention to the Dark Lady Malign as she spoke to them. *Children, listen to me. You have all done so well. I am proud of each and every one of you. The pieces are in motion and the endgame to our little charade is nigh. I have specific instructions for some of you, but if you do not hear from me otherwise, once the sun falls start your march home. When it is night make the pilgrimage to Devil's Tower!*

***

Eric did not want to abandon his new body just yet. Building one was not very complicated for a creature as ancient as he was, but he had placed too much time and effort behind this one that giving up so easily felt weak to him. He still held on to a slim shred of hope that he could resolve this issue with the vampire want-to-be demons before it caused too much collateral damage. This was not his plan, with other demons getting involved. It was the living people who were supposed to jump on the fad he helped create, not the demons that already existed. *You should have listened to Hank,* Eric thought as he raced down the highway on his Can-Am Spyder. *The little guy has always had a good head on his shoulders and when he did not fawn all over your great plan, did you listen to his concerns? Oh no, you're Metatron, the great and mighty Enoch. Why should you listen to some barely century old angel?*

One of the angelic abilities Eric had retained in his new human body was a connection to the energy flow around him. If he focused hard enough, meditating to clear his thoughts, and attempted to see things as he had as an angel, he could sense lines of positive or negative energy. Some circled the earth in strong bands, what certain mortals referred to as ley lines, but most were trails left behind by whatever angel, demon, or human had left it. Eric could follow that trail better than any bloodhound scenting a fox. It was when he found the trail left by the vampires who had visited his house early the previous morning that Eric had fired up the fastest vehicle he owned, looking more like a child's robot toy, a reverse tricycle with two wheels up front and one rear, than the extremely quick vehicle that it was. He realized that the vampires were not congregating around his home as he had feared, but heading off into the Mojave Desert for shelter. This gave him confidence in his decision to leave Maggie alone. Without the demons staying near, he could hopefully avoid them taking an interest in her.

By late afternoon the trail had become stronger and more definitive, as if something had flushed the demons from their lair early. He did not know what would have caused creatures of the night to brave the desert glare. *Perhaps they have lookouts*, he thought, *and they know you are coming. Maybe they do not wish to face you in the daylight when you are stronger*. His thoughts took on a more self-deprecating and cynical tone. *What Enoch? Do you think they're afraid you're going to hug them in a ball of warm light, until they amend their wicked ways and start playing with kittens?* It always surprised him that when he became self-critical he would think of himself as the man he was born, Enoch, and not the angel Metatron, a name he had gone by for a much longer period of time. *The impressions of our youth can run deep to our core, I suppose.*

The dry desert wind blew through his hair as he sped along I-15. Afton Canyon went by in an eye blink at the speeds he was traveling. The trail was leading him to Las Vegas, of that he had no doubt. His mind started wandering again as the canyons and landscape blurred past, *They want you to follow them, you know that. This must be a trap, but I cannot, in all honesty, think of what the trap could be. If they wanted to take my energy they would have already, so why lead me all the way out here to Vegas?*

***

On any typical day Pete would have been laughing along with the other Riders as they rumbled into Las Vegas, the humor being provided by the convertible leading the way, where three raucous voices were singing "Viva Las Vegas" at the top of their lungs: one baritone, one juvenile soprano, and one drunken Irish. This, unfortunately for Pete, was not a typical day. Though Hank was behind the wheel again - now dressed in miniature Elvis Presley imitation - this was still not enough to shake Pete out of his brooding mood. The mood had started when the Riders allowed the convertible to drive in front of them and Lucifer had turned around in the backseat, staring at Pete. No matter where Dante moved his bike in position with the others, Lucifer continued to stare at Pete. *No better way to get in a shitty mood,* Pete thought, *than to be stuck in a twelve hour staring contest with the Devil.*

The cavalcade all but flew past a highway police officer clocking traffic. Hank wiggled his fingers in an *Obi-wan*-like wave and the officer never stirred from his position. Pete could feel Dante's large frame shaking with laughter as they passed the officer "going about his business". Hank had done this several times over the last day and the Riders never said a word about it. Still unsure as to how much the motorcyclists were seeing of this side of things and how much they were not, Pete mentally asked Harmony, *Are you sure this wild card thing you were telling me about doesn't mean these guys are in on the afterlife?*

"No," she said, "Dante sees more than the others. That is simply part of being different. Among humans those who are not identical to the norms learn to be more observant. It is a survival mechanism. There is more to him, but that must be his choice to tell you; as for the rest of the Riders, their status as *Wild Cards* only means that I have no control over their actions and I am unable to influence them to keep the Balance from tipping by their actions."

That's kind of cool when you think about it. I suppose chaoticians laugh their metaphysical asses off when they find out about that, huh?

Harmony sniffed with disdain, "I have never enlisted the services of one, so I do not know, Peter. But, I think one could safely assume that, yes."

Pete watched the Vegas Strip light up like a beacon before them as dusk blanketed the valley. The sun's illumination was replaced by the colored flash and flair that had made the city famous. Approaching from the highway Pete could see all of the glitter off to his left. With Raven gone he realized that he was the de-facto leader of this odd band of champions. Nervously he thought, *Hey, boss lady, we're here, now where are we going?*

"Have the Riders exit the highway south of the Strip. Head north along Las Vegas Boulevard; you will not miss Grey. He is out and about. And one more thing, Peter?"

Yeah?

"He's in…well, you would say, 'He's in a mood'."

Oh, goody, between "The Prince of Darkness" glaring at me from the backseat and Grey being in a mood, this should be lots of fun! Look out for Pissy and Sulky, the vampire slayers.

Harmony sighed, "I know, Peter. I will not say I told you so about Lucifer, but I did. Watch him; he is clever and unpredictable. One does not cross him lightly. I will also tell Zeus so he can relay my driving instructions to Hank." With that said she retreated from Pete's consciousness, leaving him to brood alone. He had learned earlier that Dante was only mute, not deaf, so he shouted Harmony's directions over the engines' roar. The large man nodded his head, shaggy black hair flopping, and made hand motions that looked nothing like sign language to Pete. The other Riders apparently understood because they fell into place behind Hank as he exited the highway.

Whatever subliminal sense humans use to gauge danger seemed to kick into overdrive whenever the Lone Riders rode through a town. Other cars gave the motorcycle gang a wide berth on the road. Las Vegas tourists (known the world over for their self-involved vacation mentality of "what happens in Vegas stays in Vegas") gave the Riders every courtesy the rules of the road demanded. *Well*, Pete thought, *it could be just as likely they are sensing that scary-ass son-of-a-bitch staring directly at me still. Yes! You asshole!* he thought when Lucifer quirked an eyebrow. *If you read minds as well as everybody says you do, Alex, then read this, dick. "Yeah, I lied! Get over it."* Garish colored lights threw half of Lucifer's face into shadow as they stopped at a traffic light. He stared fixedly over at Pete. To his credit Pete did not back down, look away, or flinch. Lucifer's disembodied laughter flowed around Pete and Dante as the light changed to green and Hank pulled forward. Pete did not shiver until Lucifer finally turned his glare away. The laughter continued to wind around them like a serpent, even without his attention fixed on Pete.

Pete was not surprised to feel Dante shudder along with him over the biker's leather and denim. If he could see Hank pull the *Jedi mind-trick* then he definitely had to sense that malicious laugh. They had gone only a fraction of the way along the Strip when Grey – true to Harmony's word – appeared clear as day, standing atop the Luxor's sphinx. He was wearing a Stetson, his booted feet were slightly crossed, and he was waving his left arm at Pete in a jerky up and down motion with a cigarette dangling from his lips. Pete smiled, then laughed, muttering under his breath, "Asshole."

Chapter 12

Grey likes to blame so many of the actions and tendencies of the dead on their "mental conditioning", as he calls it. Mental conditioning being those holdover concepts from people's living days, where they had learned to be a certain thing or person, maybe through trial and error in behaviors. A person breathes heavily when they exert themselves in a body, so even when they no longer have lungs to process oxygen their mind, through conditioned behavior, believes that they still should pant like dogs when they move quickly. I love Grey, but he sees things in terms of nurture; nature doesn't play much of a part in his world view. The rules of nature are concrete blacks and whites. How does a man named Grey even have a chance to look at things in terms of nature?

He's lived longer, so who am I to argue? But, I believe it's human nature to think of ourselves as particular things, to assign roles and titles to who or what we believe we are.

Some people may view themselves as their jobs: he is a doctor, she is an accountant, they are construction workers, and so on. Maybe they think of themselves in terms of familial relationships: a father, brother, sister, or cousin.

I was a daughter. I never had the chance to be a mother. I am a lover and a fighter.

Do you see the tense change in there? How what I viewed myself as in the past is not how I view myself now. We are always changing whether we notice it or not.

How do young children view themselves, I wonder? They have no basis for comparison. I suppose they might see themselves as smaller than other people, or maybe they are a purer form of humanity? Without all of that mental conditioning to hold them back they can see the universe for all it is: love and hate, comfort and fear, need and satiation, all at once. Or maybe they are just a ball of genetic instincts bouncing along the road of survival? I'm more inclined to think they are the purer spirits, but I guess that could just be the inner mother in me that never had the chance to nurture talking.

I have seen this first hand though; inside information can open a person's eyes further than the guess work the masses have to wade through. It is rare for a child to stay behind. The circumstances are usually very tragic for a child under the age of reason to stay here on earth after death and not move directly back to the Source. Oftentimes when the child does stay behind, it clings closely to its mother until the pull from the Source is strong enough that it lets go of its short life. Other times…well there are other times when the child - out of confusion…or sadly out of misplaced anger - that the child stays behind, in effect driving its mother to suicide, because she blames herself for its death, and the child's spirit constantly clinging to her, reminding her of it, never allows for her to move past the loss. In some rare cases she may truly be responsible for the child's death. Believe me, that is a very hard thing to watch. I can't imagine trying to live with it.

Those labels - whether a product of mental conditioning or not - can be hard to live with. And harder still to continue with in the afterlife. Imagine what that does to a psyche to slap the term "murderer" or "killer" in that collection of how a person defines themself. Sometimes I think it would be more accurate for Grey to call it mental baggage like living people do, because it weighs you down calling yourself daughter, mother, lover, wife, or whatever. It is hard enough to just be a person, isn't it? Who are you?..............

***

"It's good to see you, Pete," Grey said, shaking his friend's hand and slapping him on the back in that distinctly American male version of showing affection without too much contact. Pete chuckled as both men stood under the replica sphinx while the others found parking spots in the garage adjacent to the enormous onyx urban pyramid saying, "You did that whole 'Vegas Cowboy' thing just to ruin any jokes I might have come up with, didn't you?"

"Damn right," Grey said slapping Pete once more on the upper shoulder for good measure, sending a shower of blue sparks from their mingled energies cascading down onto the hot desert sidewalk. It was only the two of them, as Raven had gone with the Riders to park their choppers and lead them all back through the milling labyrinthine throngs to Grey. Once everyone returned they could plan their course of action.

"Asshole," Pete mockingly groused. "Well, since all my *Vegas Vick* and *Marlboro Man* jokes are no longer an option I suppose I should ask what it is we're going to do. Last I knew we were on a trip to go see some L.A. angel named Voltron or something, but that plan seems to be shot to shit now. So, what's up?"

"Yeah," Grey replied, "things never do go as planned, do they? Once upon a time you asked me about Malign. Well it looks like you're going to finally get your chance to have some dealings with her. I'm sure Harmony has been keepin' you up to date, somewhat?" He said the last in a question that Harmony chose to answer in person. She appeared out of nowhere standing between the two men, saying, "Yes, I have."

Pete jumped a few paces back before shouting, "Damn it! I'm still not used to you saying random shit in my head lady! Now, you just pop in and out like *The Great Gazoo*? That's just wonderful."

Harmony raised a single eyebrow in Pete's direction. She looked like a different woman to both men. It was part of her connection to them that she chose the forms that she did. To Pete, Harmony looked like a sultry rhythm and blues singer, typically attired in a low cut dress or top. She had done so now and Pete was visibly struggling to maintain eye contact. Giving no acknowledgement to his struggle she said, "Peter, there are times when I believe you watched entirely too much television for you to have grown into a literary professor."

"I can multitask like no other," Pete said, dipping his eyes down for a quick glance at her cleavage, and then looking directly back in her eyes. "See, multitasking."

"Classy, Pete," Grey said laughing, "real classy."

"Yep, I ooze class from every pore, or core of my being, or whatever it is that I ooze things from now," Pete said, squinting his eyes and tilting his head in confusion at how to reword his original thought. "Never mind. All that matters is that I ooze class. So, what's the plan people, or person and entity of power, or…aw hell, forget it. I give up."

Smiling, Harmony shrugged her shoulders, saying, "I honestly do not have one. We know what Malign is doing, but we do not know why. Nothing has changed; as far as the Balance is concerned you can continue to travel out to Los Angeles to speak with Metatron if Hank still wishes to. In either case that may be the wisest course of action. The two are obviously connected in some way."

"No," Grey said sternly, his voice resonating with finality.

Harmony turned to face him. "Jasper, there is obviously a connection between Malign and Metatron. Both are involved in this vampire nonsense-"

"Not that," Grey cut her off. "Yes, they are connected, of that I ain't got a doubt, but our best course of action ain't to go to L.A. We need to take out the demons she has pretendin' to be vampires here, first, so they don't have the opportunity to jump us later."

"Look, I know I'm still technically the new guy," Pete said, "but, um, it doesn't feel like the vampire demon things are tipping the Balance to me, so are we allowed to do that?" He directed his question more to Harmony than Grey. She only shook her head, but Grey answered instead, "No they haven't tipped the Balance and, no, we can't launch a preemptive strike, but…" He gave Harmony a lopsided grin before he finished, "Would destroying them tip the Balance in the other direction? Because it don't feel like it would to me."

Harmony's nostrils flared, her eyes flashed from several shades faster than Pete could name the colors, and she pointed an index finger sharply at Grey's chest. "Jasper Reynolds, even you would not dare! That is not the task I have charged you with. You cannot manipulate the system like that."

"Oh yeah, darlin'?" Grey answered, folding his arms across his chest. "You just watch me. It seems like a *gray* area to me." Pete snickered and started to laugh at Grey's pun, but he cut it short when Harmony directed the anger of her gaze in his direction.

Harmony looked from one man to the other, fury coloring her eyes. After a moment where the only noise came from the passersby she shook her head saying, "You two are perfect for each other, obstinate and contrary to the core."

"No we aren't," Pete said smiling. Harmony tried to smile back, but failed. She placed a hand on each of their shoulders and said, "Please, be careful. It is one thing if you were to fail. I could accept that, but it is something altogether different if one of my soldiers were to tip the Balance with their actions. I do not know what would happen."

They stood quietly ruminating on that dire confession waiting for the others as pedestrians continued to walk and jostle their way around the three of them standing out in front of the Egyptian-themed resort. Pete took a moment to watch the crowd, for the first time seeing how many demons there were mixing in and among the throng. The out of place bright saffron robes from a passing cluster of Buddhist monks caught Pete's eye. The orange-clad men would have seemed out of place in the city of vice during the daylight, but they were even more at odds in the night because they had an accompanying sphere of angels hovering around them, keeping the corrupting demons at bay.

As if cued to Pete's thoughts a scantily clad woman wandered over toward the monks from a group of other similarly dressed ladies. Unbeknownst to her, she had a small demon draped around her shoulders like a mink shawl, lovingly rubbing its tiny rodent hands over the tops of her breasts and licking its forked tongue under her earlobe. It flashed fierce red eyes at Grey, Harmony, and Pete, but hissed loudly when the woman wandered too close to the monks. She held the camera from her phone out to capture a picture as she draped her arms around a pair of them. The monks allowed her to do so with serene smiles on their faces, as if humoring a child.

The woman had barely been among the monks for more than a few seconds when an angel disgorged itself from the protective sphere. It flew across the short distance, wrapping itself around the demon that clung to the woman's neck while the black creature hissed and thrashed. The woman lost her balance, tripping and falling onto the pavement, breaking the heel off one of her knockoff pumps. Pete jumped back as the angel and demon struggled. Grey and Harmony both watched with clinical detachment when the ball of light and shadow that had recently been two separate creatures dispersed in a wave of energy. The tourists on the street barely noticed the spill over, only a strong out of place wind that most dismissed as cool air currents blowing out from constantly opening casino doors. The wind ruffled the hem of one of the monk's robe as he leaned down to offer the woman a hand up. She took his proffered hand, smiling, and another angel dislodged from the sphere and attached itself to the woman, looking to Pete like a small child riding piggy-back along the woman's shoulders. The angel was lovingly wiping away the grime that the demon had left behind. The woman's friends were shouting for her to follow them; they had bars to hop, money to spend, and asses to shake. The woman - *not much more than a girl really*, Pete thought - begged off saying she had twisted her ankle and she wanted to go back to her room to put some ice on it, but she would call them later if it felt better. She had barely stopped speaking by the time her friends were gone and onto their evening's activities, showing little or no regard for their friend's injury.

Both the woman and the monks had wandered off, she with her new companion and them less two, before Pete looked at Grey and Harmony saying, "What the hell was that?"

"That, Pete," Grey said, "was people, both dead and livin', making choices."

"No shit Sherlock, really?" Pete said sarcastically. "What I meant was I thought you told me angels couldn't do more than just hug people and send them happy-happy thoughts about fluffy clouds and puppy dogs. You know, shit like that."

"No, Peter," Harmony corrected, "angels can make sacrifices, just like they could as human beings."

"You mean that…that angel just committed itself to oblivion, all to stop one demon and help some skank to see the light? Seriously? Man, I don't get this job sometimes."

Harmony continued her explanation, "Peter, to that person, the sacrifice was warranted. No one knows how far the ripples of a single action can travel. Also, if that angel was a Buddhist in life then perhaps it did not see its sacrifice as anything noteworthy. If there is no ego, then there is nothing to sacrifice."

Grey snorted before saying, "That, or if the angel is strong enough it could pull both it and the demon back to the Source, allowing them to be *reincorporated* I guess you could say. Back at the Source they will be who they were, without the corruption from this world to taint them. That's my theory at least. I don't know if it would work though, because I've never seen it firsthand."

"Seen what firsthand?" a belligerent Irish accent asked. "I thought you'd seen and done just about everything, Grey."

Gabe was leaning around behind Raven, with a bottle of something he must have pilfered from one of the casino's bars in passing in one hand and his other arm wrapped affectionately around Hank's shoulder. Zeus loomed over them as the rest of the Riders piled up behind him. Lucifer kept to the fringes of the group and any other demons that had been congregating in the area fled when they saw him.

"No, not everything, Gabe," Grey answered in a drawl. "I've yet to see you bed as many women as you claim to have."

The Irishman shrugged saying, "Fair enough, Grey. So, we going to paint this town red or what, mate? Maybe live it up a little first or are we just going to work, Mr. Boring? All work and no play make Gabe a dull boy, eh?"

Instead of answering him Grey shot a small ball of light from his outstretched fingertip, a quick draw cowboy using his right hand as a mock pistol. The small bullet of light spun across the distance separating them, invisible to those who were not yet dead, and the bottle Gabe was holding exploded into a thousand pulverized pieces of glass and wisps of alcohol vapor. Gabe stood dumbfounded staring at his empty hand as Grey started walking up the Strip with the crowd. Pete chuckled, following his mentor, while Raven steered the others after them, slapping Gabe on the shoulder in passing saying, "Come on dull boy."

"But, he just…" Gabe stammered pointing to his empty hand.

"I know," she said. "He does that kind of thing."

"That's just not right…" Gabe said, but followed the others when he realized no one was left to listen to him. They had all followed Grey. "Just not fair," Gabe mumbled to himself trudging behind the group.

***

"Look, Grey, there's another one!" Pete yelled to his friend, rapidly smacking him on the upper arm to get his attention.

"Yeah, Pete," Grey said in resignation as they strolled in and around the patrons of a vampire themed nightclub they were searching through. "I saw the last four that you pointed out, too."

Grey had decided that they would have a better chance of rooting out all the vampires Malign had placed in Las Vegas if they split up into groups, covering more ground in a shorter period of time. Harmony had reluctantly agreed to act as a supernatural walkie-talkie, as Pete had put it, spreading the metaphysical muscle around into three groups with the Lone Riders providing human backup. It was the only way Harmony would sanction the hunt. She wanted to keep a closer eye on things since this was not - technically speaking - an issue for the Balance. Grey was going to go through with it no matter what. Pete could tell that by the tone of the man's voice, so Harmony's go-ahead was really an afterthought or way for her to save face.

The groups had been broken up into Grey and Pete with Dante and Bulldog, heading north, while Raven, Gabe, and Lucifer took five of the Riders to reconnoiter the center of the Strip. Finally Zeus plus Hank and the last five Riders went to scope out the south end.

"Jesus!" Pete exclaimed, "there's another one! They're all over the place!"

"Yes, Pete," Grey said in exasperation, "we see it. I had the same problem in Santa Fe. I get it."

"But they're everywhere man!" Pete yelled, whipping his head around from side to side to keep more than one in his line of sight. "How the hell am I supposed to look for vampires when every other woman walking around this place has a nipple poking out of her shirt? Look at that one!" Pete exclaimed gesturing, "I don't think that even counts as a shirt, does it?"

Dante and Bulldog both laughed while Grey shook his head. An ear piercing scream from the back of the club broke up the men's moment of levity. All four turned to look in the direction of a loud crash that followed the first and preceded a second scream, this one accompanied by a few male yells and shouts, too. A demon, standing well over seven feet tall, hunchbacked with black bat-like wings and fangs dripping blood, had flipped over a table in a rear corner of the club, and it was darting down bird-like, ripping and chewing at a young woman's throat.

"Shit!" Pete yelled and jumped up onto a table as the terrified crowd started to press toward the nearest exit. Dante and Bulldog followed suit, climbing up and scuffing the polished bar with their road worn boots. Drinks were scattered everywhere as the two human men went for their weapons. Bulldog had procured handheld ultraviolet lamps somewhere along on their trip that - surprisingly to Pete - actually worked against the demons. *Who would have thought that some of the vampire legend's weapon paraphernalia would work on demons too*, Pete had thought when the gang's leader had flashed his torch around and several demons that were nearby fled as if the sun had come up when the burly man had turned the flashlight on in demonstration. Both men pulled out the UV flashlights now as the demon chewed at the dead girl's neck. It hissed sharply when Dante's light burned into its shoulder. The demon picked up another table, scooping it up like it weighed nothing, and hurled it at the bikers, causing them to drop their lights as they jumped out of the way. The table proved to weigh quite a lot as it shattered the bar and continued on, exploding into the wall of bottles and the mirror behind the counter.

Pete launched himself from the tabletop, throwing a ball of red light at the demon while in midair. It was the demon's turn to dodge and it dropped the woman it had been munching on as it dove out onto the dance floor to avoid Pete's missile. Though the deejay had abandoned his post with the rest of the screaming mob, the sound system continued to thrum away in a deep bass and rumble. Spotlights, black lights, and strobe lights all flashed a seizure inducing effect on the empty dance floor as the vampire rolled with the momentum of its leap, landing in a crouch. The vampire demon was still looking down when a pair of worn cowboy boots stopped a few feet short of its face. The demon's head snapped up and it flashed its fangs, hissing at Grey.

Grey smiled down at the demon and said, "Hello sunshine. Want to dance?"

The demon started to hiss another response, but Grey struck faster than it could articulate. He wrapped his right hand around the monster's throat and squeezed. Blue light flashed from his fingertips as he sent power down his arm into the creature. Being the larger in size the demon tried to climb to its feet in hopes of breaking Grey's hold. Grey grabbed its right wrist with his left hand and swept the vampire's legs out from under it, forcing it onto its back on the dance floor as he pinned it there with a flood of energy. It screamed and thrashed to the club's techno music as Grey finished it off. Pete, Dante, and Bulldog had all regained their feet and had climbed the edge of the raised platform to watch as the demon exploded in a shower of shadow and gore.

"Christ!" Pete swore. "Why the hell did that thing show up in a body like that, in the middle of a damn nightclub, too?"

Grey still held his pose, crouching over the ichor splattered platform. He turned his head only partially before he answered Pete. The strobe lights flashing lent an eerie, almost maniacal bent to his profile as he said, "Because Malign has them so worked up they think they can brazenly flout the rules and get away with it." Inside his head he thought in Harmony's direction, *I told you so darlin'*. She either chose to ignore him, or she was busy communicating with the others because she remained silent.

Both Dante and Bulldog had only seen minimal usage of any of the Balance warriors' power up to this point. Though Raven's earlier highway acrobatics had been impressive, it was something else to watch Grey work, up close and personal. The two bikers stood tall in their leather, denim, and road grime, with the wide-eyed expressions of children who had just seen someone pull down Santa Claus' fake beard. Bulldog spoke out the side of his mouth to Dante, "What the fuck did we get ourselves into, brother?"

Dante solemnly shook his head and shrugged his shoulders.

***

"Get back here and fight like men, you pussies!" Gabe yelled at the retreating backs of two teenage boys pretending to be vampires. He turned to the crowd of young women dressed in variants of the counterculture theme, mainly blacks and fishnets, and with a smug smile said, "You see, ladies, I told you they weren't real vampires!"

He ran the back of his hand down the cheek of the closest young girl saying, "You see, love, a real vampire would have burst into flame when his skin came in contact with garlic." She giggled coquettishly at his attentions.

"Oh for God's sake!" Raven exclaimed, "We don't have time for this!" She slapped Gabe's hand away from the girl's face and grabbing his wrist, she drug him away by the other hand as he shouted, "Alas, my dears, it was not meant to be," to his adoring masses.

When they were far enough away that the group of girls could no longer be seen waving to Gabe's retreating back, Raven turned to him and said, "Did you really have to rub pieces of garlic bread in those boy's faces?"

"Of course, I did," Gabe said placing a hand over his heart. "It is my solemn and sworn duty to protect the innocent women of the world so that I may corrupt them. Those fools were claiming to all those pretty young girls that they were *real vampires*, so it was my charge to prove them false, love. It needed to be done. It could not be helped."

"Fine," Raven said, "but did you really need to keep chucking the rest of the loaf at them as they ran away?"

Gabe sniffed, holding his head high, "It had to be done, love. There was simply no avoiding it."

Raven laughed. No longer being able to feign disapproval she said, "Well, I guess if there was no avoiding it. You did what you had to do."

"Exactly," Gabe agreed. "They should count themselves lucky that I didn't fetch one of those Elvis impersonators who marry people to bless me some holy water to douse them with."

"Death by Elvis?" Raven asked. "You are a cruel man, Gabriel O'Connor."

"Aye, love, it's a dirty job, but somebody has to do it."

They were laughing, taking a moment away from the seriousness of their chosen paths when Lucifer dropped down between them, startling Gabe so much he staggered backward yelling, "Jesus bloody Christ, Lucy! Can't you just walk up to people and say hello like a normal person, for fuck's sake?"

Lucifer smiled at Gabe, but turned to Raven saying, "Grey destroyed one in a nightclub. If you two would stop laughing for a minute you would hear the sirens. Apparently the moron was ballsy enough to form a body and murder a woman in front of a crowd of people. I took the liberty of sending our parcel of Riders to go see if they can lend the others some assistance."

"Damn it, Grey," Raven muttered as she looked in the direction the nearest emergency vehicle was heading. "Do you always have to be right?" Turning to meet Lucifer's gaze she said, "Fine, this is what we'll do. There have to be others…" She trailed off as screams erupted behind them. It was a woman's voice wailing in terror from the direction of the young vampire groupies Gabe had been so recently wooing. Not waiting to see if either man followed, Raven ran in the direction of the now multiple voices screaming in agony and fear.

***

The lights of Las Vegas shown out like a beacon, illuminating the trail of darkness left by the demons to Eric's vision as he pulled off the highway. He parked in an open lot along the south end of town where there were more shopping malls than casinos before it became the area known as the Strip. He had just turned off the engine to his Spyder when he heard a nearby shriek. He snapped his head around at the sound and saw one of the vampires he had been following swoop out of the night sky in his direction. Eric gathered light and energy around himself to form a defensive shield. He closed his eyes, bracing for impact as the vampire dove, but when he felt no clash and shutter of power he looked again, in time to see the vampire fly right past him. It screamed in his direction again as it passed, heading for the open desert.

      Confused, Eric looked in the direction that the vampire had come from to see a giant Viking charging down the sidewalk, arms pumping as he ran with a huge grin on his bearded face, followed by what appeared to Eric to be a biker gang dressed for the road in leather and denim. Orange lightning and bellicose laughter flew from the Viking in flashes and shouts that shot off into the night after the vampire. As the group raced past Eric he could see a familiar young boy hanging from around the Viking's shoulders, riding piggy-back, arms wrapped tightly around the large man's neck. The boy turned to face Eric as the mob chasing the vampire passed. He smiled and waved a hand in Eric's direction as Eric asked, "Hank?"

Chapter 13

Fear is a very intimate and personal emotion. What scares each person can be utterly different. There can be universal fears like death and fire; those are animal ideas, meat worried over its continued existence. The smaller individualized fears can differ greatly. It shows you just how fragile the human psyche really is, doesn't it? Someone may appear strong on the outside, but they crumble like a house of cards when they are forced to face their fear.

Fear is also individually tailored. We like to dub certain fears or phobias as irrational, but is that fair? I mean, to the person the fear belongs to it seems perfectly rational to be afraid of whatever it is that scares them: spiders, snakes, heights, open spaces, maybe clowns, fat people, or bad hairpieces. The object of the fear doesn't matter at all, but for the fear itself! I say FDR was right; I was never one of his citizens, but that does not make his statement any less valid.

Pete would probably have something to quote from "The Jedi Code" about fear leading to hate or something along those lines. I don't buy that and I'd tell him that not everything that comes out of the mouth of a green puppet is a God's honest truth nugget of wisdom. Fear and hate only have the loosest of connections.

Hate is a totally different and unrelated mindset at its core. Sure, people who are afraid of spiders and snakes might learn to hate arachnids and serpents, but does the agoraphobic really hate the shopping mall and all those people stuck so close together? Well…maybe that is a bad example, because I hate the mall, too. How about a fear of heights? Does a person scared of heights hate mountains? Do you see my point?

Hate - I know hate. It has nothing to do with my fears. My fears have always been the simple human fear of loss: loss of people, places, and self. My hate has bubbled up from a different fount and always has. I hate the injustice that the universe is rife with. When a child dies, I hate that. When an animal is fed gourmet food that costs more than some people make in a week of hard labor, I hate that. When an adult uses their authority to corrupt or harm a child, I hate that. When countries of abundance flout their riches by inventing a game called competitive eating while others starve, I hate that. When a populous is easily swayed by some talking Ken doll on television, I hate that. I could keep going, keep listing my hates, but I think you may have some of your own that you'd like to mentally add to the list, too. Do they have anything to do with fear? I didn't think so.

Once I was told by a very powerful, very evil demon that we were much alike. He said it was a shame that Grey had met me first, that my hate and his were similar, and that I would have been better suited to his side of things. There are times when I am so angry that my hate feels like a tangible force. It is at those times that I wonder if that demon wasn't right. And do you know what?

That scares me…………

***

Raven pressed past the throng of bodies, running away from the screaming women to see two huge vampires huddled over the limp body of the girl Gabe had touched only minutes earlier. She did not hesitate or even slow her charge as both vampires started turning upon hearing her approach. With a gun in each hand she fired before either vampire could completely face her. One staggered under her barrage of lavender bullets and fell back to the sidewalk, lying on its side twitching, next to its victim in a similar pose. It shuddered, then dissolved, poring leftover energy out in a puddle that oozed into the pavement. The tar-like gelatin remains of the demon dripped into the Strip's gutter that was already overflowing with leaflets for prostitutes and cheap vacation homes.

The other vampire had taken wing while its cohort took the brunt of Raven's fire. It hovered over the street, as frightened and confused tourists ran about in a panic screaming or recording the scene with their cell phones and cameras. The vampire swooped down, dodging fire from Raven's guns and picked up a tourist who had been filming it. The tourist looked to be a man from a South American country to Raven. It was hard for her to tell for sure because the vampire launched the man - still clutching his camera - directly at Raven. She ducked as the man flew by and knew that Gabe had caught up to her when she heard the impact of bodies punctuated by a muffled Irish accent say, "Gerr the fuck off'a me!"

The vampire had expected its human missile to deter the woman with the guns longer than it had because it was still hovering in the same place, staring wide-eyed at her when she opened fire. It shrieked like a banshee as her ammunition tore hole after hole through its black flesh. A final round punctured the creature's head and its body lost cohesion midair, spilling negative tar-like goop all over a group of the Asian tourists who had continued to snap pictures of the monster throughout the fight.

Pete, as well as Grey and the other Riders, had run up in time to see the last moments of combat. They all stood watching Raven as she held her pose, still in her shooters stance, vigilant for another attacker. Grey stepped forward and started yanking tourists to their feet. He ran a hand across their bodies to clear off all the residual negative energy, then patting them on the shoulder and handing them the nearest camera, whether it belonged to them or not, he sent them away with a smile. Pete shrugged his shoulders and stepped over the tourist groaning at his feet to talk to Raven. He said, "Damn girl! You took out two?

These guys are tough. Grey nailed one in a dance club. Bulldog and Dante cornered one behind a bar and I had to finish it off. Where was your backup?"

"I believe it's obvious she didn't need any," said Lucifer's voice from directly behind Pete's right ear. Pete jumped several feet, almost landing in Raven's arms, as she steadied him. "God damn it man! You have got to stop doing that! Between you and Harmony I'm the jumpiest damn ghost around. It's a good thing I can't pee myself anymore. Christ!"

Having finished helping redirect the tourists Grey walked over saying to Raven, "Good work, darlin'. That's already one more demon than I saw here last night. There ain't no telling how many more are hanging around, but it's a start."

Gabe staggered over to the growing congregation as the Riders approached from the other side, giving the group the appearance of a supernatural football huddle with Grey leading as quarterback. The Irishman had finished dusting himself off and was busy twisting the foil wrapper from the top of an abandoned bottle of liquor he had pilfered from the bag of a terrified tourist. Pulling the cork out with his teeth he looked up and muttering around the oral obstruction asked, "So, what did I miss?"

Grey just glared at him, but Pete chuckled answering, "Four down, nobody knows how many left to go."

"Right," Gabe said nodding his head and taking a swig from the bottle. "Well, captain, what's next?" he asked Grey, being sure to keep the bottle tucked away under his arm, out of path of any more supernatural finger bullets.

Grey did not have the opportunity to respond. Harmony's voice echoed urgently in the minds of all those who were in her charge, "Zeus needs help. He has chased one of the demons too far out into the desert. It was a trap and in his exuberance he fell right into it. Hank and Metatron are shielding the Riders, but Zeus cannot stand alone against so many for long."

Looking in turn at Pete, Gabe, and Raven, Grey barked out a sharp order of, "Go, now." Each of them vanished, without arguing, in a flash of light that had the rest of the Riders making noises of astonishment. When it was only he and Lucifer left from their side of the flat-line, Grey placed his hand on Lucifer's upper arm saying, "Alex, I do not ask you this for my people, but for theirs." Grey nodded his head in the direction of the Lone Riders who were stirring, trying to understand what they were missing out on.

Bulldog had stepped forward to overhear the two men. It was obvious by the extra creases and look of concern on his bald brow that he was not used to being so impotent in the affairs of his people. He asked, "What's going on guys? What did we miss out on?" His gravelly voice hitched a bit at the end.

After a pause and deep breath Lucifer nodded at Grey. Turning to Bulldog he said, "Your friends - and his - are in danger. The others went and Grey here will go to help them, too. We cannot follow by their means, so I will go with you to fetch your motorcycles and lead you to your friends." Looking back at Grey he continued, "That is what you were going to ask of me, was it not?"

"Yes," Grey agreed. "Yes, it was. Can I trust you, Alex?"

"If you believe using my birth name will appeal to my human side, *Jasper*, then you are sorely mistaken. I will do as you ask though, no matter what pathetic psychological ploy you may attempt."

"Not your human side, Alex," Grey said, folding his arms across his chest. "No, I'm appealing to your ego. Your legend. There has to be a part of you in there that wants to play the hero again or else you wouldn't have done so many of the things that you have. What do you say? Do you want another chance to be great?"

Grey did not wait around to hear Lucifer's answer. He turned and vanished in a flash of light like the others. Bulldog and his Riders milled about while Lucifer stared for a moment at the spot where the cowboy had vanished from. After a quietly grumbled, "Asshole," Lucifer turned to the motorcycle gang's leader saying, "Your friends are waiting. Let's go."

***

Grey walked into the sun-dappled meadow that was his connection to Harmony, just as the others were leaving. He jogged over in the direction they had vanished, only to go nowhere. Harmony blocked his path. She stood, arms folded across her spare frame, flower print sundress rustling around her tapping foot. The top of her head was a smidgen shy of parallel with his sternum. Grey grinned down at her and said, "I've been a bad boy again, huh, darlin'?"

"This is not a laughing matter, Jasper," Harmony said in a strained voice. "My knights are charged with keeping the Balance, not playing God. You are playing with forces way beyond your scope of control."

"Ain't I always," Grey said, matching her cross-armed pose. An edge of anger was creeping around his dismissively cocky demeanor. "What's new about this? We both need Lucifer's help, so I got us his cooperation. We both know Malign has got something up her sleeve, so I'm forcing her hand. I ain't tipped the Balance yet so don't tell me I'm wrong."

"No," she agreed, "but you are doing so for your own selfish reasons. Whereas before you would bend the rules for me, this time you are bending them for yourself. Not to mention that you are setting a bad example for Peter. I do not want him thinking this sort of ruse and charade is how we do things. You want to destroy Malign, but just as you finally told Raven, you cannot do that without creating a power vacuum. Unless, of course, you had another very powerful demon sitting on the sidelines ready to take her place."

Meeting her gaze Grey mulled her words over a bit before saying, "You know, darlin', for supposedly being able to read my mind, you don't know shit," Grey walked past her. Harmony did not stop him or rage in a torrent of emotions as she had in the past. She only dropped her chin to her chest and quietly said to Grey's retreating back, "Not your mind, Jasper. Your heart."

Grey paused, turning his face partially toward Harmony so his profile was all she could make out, and said, "There ain't no difference." He continued on his march, vanishing in a flash of light to go aid his friends. Once again the two of them parted ways with raw emotions and tears from a creature who could never truly need to cry them.

***

The transition from idyllic prairie meadow to the seventh layer of hell was staggering even for Grey. The desert night was filled with the shrieks of demons masquerading as vampires and the shouts of his friends, plus the yells of the Lone Riders trapped within a sphere of light being fueled by Hank and another who – to Grey – looked to be the angel Metatron. Some vampires had caught on fire from either Zeus' lightning bolts or the humans' ultraviolet flashlights; Grey could not tell, but whatever the cause for combustion they were running about like bipedal torches. The ground under his feet crunched and he looked down to see that for miles in any direction the sand had been fused to glass. He looked back up. His focus drawn to the sound of a demon howling in pain accompanied a raspy Irish voice belting out U2 lyrics. The vampire flew past him, only missing a collision by a few feet. Gabe had one of his hands wrapped around the demon's neck as he rode upon its back. The other was up in the air doing a passing imitation of a bull rider at a rodeo. The absconded bottle of booze was still clutched in his free hand. Gabe waved it at Grey in a salute as they flew past and shouted, "Not bad, eh cowboy?"

Grey shook his head and yelled to the night at large, "I leave y'all alone for two minutes and all hell breaks loose. Jesus!"

Raven ran past firing both guns, tearing a swath of destruction through the vampire mob. She looked over her shoulder and shouted at Grey, "Less complaining and more killing, old man!"

Grey raised his eyebrows, "Old man, huh? Well now, I can't have that, can I? It's alright for me to say it, but young'uns calling me old? That just ain't respectful enough, not by a long chalk."

There was no easy way for him to tell how many demons there were out in the night. For every one that flashed a fang or red glowing eye his way, there had to be ten more out there waiting for the right moment to strike.

Hysterical mobs may seem detrimental to the ecumenical equilibrium of the living world, but they have little to no effect on the Balance. Having caused enough damage back in town, Grey did not really care how the mortals explained away what happened this night in the state of Nevada, city or desert. Coming to that conclusion, he started pulling in energy, neither from the warm earth beneath his feet nor from Harmony - as she at times would guardedly dole some out - but from the Source of life. The Source was an infinite pool to dip into, but one that could just as easily drown the inexperienced. Grey was not what anyone would consider inexperienced.

Life flooded his core; it coursed up and down his limbs, crackling and snapping like a downed power line. He flavored it with the smallest spice of his anger and hate of Malign. When he felt that he would lose control if he held on a moment longer, Grey bellowed into the night sky and slammed his fists into the ground. Shards of sand-made glass erupted up in front of the wave of power Grey released into the earth. Every demon in the wave's path dissolved on contact, no protracted explosions or movie special effect vampires staggering about on fire, just simple evaporation, never to be seen again. The wave crested over the warriors who were a part of the Balance, granting them added strength, and continued on to reinforce the angels' shield.

      The tidal wave of energy lost size and aggression the further it went from its epicenter Grey. The night grew eerily quiet compared to what it had been only seconds before. A shout of encouragement rang out from the Lone Riders when the angels safely dropped their shield. Pete started to build a slow round of applause, the kind he grew up watching everyone on television perform after a dramatic deed. He had not slapped his palms together more than half a dozen times when a feminine laugh carried on the wind blew across the desert from behind Grey. The laugh was soft and silky; it held the essence of an aphrodisiac, a power and life unto itself. Taking a deep breath of the burned and acrid desert air Grey turned to face the direction the laugh was coming from. The feminine laughter slowly built to the high ear-splitting pitch of a siren, and then suddenly dropped to the lowest octaves of a gruff baritone or bass. The night continued to rumble laughter at Grey and his friends as the deep red light from hundreds of eyes shined back at them.

Chapter 14

Women and vampires. Sure the two have always gone hand in hand to a certain point. From Stoker's fabled "Dracula" seducing and feasting on virgins, to the Catholic Church pushing the legends forward as a lever of guilt against promiscuity. Lucifer told me once that Dracula was only marginally based on Vlad Tepes. The horrifying acts of a man called "The Impaler" were much more impressive than the real demon that was the driving force behind the legend, which was some Yugoslavian gigolo named Yanni.

The connections are there, I don't deny that, but it seems that the current vampire fad in what is now a world culture has taken things too far. There used to be an unwritten set of guidelines men could use for gifts to woo a woman in courtship: flowers, confections or chocolates, jewelry and wine. It seems an odd jump to go from candy to books or movies about blood sucking creatures of the night, but hey, that's just me.

I say let's delve into the psychology of it for a moment. Women the world over have always been valued for their beauty more so than their minds. Please, I'm generalizing, so don't get all agitated thinking of examples to prove me wrong. Women are prized for their looks, end of story; wars have been waged over men's desire for women. Hell, just for one woman even, if mythology is to be believed. Do you think Helen still had the face to launch a thousand ships after a few decades of popping out Paris' kids? Beauty has a shelf life and as such women who have only been valued for their appearance would do anything to keep it that way, to stay young forever. If I'm wrong then why did humanity invent plastic surgery?

Enter the vampire mythos, a quick and easy way to youthful looks without the cost of liposuction. You ever notice how the new vampires never look their age either? Only in the old myths and legends do they stress the whole undead corpse image, because that would be just icky for a teenage girl to sleep with a guy who looked like his hundred years of life wouldn't it? Come on, that's why it's so gross every time Hugh Hefner marries another twenty year old blond bimbo, right?

Would you make a deal with the Devil for immortality and beauty?

The only catch or fine print is that you can't go out in the sunlight, eat Italian, Mediterranean, or any other cuisine that goes heavy on the garlic, no more going to church - gee twist my arm - or just be on your guard for whack jobs chasing after you with wooden stakes? I like a good pizza, but so far I could get behind those conditions in exchange for eternal life. The blood sucking also seems to stick to the female erogenous zones, too. Vampires nuzzle and drain from the neck, wrist, or inner-thigh. You never hear of a vampire going after a scalp wound - those things really bleed, right? Or, how about the brachial artery, no? We don't want to risk having skipped the shave and have stubbly pits for Count Hottie if he decides to lift our arms, now do we girls? I suppose the European vamps would just be used to that by now anyway. So, you gain supernatural beauty and immortality, for giving up the tanning beds, Sunday service, and hummus, right?

Not such a tough choice really. Move to a big city where people go missing all the time and you have twenty-four hour dry cleaners for the occasional blood stain that just won't come out. I can see why so many women want to be seduced and live forever, who wouldn't? But with that sensual desire and sought after seduction comes another change to the legend, to make it more palatable to the modern mind.

Today young women aren't having their throats ripped out and their blood feasted upon. No, that's just too scary of a fantasy. Slow down there Count Overbite, some of us aren't into the whole Sadomasochism scene. We need a softcore version of that hardcore fantasy. So, let's eliminate that icky scary blood stuff and now the world has vampires that leach a woman's emotions. I've heard them called "psi-vampires" or "psychic vampires". They feed off of your life force, energy, and emotions. Really? No wonder these creatures go after the ladies, am I right? I didn't get to have children of my own before I died, but I still had been having my period for enough years to ride that hormonal roller-coaster. How do you get a psi-vamp turned on? Whisper sweetly to him, "I'm ragging it."

Jesus girls! Wake up! If a guy wants to drain you of your energy, emotions, and life force he won't sparkle in the sunshine, he'll just marry you…………..

***

The deep and disquieting laughter gradually faded away into the dark desert night. Malign flowed up from the ground in front of her pet vampires. She was once again dressed to the nines and would have looked out of place at any celebrity award show, only in that she would have embarrassed all the famous women with her beauty and grace. Walking along the front lines of her demon army she trailed a hand lovingly along the wings of her infantry. She spoke, without need to shout or yell, since her voice carried over the still night with a power of its own, "Oh, Jasper, aren't we having some fun now, hmm?"

"Depends on your definition of fun I guess," Grey said looking around behind him. "I just toasted, what, a couple hundred of your little fanged freaks? Yeah, I'd say I'm havin' fun, a real *blast*. How about you, Malign?" He winked and gave her his best lopsided grin.

She grinned back, "Oh, well played cowboy, but what do you have left? I can only imagine you'd be having stamina problems about now." Her voice dripped with saccharin sweet mock sympathy. Placing a hand conspiratorially to the side of her mouth she continued in a whisper, "I hear it happens to everyone at some point."

"Fuck this!" Raven interrupted. "Can I shoot her this time or not, Grey?" She had walked up behind him and had her right hand weapon trained on Malign, following her every movement as she strolled along. Grey chuckled, "It won't do no good. She'll just flee down below again."

"It will make me feel better," Raven added. "Is that enough *good* for you?"

"Yeah absolutely, go ahead, knock yourself out, darlin'." Grey had barely finished speaking when Raven opened fire on Malign. Instead of fleeing and proving Grey correct she gracefully stepped behind the front row of demons, allowing their hulking mass to absorb Raven's barrage. Three demons crumpled and fell at the she-devil's feet, making pitiful mewling sounds. Raven brought her second firearm into play, doubling the amount of energy she was sending at the vampires. Malign stepped behind the second row and the monsters filled in the gap left from their fallen compatriots. When more than a dozen had perished the army of vampires started to stir in agitation. One vampire began to edge away from the ranks, looking askance at his mistress, hoping she would not notice him fleeing. Malign's eyes focused on the cowardly demon and her voice thundered out at all of them, "Shut up! Stop whining! And stand still you pathetic filth!"

The demons stilled and grew quiet as Raven continued her slaughter. The others had wandered over to stand behind her and Grey as they faced the vampires. Gabe spoke up over the cries of the fallen monsters, "Jesus bloody Christ! That is one cold, sick, twisted fuckin' bitch."

"Stop," Pete said quietly, but no one responded.

Grey stared ahead, eyes burning in the reflected light of Raven's bullets. He did not acknowledge that Pete had said anything, that there was anything going on outside of the norm. Seeing that he was not receiving a reaction from anybody on his side, Pete yelled, "God damn it! I said stop!" He reached out and slapped Raven's hands down. She flashed a look of pure hate in his direction. Pete did not back down. He stalked to Raven and towered over her. "Look at yourself. This is what she wants. Both of you!" Pete accused and punched Grey hard on the shoulder like a big brother playing bully. "You've all told me how much this bitch likes to fuck with people. She knows you both hate her, and rightly so, but you are destroying creatures that are just standing there, mowing them down like cattle. Fuck, another couple of minutes and you two jackasses might have tipped the Balance for her."

Raven's clouded look of anger melted and she whispered, "Oh."

Pete looked at everyone, face to face, as realization dawned. He shook his head saying, "I can't believe I'm saying this and it hurts my inner grammar monster to do it, but *no-duh!*" Then in a passing imitation of Raven's voice he said, "Oh, gee would the evil crazy ass white she-devil try and manipulate us? Never. She'd play by the rules."

He would have continued, but Malign's voice piped up from the rear of her army, "Very good young man. It appears Jasper chose you well. Tell me, did your intellect come naturally or are you overcompensating for affirmative action, hmm? Do you need to prove to the world - even in death - that you aren't just another dumb nigger? Is that what drives you, boy?"

Pete did not turn around. He continued to look into Raven's blue eyes. He smiled and said, "See, I'm not rising to the bait. I'd really, and I mean really, love to shoot the stupid bitch with a gun right now, too. But," and he looked to Grey as he said the next, "I am not going to let my past cloud the here and now."

Grey nodded and surprised everyone by pulling Pete into a hug, as he thumped Pete on the back he said, "Well done my friend. I knew you'd prove your mettle. Of course, we can't just destroy demons that haven't done anything to tip the Balance. That was one of the first lessons I taught you." Grey paused and pointing to a growing light behind the vampire army, continued saying, "But he can."

Lucifer was driving one of the Rider's choppers. He was leading the charge of the remaining seven motorcyclists into the rear of the vampire army. Dante and Bulldog had strapped as many ultraviolet lights as would fit to the handles of the rides, scattering the vampires with the burning light. Lucifer raised his flaming sword into the air like a general leading his troops and brought it down as he plowed into the vampires, lopping heads from winged shoulders. Whatever hold Malign had over the demons broke when the motorcycles barreled into them; some took to the air and flew away, others dove into the ground seeking sanctuary, and others were simply run over. Gabe yelled over the roar of man, machine, and demon, "Lucy, you fuckin' showoff!" as Lucifer continued to decapitate every passing vampire with graceful swipes from his flaming sword.

"You're just jealous that I look so good doing it," Lucifer's disembodied voice said next to Gabe in a conversational tone as the demon rode his motorcycle over a pair of downed vampires. He spun around, pulling his chopper up into a wheelie, and saluted his traveling companions with his sword. Grey could see the warrior the man once was shining through momentarily, as his silhouette was limned in the firelight.

Malign rose up behind him, no longer dressed for the Oscars, but a thing out of H.P. Lovecraft's worst nightmares. She was hunched over and still standing twice as tall as a man. More ape-like than human she bellowed, swinging a massive fist at Lucifer, launching both him and his chopper into the air where his motorcycle exploded from the concussive force, sailing over Pete's head like a massive metal comet. He turned to Grey and said, "If Kong there goes back to Vegas and scales New York, New York, I'm out."

Grey chuckled saying, "Oh, I don't think that will be a problem."

Lucifer flew out of the twisted machine wreckage, a winged Greek god, alabaster skin illuminated from within, a corona of indigo radiated about him, ebony crow feathered wings spanned from his shoulders, blending in with his now shoulder-length black hair. He was bare to the waist wearing a long flowing cream colored kilt-like undergarment. His baritone voice roared across the night as he shouted, "Malign!" Sword raised and doubling in length to match his now larger foe, the fallen angel soared through the night.

"Oh shit!" Pete exclaimed as the two demons clashed. The ground under his feet rumbled with tremors. Sticking his arms out to maintain his balance, he turned an accusatory glare at Grey. "You planned this, didn't you?"

Grey shook his head, watching the battle. Most of the vampires had fled or been destroyed. The ones that had stayed by their master's side were being dispatched by Raven, Gabe, Zeus or the Lone Riders. Pete said, "Bullshit, you knew. Look at you all smug. Nice poker face, Grey. Why don't you just complete the whole mastermind image and pull out a bag of *Jiffy-Pop* and roast it over a flaming vampire."

"Pete," Grey said in mock indignation, "I don't know what you're talkin' about. This is just two demons, who happen to hate each other, duking it out. Not even really our business, as you pointed out. Whoa! Did you see that?" Grey asked excitedly as Lucifer preformed a roundhouse kick, knocking Malign from her feet and making the ground rumble again when she landed.

"He is still beautiful," Eric said speaking for the first time since the battle began. The angel stood raptly watching the battle beside Grey and Pete continuing, "No matter what he has done and in whose name he has done it. He is beautiful."

Pete turned quickly at the sound of an unfamiliar voice. With eyebrows beetled in question he asked, "And who the hell are you?"

"Pete," Hank said from around Zeus' neck, as the two of them joined the gathering at ringside, "this is my friend Metatron. He's going by the name Eric, for now."

"The Voltron angel?" Pete asked. "The guy we came all this way to convince that the vampire fad may *not* be such a great idea to endorse? … Here? …Sure, why not. That makes perfect sense. So, what do you think now, jackass? Still a good idea?" Pete gestured to the carnage and destruction spread across the desert.

Eric looked contritely at his feet and kept his gaze downcast as he said, "No, I was wrong. I let ego color my judgment. I should have seen what was happening and stepped in sooner. It…it wasn't until the monsters tried to harm someone I cared for that I saw my folly. That is no excuse, I know. Every life should be precious, but I am only a man, flawed and weak. For what it is worth, I apologize."

Pete rolled his eyes, "Yeah…well…don't let it happen again, alright?"

Eric smiled saying, "Of course."

Grey snorted, "Typical angel, can't even let a man enjoy a much deserved 'I told you so'."

The battle of titans raged on. The others both living and otherwise had gathered in a cluster with Grey and Pete up front. They looked so small and helpless compared to the monsters fighting in front of them, like a small band of primitives paying homage to their deities. Desert landscape was transformed into lifeless post-apocalyptical wasteland as negative energy liberally spilled over into the physical world. To the group at large Zeus asked, "Um…what do we do?"

"Nothing," Grey said, "we let them…" He trailed off as Lucifer was knocked backward, crashing and crumbling a canyon wall in the process. Malign vanished, no retreat to the underworld, no running or fleeing; she simply vanished. Stumbling back to his feet Lucifer shouted, "Coward! Come back and let us finish this!" His words echoed into the empty warzone.

Looking at Lucifer, as he stood there panting and agitated, Grey muttered a low, "Damn."

With battle lust still raging high and his foe no longer before him, Lucifer turned his ire on the only other creatures in the destroyed desert. Deep indigo burned from his eyes as he focused on the crowd. He raised his sword high into the air as his black feathered wings flapped and the flames dancing across the naked blade changed from red to a blue matching his eyes. Lucifer bellowed an inarticulate war cry and flew toward the group. Pete whispered, "Oh shit."

Eric raced out in front of the cluster of people – who to his logic would not have been there if he had but listened to his friend – and pushed as much energy as he could into a barrier protecting those who he had put in harm's way. Lucifer crashed into the shield with a blinding flash of light and shadow. Falling to the ground the former angel shook his head to clear it and faced the man who had stopped him saying, "Metatron? What are you doing here?"

Eric smiled, "That is a long story old friend. Would you please calm down so that I might live to tell it to you?"

***

Dawn was breaking over the sands as the Lone Riders drove back into Las Vegas. An exhausted Lucifer rode with them. Eric had gone back for his Spyder and had offered to let Zeus bring Hank back to town via it, while he walked with the other warriors of the Balance. Grey had instructed all those going on ahead to pick a resort to check into and they would meet them there to regroup, recover, and plan their next course of action. As they drove off Pete heard Hank say, "Let's go to the one that's a circus. We can, can't we?"

Zeus revved the engine and tore off before Pete could chime in. Into the cloud of dust that the reverse tricycle left in its wake, Pete muttered, "I hate clowns."

When the only ones left were those who were walking, Grey took the lead, tilting his head back, letting the rising sun warm the right side of his face as he slowly ambled on, hands in his pockets. Pete, Raven, Gabe, and Eric followed him. He was more than content to enjoy the silence. It gave him an opportunity to reflect on a gamble that failed and how whether it was his reading of the cards that caused the failure or if fate just dealt him a bum hand. *You had to try*, he thought to himself. *It was worth a try at least, without losing anybody from my flock I'll take it as a win just for the satisfaction of seeing that bitch run from someone other than me.*

Grey knew his peace and quiet would not last long. It was always a temporary respite to retreat into his thoughts when he was with Pete, Raven, or Gabe, or as that twisted sadist, Fate, would have it this time, all three of them. They had not covered more than a quarter of the distance back to the city when Gabe could no longer hold his tongue - to be fair Grey was surprised he had lasted as long as he did - "Oi! Angel boy, this was a real nice fuckaroo you caused here, eh?"

"Let it go, Gabe," Grey said trying to hold the silence for even a moment longer.

"No, Grey, I don't fuckin' think I will," Gabe continued, building up steam. "This kind'o shite burns me, mate! Some high and mighty, holier than thou, peace and love, tree hugging hippie gets to play God, manipulatin' people. And when it blows up in his face he gets to say, 'Ever so sorry chaps,' and all is fuckin' forgiven?"

"That's the job, Gabe," Grey said continuing to walk north, never breaking stride.

"Fuck the job, Grey!" Gabe yelled, really getting into the flow of his ire. "What kind'o fuckin' Balance is that, huh?"

Pete tentatively added, "Hey...um, I can't believe I'm saying this, but I agree with Gabe."

Grey stopped and the three of them had been following so closely that they almost ran into his back. Eric had fallen slightly behind the group as Gabe had ranted. Grey did not turn around. He stood enjoying the warmth of the sun saying, "Raven, darlin' how about you?"

She kept her head downcast even though Grey stayed facing away from them. She did not say yes or no, only, "I'm sorry, Grey."

"Fuckin'- A right, love!" Gabe shouted, "Union solidarity, the local Balance 516!"

Grey spun around so fast all three of them jumped back. Pete even tripped and fell on his behind. Grey did not yell; if anything his voice dropped lower and quieter into a menacing growl, "And what would you have me do, Irish? String him up and take everything that he was? Bleed him dry into the earth? Or maybe I should feed him to Malign and her vampires? A sort of poetic justice since he unwittingly helped her grow that bloodsucking army of hers, because even you can't be stupid enough to think that what we just faced was all of them. What we fought wasn't shit!"

"N-no, I just thought...," Gabe stammered.

"No!" This time Grey did yell. "You didn't think! But apparently you think you know better than me how to handle things, right? Or, for that matter, better than Harmony?"

"Grey…," Raven started, but he interrupted her. "No, Raven, you listen. All three of you listen to me. You have to realize why things are the way they are because someday I'll be gone, and don't get all up in arms about that. Y'all sure as shit ain't ready for me to leave yet, ain't that the truth. But, by the same token, shit happens so you can't count on me always being there. Harmony is what she is because she does not let herself, no *itself*, be controlled by its conditioning or emotions or ego or whatever the fuck it is that drives most you on. Injustice pisses me off just as much as all of you, don't think that it don't, but I learned long ago to use that anger properly. I don't let any of you in past my defenses, to get too close to me, to see me. Do you know why?"

The three of them stared: Pete wide-eyed, Raven glassy-eyed with emotion, and Gabe fire-eyed with anger. Raven said, "No, Grey, we don't. We never have."

Harmony's voice echoed rapidly through Grey's mind, *Jasper, I do not know quite what it is you are doing. Though I appreciate the asexual defense, I caution you not to take this beyond what they are ready to hear. Look at them, all three are really just children, adoring in their own ways. All want to impress you, do not ruin that. I beg you.*

Grey sighed before saying, "Because…look how worked up y'all are over Eric's failed scheme. Sure, a few folks died as a result, but people die all over the world every damn day and for a lot less than some pompous angel's attempt to thin the herd. That's my best guess as to why he was doing what he was doing. Is that right, Eric?"

Not wanting the focus to be drawn back to him, Eric only nodded in response. Grey said, "Now, imagine if I had died last night at the hands of Malign? Do you think any of you would have let Eric walk more than two steps away from that? What if I did let you in past my defenses? Let any of you become as close as y'all seem to want." He looked at each of them in turn. "Imagine what I would do if it had been one of you that had died last night instead? Do you think *anything* would have walked away from that?"

There is no adjective to describe the silence that fell over the desert morning; it would have made a tomb look like a wild kegger or the silence of the grave look like *Girls Gone Wild*. Grey turned his back to them once more, a brother, a friend, and a daughter. As the hot morning wind drifted over to them, he walked away saying, "Just do the damn job."

Chapter 15

Everybody lies. It doesn't matter if you are living or dead, angel or demon, man or woman, everybody lies. We lie to make ourselves sound more impressive, we lie to make the hurt go away, we lie to hurt, and we lie to keep others from hurting. We lie.

There are times when we lie because the truth is too horrific to face. There are times when we lie - and even as we tell the lie - we know that there will never be a point where we can rectify, undo, or at least color that lie with some truth. It is set in stone forever, until the stars grow cold. I've told such lies. I think if ever there was a moment when my soul was in danger of damnation or 'demonification' - I'd guess you could call it - it was when I lied to my little sister Elizabeth. The SS had come for us in the middle of the night; the favorite time for governmental bullies to strike, when people are tired and unprepared for a fight. A neighbor had told them where we were hiding in hopes of saving his own hide. He didn't, of course. That was the worst part of the war; so many thought to save themselves or their family alone, when if we'd all banded together at once, it never would have happened to begin with. I guess all wars are like that, aren't they?

My parents had been violently roused from sleep. I hadn't slept well since the war started; sometimes I think that's how it is for all the youth of an oppressed people. They burn with the fire of injustice and the old are broken and tired and just want to sleep. I scooped Elizabeth up in my arms so the SS goons wouldn't hurt her. My father tried to stop them and earned a fractured jaw for his trouble. My mother shrieked and was jabbed in the stomach with a rifle barrel when she ran to his side. Elizabeth was in tears. She buried her face in my nightshirt and I could feel the dampness of her tears soaking into my skin, a warm contrast to the cold night air. I rocked her as we were loaded onto trucks like cattle. My mother sobbed clinging to my father, while their two daughters took what comfort they could from each other. I remember…Oh God, I remember to this day saying to her, "It's okay little, Lizzy, it will be alright. We'll be safe soon."

Of course, that was a lie. We never were safe again. She died three days later. Maybe…maybe that wasn't such a lie after all. When it was over she was, and is, safe. I believe that. She had to go through a hell no child should, but at the end she was safe. She has to be. I couldn't very well tell my six year old sister that we were going to die could I? I lied, whether justified or not, I lied. Someday I will tell her I'm sorry. Someday, maybe, before the stars grow cold, she'll learn how sorry I am………..

***

"See!" Pete yelled, "that's why I hate clowns!" as the clown capered around him and Grey on the casino floor. They had left the others to find their own ways to wind down and were headed to one of the quieter eateries in the resort for a bit of respite and palaver. Most of the Riders had opted for sleep. A few like Dante and Bulldog were too keyed up for rest so they accompanied Hank, Zeus, and Eric to the pool. Gabe had sworn off that option, neither wishing to be in the company of angels nor, as he emphatically insisted, did he want to see Zeus in swim trunks. Raven had promised Lucifer she would watch over him while he rested so no other demon could take advantage of his weakened state. That left Grey and Pete on their own and knowing the older man as well as he did Pete suggested they get something to eat. It is what Grey would have done anyway plus it would give Pete the chance to pick his friend and mentor's brain as to what would come next.

The two strolled through the casino trying to find a quiet, non-buffet place to eat. That was when the clown started to circle around Pete, honking a horn every time Pete's right foot touched the gaudy casino carpet. With the clown's noises and antics the three of them had started to gather a following. Whenever they passed a parent - who had brought their child down for some juvenile entertainment during the daylight hours so they could have their own adult dalliances come nightfall - the child would laugh at the clown as he honked and made goofy faces behind Pete's back. Many of the children had dragged their parents along behind them so by the time they reached a quiet lounge, tucked away in a back corner of the resort, Pete, Grey, and the clown had more than a dozen observers. Pete turned around and sharply barked, "Look! We're going to eat now, so just shoo. Go on, go." He waved his hands away to try scattering the clown and crowd, even jumping at them a bit like a beach picnicker trying to scare a flock of insistent seagulls.

The clown turned to the crowd and imitated Pete, drawing a new round of giggles from the children, as its floppy rainbow wig bounced along with the cadence of its miming. Chuckling a bit himself Grey said, "Jesus, Pete, I thought all these Vegas places had gone to the spandex, glitter, and lightshow type circuses. Leave it to you to find the only classic clown for miles."

"Are you laughing, Grey? I know you wouldn't be laughing if it were you, because this isn't funny man," Pete growled. Turning on the clown, Pete repeatedly poked a finger sharply at the clown's polka dotted chest punctuating every word saying, "Look, pal." But every time Pete poked, the clown squeezed a Whoopee cushion which it was clutching behind its back. The children roared laughing with every fart and putt from the pink rubber novelty. A few of the fathers started laughing too and the mothers smiled indulgently. When Grey started laughing along with them, Pete had had enough. He shouted, "Fine! Have it your way."

The next time the clown squeezed the Whoopee cushion Pete slipped a bit of extra energy into it, filling the cushion with more air than it could hold. It exploded with a resounding bang that had a few security personnel scurrying over to make sure the noise was not a firearm. Every face in the crowd flinched then looked accusingly at Pete, as he smiled smugly, yelling at the clown, "There! How do you like it?" The clown started to cry.

"You're mean!" one little boy shouted. He deftly twisted out of his mother's restraining wristlock and went over to hold the clown's white gloved hand asking, "Are you okay?"

The boy's mother glared at Pete. Every face in the crowd glared at Pete. The clown continued to silently cry, as the little boy patted its hand reassuringly. Muttering under his breath, Pete said, "Grey, what do I do here? I need a little help man. This could turn ugly."

"Hey, I'm with the kid, you anti-clownite," Grey said folding his arms across his chest. One of the security officers had finished speaking into a walkie-talkie. Heading over to Pete he asked, "Sir, is everything alright here?"

"Yeah," Pete said stepping over to the security guard, turning his back to the crowd and silently sobbing clown. "Look, it's no big deal. I just-"

Pete was interrupted by a rubber chicken smacking into the back of his head. The chicken made a loud squawk upon impact, but fell limply at his feet as he spun around glaring heatedly. The clown was staring wide-eyed with surprise and shook his head at Pete's unspoken accusation, pointing at the little boy who was staring defiantly back at Pete.

"Sir," the security guard said. "This is a family resort. I'm going to have to ask you to leave, please." The "please" carried the weight of an order, not a request. Pete looked for some support from Grey, but the cowboy must have slipped away when no one was looking because he was nowhere to be seen. *Where the hell did he go?* Pete thought to himself, as the security guard said, "Sir, please."

"Fine," Pete said absently, still scanning the crowd for his friend. Then he spotted Grey, sitting at a far booth in the diner, sipping a cup of coffee. Sensing Pete's eyes on him Grey looked up and gave him a small twiddling finger wave, until the waitress returned, blocking him from Pete's view. "Sir!" The security guard demanded, this time placing a hand on Pete's upper arm in an attempt to escort him out.

"Okay, fine," Pete said, shrugging the guiding hand off. "I'm going." And he stomped off in the direction of the nearest exit. He had only gone a step or two when his right foot touched carpet and the honking started up again. The children started to cheer. Pete walked away, honking, mumbling, "I hate clowns."

***

"We failed you mistress," Gregor hissed, groveling at Malign's feet, as she sat atop another throne of darkness. "I am sorry."

"I typically reward failure with annihilation, Gregor," Malign said. "You know that."

"Yes mistress. What I am is forfeit. I will not struggle," Gregor said, lowering his forehead to the stone floor in obeisance. Malign smiled at his attitude and posture of deference saying, "And that, Gregor, is why you will live."

"Mistress?" the vampire demon asked, without raising his head.

Malign stepped down from her seated position of authority and paced around him, deep in a cavern under Devil's Tower. She said, "The failure was not yours, Gregor. I had not anticipated Lucifer's participation in this little endeavor of mine. I should have. It seems that after all this time there may still be a sliver of the man he was within there somewhere. I had assumed I'd taken that from him long ago. He was not strong enough to take me last night. I felt that, but I could not risk him weakening me to the point where another lesser foe could end me. That would be embarrassing. He is resting now I am sure, but I do not know where. Lucifer is not of interest to me, Gregor, but another angel I may corrupt is though. That is your opportunity at redemption."

"What is your command mistress?" Gregor said looking up at her for the first time since he was told he would not be punished as expected.

"The puppet is with the Balance tools now. Go fetch me the boy angel that your brethren failed to bring me before. I want that child, Gregor. Do you understand me? In this there is no room for failure. If you do not bring me the boy, you will be destroyed, not incorporated or devoured. I will tear you apart and let the world reclaim the pieces. Am I understood?"

"Yes mistress."

"Good. Now if you cannot find them then find someone who does know where they are, someone who knows that pathetic little human playground in the desert. Risk the sunlight if you must; it would be a simpler fate than what I would do to you if you fail. Go!"

***

Down below Vegas, below the casinos, below the flash, below the glitter, there are places where people who seek out more unseemly entertainment, in a city that already caters to indulgences, may find what they are looking for. These are places, small rooms and staffed establishments that you will not find on the tourist maps. Here is where the people go seeking surcease - if only for a moment - from kinks and perversions that keep them up at night. Here, there be monsters.

Monsters, both living and dead, for there were more demons down there than men, lurked in every shadow. Lucifer had chosen to curl up in the corner of a den catering to extreme sadomasochism. The cries and whimpers of the tortured had sung him a lullaby that had him dozing in a state of meditation, regaining his strength. Raven stood by him, watching the living men indulge themselves in the pain of others. Smaller demons scampered about the floor space, drinking in the violence and negative energy, dancing Gene Kelly-like as the sorrow rained around them. "You chose this place to rest on purpose, didn't you, Alex? It was only after I agreed to guard you that you said where you wanted to go," Raven said to the prone form lying beside her.

"Perhaps," he whispered. "Does it remind you of your death, with all those fools partaking over there?" He lackadaisically waved a hand in the direction of the room's patrons and participants, both willing and unwilling.

Raven kicked him lightly in the side and said, "If you call me 'Clarice' or ask for a nice Chianti, I will leave you here for the vultures."

"Ha," Lucifer laughed, rolling onto his side to look at her. "Fair enough, Raven, you have more than earned my respect. I did not choose this place to torture you. It is easy to regain strength among the wicked, and the demons who often hang about such places would never be a match for me, undefended or not, even at my weakest."

Raven did not dig for a further explanation than that. There was always more than one reason the man, who the world thought of as Lucifer, did the things that he did. To her it felt like hours went by, but in a place where the sun never touches, time can be a slippery concept. The faces in the crowd changed but the torture stayed the same. She turned to Lucifer and asked, "Why have you cooperated, Alex? This whole time you could have walked away. Harmony is not a god. We all have free will. Gabe can barely take care of himself, let alone keep an eye on you. Why stay? Hell, you aren't even one of us."

"I was," Lucifer said, "a long, long time ago. When I first died, Harmony came to me and said I was what she had been looking for. I would be her greatest soldier. She made me - a man who had toppled empires - feel like I was something greater than the world already considered me to be. Perhaps… perhaps I wanted to feel that way again, even if it was for only a short period of time."

Raven stared at him. Her mouth hung wide open and all she could do was blink. Lucifer sat up onto his elbows and leaned his back against the stained concrete wall saying, "I take it by your shocked expression you knew none of that."

"But…I thought you were an angel," Raven said. "That's where the whole fallen angel mythology came from, right?"

"It is and I was," Lucifer agreed. "I left Harmony's employ when I grew tired of never doing anything except leaving things as they are. That, Raven, is what has Grey so wound up and agitated most days. To his credit he has lasted much longer than I did. Or any of his predecessors come to think of it."

"Jesus," Raven exclaimed. "Does Grey know any of this?"

Lucifer shrugged, "I would not see how he could. I doubt Harmony would tell him, but then again, never underestimate him. You know that. I wouldn't be surprised if that clever old cowboy hasn't figured most it out for himself."

"Jesus," Raven said again.

"And," Lucifer added laying back down, "do remember child, I am the Devil after all. I could just as well be lying."

***

"Cannonball!" Zeus shouted, running from the farthest edge of the pool and wrapping his gigantic frame into a compact sphere to go plunging into the deep end. The children who had been playing with Hank all cheered when Zeus' splashdown rivaled any of the pool's jets or mechanized wave action features. Glowing lights from tiny lesser angels skimmed the wave crests that rippled out from Zeus' epicenter, like chipmunk-sized surfers.

Dante sat with his feet dangling in the shallows, jeans rolled up past his thin boney ankles. Bulldog and Eric were sitting in lounge chairs behind him talking incessantly. It was a curiosity to Dante that Bulldog found it so amazing when the perfectly manicured and coifed man told them he was an angel. His friend continued to waste words, as Dante thought of it, asking questions about life and death. *People never appreciate what it is they have unless they do not have it,* Dante thought, then quickly berated himself. *You shouldn't think that way about your friend, but it's hard. I'm not jealous; no, I just wish they could see things through my eyes.*

Dante watched all the children playing with the big man and his little brother. *Another angel if my eyes are telling me the truth,* he thought. *All those tiny lights flashing around them must be some type of angels, too. I always thought they were fairies or pixies or something. I still don't know what the hell the big guy and his friends are though. The dark one confuses me, too.*

"Hey!" Bulldog's raucous voice intruded on Dante's thoughts. "Didn't I see in a movie or something that you angel guys are…well you know? Pecker-less?"

Dante chuckled and did not listen closely enough to hear whatever attempt at decorum the angel strived for with his explanation. Dante went back to watching the small angels fly about with the children. He had seen so many like them over the years. They never spoke to him like Eric and Hank had, but they did come and visit him, especially in the years when he was at the orphanage; those were times that Dante did not like to remember too often. But, like all bad memories, we cannot often shake them and they come back to us no matter how hard we try to block them out. It was mostly flashes and images for the mute man: a heavy hand, faces yelling and taunting, tears at night, a small lavender light drying his eyes, more dark thoughts, red eyes under the bed, another beating, more cruel names *Half breed* and *Chief Cat-got-his-tongue*. The demons from Dante's past continued to distract him from the demons that were creeping up on his new friends in the shadows right then.

Chapter 16

Promises...I wonder if somebody makes a promise and it doesn't come true, then does that make the promise a lie? Or is it the person who becomes a liar and the promise - no matter what vein it may have been made in - is left unsullied?

I've made promises I couldn't keep. We all have, but then again, as I've said before, we all lie too. So, if you want to pretend that you've never made a promise you didn't keep, then you're already a liar. Go ahead.

To have and to hold, for better, for richer, for poorer, in sickness and in health, for as long as you both shall live - yada yada yada - you may kiss the bride and get what you want for now, but we don't really mean to hold you to these promises, don't worry. You can back out at any time, with the aid of your own personal psi-vampire, I mean lawyer.

Yet I have seen husbands and wives who pass on before their partner, wait around - sometimes for decades - until their lover dies as well. Now there are some people who take their promises seriously I'd say.

I think it might be interesting if we could gather a tally as we go through life and afterlife, a scoreboard of all the times we make a promise we don't keep. I know that sounds like something children are taught in religion class, right? God keeps a scoreboard of all your rights and wrongs. I don't mean it like that. What I want is a sort of public profile these broken promises could be viewed on. That way if somebody says to you, "I promise I'll do this or that," then you can bring up their scoreboard and either say, "Hey, look at that; maybe you will," or you can laugh in their face and say, "Yeah, right. Look at this; you couldn't even keep a promise you made to the woman you loved. Why would you keep one you made to me?"

That sounds jaded I know, but it is so hard at times for me when I see someone make a promise that I know they cannot have any possible way of keeping. It's hard to see them lie to save the hurt on a friend's face. Maybe we should all just be a little more careful about what we promise other people............

***

"Psst!" The whispered hissing came from under the table next to Grey as he finished his meal. "Psst! Hey, Officer Badass, over here!" Grey looked over to see the diminutive form of Eduardo crouching under the neighboring table, looking even more like a dark side version of a hamster in the bright fluorescent light, waving and gesticulating. Chuckling Grey said, "Already wanting to cash in that IOU, Eduardo?"

"No, no sir, Officer Badass," the small demon said, shaking his head. "Eduardo is sorry. Eduardo didn't want to do it, but they made Eduardo. They said they'd eat Eduardo if he didn't help. Eduardo doesn't want to be eaten. Well…the fun time naughty eaten would be okay, but this was the evil bad vampire type of eaten, you know?"

Taking immediate and intense interest in the tiny demon Grey asked, "What did you do, Eduardo?"

The tiny demon started to fidget and he nervously said, "Eduardo didn't want to, honest. Eduardo wanted to come get you as soon as he could, but they kept Eduardo until it was too late."

"Too late for what, Eduardo," Grey said, anger dropping the octave of his voice to a low rumble. The few other diner patrons turned to watch the lean, dangerous looking man crouch down and start yelling to the empty space under the table next to his booth. A loud explosion that rattled the ice in every glass and jingled the silverware on every table turned their focus elsewhere. "F-for that," Eduardo stammered. "Eduardo knows the IOU is off. Eduardo knew that Officer Badass has a reputation for coming back and finding out who did what. Eduardo didn't want you to come looking for him. Eduardo thought it would be better to just come clean."

Harmony's voice spoke up quickly in Grey's mind, "Jasper, you have to go now. Zeus is going ballistic. I sent Gabe and Pete to stop him already, but they cannot do much more without harming him. Jasper, Malign's vampires took Hank. Another vampire tried to do the same a few days ago, but Raven stopped it. At the time I thought it was a random occurrence, but apparently Malign wants him for a reason."

"Shit!" Grey swore. "I'm on my way."

"B-but, Officer Badass," Eduardo stammered. Grey had started to walk away from the booth, but he swung back viper quick and snatched Eduardo out from under the table. Chairs and table toppled over in a cascade of plastic, wood, and cutlery when Grey pulled the demon out from his shadowed sanctuary. The tiny creature did not fight or struggle, as Grey held it by the throat. It stared at Grey with liquid black eyes. Eduardo swallowed audibly and said, "But Officer Badass. Do you know where they took the boy? ... Because if you don't, Eduardo does."

***

"Let me go, Pete!" Zeus roared, as his friend did what he could to restrain the large man. Gabe was wrapped around Zeus' ankles like a toddler trying to stop daddy from going to work while Pete held him in a bear hug from behind, his hands barely reaching around to encircle Zeus' bulk.

"Sorry, Zeus," Pete grunted around the effort. "But, Harmony told us to keep you from causing any more destruction."

"They took my brother, Pete!" Zeus yelled.

"Aye," Gabe said from bellow between grunts. "We know mate, sorry. If the boss hadn't told us otherwise, we'd be chasing the black hearted fuckers right beside you now."

"What happened?" Raven asked appearing in a flash of light at poolside. She was looking around at the destruction. All the other aquatic patrons had vanished. Plastic lounge chairs were twisted and melted around the charred concrete. Shade umbrellas were turned inside out and several were imbedded in the resort's exterior wall like giant darts. The shallow end of the pool was slowly turning a bright pinkish hue, radiating to a darker red where Dante's body lay leaking out the last of his blood. Bulldog was cradling his friend's head in his lap and weeping loudly. His beard hung low over Dante, soaking up the chlorine diluted blood. The only other creature she could see present was Eric, as he tried to heal the gaping wound in Dante's neck. Around his grappling Pete yelled, "I'd love to explain…but…damn it, Zeus, stop struggling! … I'm a little busy at the moment."

Pete could not tell if it was exhaustion over the recent battles, sorrow due to loss, or just the sound of one of his oldest friend's voice, but the big man went limp. Zeus stopped struggling and crumpled in a heap next to a profuse pile of melted polyethylene. Gabe and Pete let go of him as Raven rushed over to grasp his hand in hers. He looked up with tears streaming down his eyes and said, "I couldn't save him before, Raven. How can I fail him again?"

Grey's raspy voice answered, "You won't, son," preceding him as he appeared much as Raven had only moments before. "I know where they took him, Zeus. We'll get him back, I promise."

Raven shot her head up at the confidence in Grey's voice and her eyebrows rose in an unspoken question. Grey did not acknowledge her, but crouched down on the other side of the weeping giant. He grasped Zeus' free hand in his and said, "Get to your feet, son. We got time to catch up, don't worry. We'll-"

He was interrupted by a wail of grief from Bulldog as Eric shook his head saying, "I'm sorry, there is nothing more I can do."

"Sorry," Bulldog raged. "Sorry? You're sorry? You're a fucking angel, God damn it! Ain't that what you people said? He got his throat ripped out saving the *real* living kids that were in the pool from those fucking monsters. Monsters that were here because of you!" He glared at Eric then looked around at every face. All of them relative strangers that he had just met in the last few days, while the one face he did know was lying in his arms, pale and growing lighter by the moment, staring up at him with lifeless eyes.

Bulldog could not see or hear what the others could. He had not been born with, or given, the gift of vision like his dead friend had been. He looked away from the gazes of people he did not know, who he had not shared years of his life with, and back to the man he had been proud to call brother. Bulldog could not see or hear Dante - the energy, mind, and spirit of the man - standing behind him shouting, "I'm still here man! Right here behind you!"

Dante glared at the others, "Why can't he see me? ... My God! Y-you can hear me can't you? Pete, Pete, please, what do I do?"

Pete shuffled uncomfortably, not wanting to meet Dante's questions face on he looked over to where his body was lying in the pool. He could hear sirens blaring in the background, as emergency vehicles responded to one of the many catastrophic calls they had received in the last twenty-four hours. When he spoke it was in a whisper that only the dead could hear, "Dante, man I'd like to help you, but that's not really our area. And, yeah, we can hear you man, loud and clear. You have one of the strongest voices I've ever heard."

Dante looked pleadingly at them. "Not your area? What do you mean, 'Not your area'? What am I supposed to do? You're saying for the first time ever my friends could hear me, but they'd have to be dead to do so? What kind of sense does that make?"

Grey stepped over to Dante's spirit saying, "It don't make any sense. I'm sorry, but that's life and death. Neither makes much sense from the perspective of those that go through both. We don't get to see the big picture. We get stuck with little glimpses like this and the universe tells us to make do. You can come with us friend, join us if you like. The boss lady tells me you're somethin' special. What do you say?"

Dante closed his eyes and shook his head, "I'm sorry mister. Thanks for the offer, but I'll pass. I'm not stupid. I know I may have been wrong in my interpretations of some of the things I have seen over the years, but I have seen them. If I stick around my friends then at some point they may see me - or heaven help me - they might hear me."

"That's a risky proposition friend. There ain't no guarantees," Grey said. "Seek shelter at night and watch your back. But, know that if you change your mind at any time, all you got to do is say so."

Dante nodded in understanding and sat down next to Bulldog and his own dead body. The rescue teams burst through the doors, only to see one biker holding the lifeless body of another. All of them that were past the mortal coil had let go of their physical shells, even Eric was gone, and the glowing angelic form of Metatron remained among the Balance soldiers. He looked over at Grey and said, "I am going with you."

Gabe spoke up before Grey, saying, "Don't you fuckin' think you've done enough." He pointed over at Dante and Bulldog as the EMT's pried the body from Bulldog's arms and their police escorts handcuffed the biker's now empty arms. "Sweet Jesus, those blokes think he did it?"

Harmony's voice resonated around the pool for all the dead to hear, "The mortal authorities have to be cautious, Gabriel. They will not know what happened even if they review the security footage. The extra energy surged through all the electronics. I do not know what will become of Bulldog and I regret that, but we must act now, where we are needed."

"What about him?" Gabe said gesturing toward the glowing Metatron. "He comin' too or not? I think things have been *Touched by an Angel* enough already for this cluster fuck! We don't need his help."

After a second's deliberation Harmony said, "Sorry, Gabriel, but yes, he may go. Everyone deserves a chance to rectify their actions. Let us hope he can. Only I cannot escort him as I would all of you; his presence, ironically enough, would un-Balance me. So, either way I do not believe he would arrive in time."

"What if I went with him?" Lucifer asked from the shadows where he had been hiding for how long, no one knew.

Harmony sighed, "There is not much time for argument. Fine, Alexander, if you accompany him then Metatron may come as well. But please, hurry." A glowing wall high enough to encompass Zeus' seven feet flared into existence when Harmony stopped speaking. It obscured the police officers and medical staff that were attempting to figure out what had happened.

When everyone started to walk toward it Pete said, "Wait, I don't even know where we are going?"

Grey laughed, a dry uncomfortable sound that expressed more pain than pleasure. "To Devil's Tower, Pete, where else?" And he continued his agonized laugh as he walked through Harmony's gateway.

Chapter 17

Lots of religious scholars, scientists and plain old housewives say that the mind and body are codependent. It's all just mind over matter. I don't know, maybe they are right. If they mean the mind as in the physical meat of the brain, then they are certainly correct. But, neither mind nor body can function without the spirit. Some call it the soul or the poets like to say the heart, again not the tangible organ, but the metaphorical heart. There are living, breathing people who have both mind and body, but they aren't alive. Maybe you have been lucky enough to only read about such people, but they do exist, trust me. I don't mean grandpa suffering from Alzheimer's staring with a vapid gaze out a window to a past that only he can see. No, I mean young people who have lost or never found their mind, but their body functions just like it should.

Why is that? There never is just one answer to things; God how people forget that at times. A person may not be alive because something in their environment caused them trauma. Maybe it was physical intentional abuse, or maybe negligence, but at some point in their life something caused that trauma………or it could always be demons.

No, seriously.

I don't mean to imply possession. No head twisting, pea soup type stuff but the constant prodding and poking to a living psyche by a demon can cause damage if the person does not have a strong enough innate power of will. There has to be both the weak and the strong for there to be a Balance. Sorry but that is kind of a job requirement that I have to plug that in there every now and again. It's my version of asking, "Do you want fries with that?"

The weak willed can be influenced by demons; it does not make them evil. It only makes them weak; what they do with that influence - ignore it or act on it - that is up to them. I met a group of boys who, once the demon influencing them lost its hold on them, were able to function and turned out to be decent kids. Maybe it just took longer for them to grow up, who knows? Iconic Linda Blair possession aside that is why demons typically go after youth, their minds are not solid enough yet to protect them from influence.

Funny how if the living knew half of what went on beyond the veil of death they'd be teaching their children the Method of Loci instead of religion. That is the first thing Grey teaches any of us who go to work for him. I can personally vouch for the effectiveness of creating a memory palace to retain all that you are. If young children had a place to retreat to when a demon was trying to influence them they could retain their mind, their body, and grow into their spirit. The spirit is what they would really be protecting, that energy that is distinctly them and no one else. That's what makes them fall under the category of "alive" in my book.

It's sad though, to see things how we do, almost always dealing with the worst case scenario. Because, though it does happen in the opposite way sometimes, mostly as warriors for the Balance we clean up the mess left by some demon.

Sometimes I wonder…maybe some child sitting there, staring out a window at his own inner world, is fighting a demon from telling him things, suggesting horrid actions. Maybe that boy, who looks like he isn't really alive, really there, maybe he is saving the world from himself……….

***

Seven distinct individuals walked into seven different versions of Harmony. She was waiting for them, appearing to each of them as someone else, but it was Zeus that she rushed over to and embraced. *Huh*, Pete thought. *I wonder how she looks to him. He isn't stooping to hug her like he should if he saw her as the same height I do.*

"Francis," Harmony said. "We will get him back. Do not worry. It may sound cruel to hear, but they want him for a reason, Francis, or else they would have just devoured him then and there." She stroked the side of his face in a calming maternal gesture. She looked around at the others saying, "Seven of you. Well I suppose that is fitting for where you are going."

"Yeah," Pete answered. "Devil's Tower, as in mashed potatoes 'this means something' and *beep beep beep boop boop*." He made up and down waving motions with his right hand to accompany the sounds.

Harmony sighed, "Yes, Peter. But, there is more to that place than Mr. Speilberg portrayed. There is power there, dark and ominous power. There are many such places around the world like it, but few rival Devil's Tower for raw energy. *Mato Tipila*, 'Bear Tower' to the Lakota, who tell the legend of its creation through the story of seven girls who were playing a distance from their village when a giant bear came upon them and chased them to a rock. The rock was not tall enough to save all the girls, so they prayed to the rock's spirit to take pity on them and save them from the bear. The rock's spirit heard the girls' prayers and grew to an enormous height as the bear thrashed attempting to climb the rock, breaking its claws, digging deep furrows into the rock's side trying to reach the seven girls, explaining the striated outer appearance of Devil's Tower."

"So," Pete asked, "The bear was some kind of demon who left the area tainted with negative energy or something?"

"No, Peter," Harmony said smiling. "Devil's Tower is a monolithic igneous intrusion, the inside of a worn away volcano. I only told you that story to explain my comment about the parallel with the seven of you - seven children, seven soldiers. The Lakota's legend has nothing to do with its font of energy. It is a place of power because before humans walked the earth, when the continents were still locked together, that volcano was responsible for the extinction of an entire race of sentient lizard people who had started to evolve from the dinosaurs."

"Holy crap, seriously?" Pete asked while the others started to laugh. "Oh, I see, poke fun at the rookie, still. Ha ha."

Everyone was laughing to some degree or other, even Zeus was smiling around his sorrow. Harmony walked over to Pete whispering, "Sorry, Peter, but he needed that and besides how many times do I have to tell you? I do not know everything. The place simply has power and Malign likes power. That is all I know."

She touched Pete on the shoulder kindly and turned to the others saying, "I cannot take you to the summit. There is something about the place that is blocking me from doing so. It may be Malign or it may be whatever fuels that place. I can take you as far as the paved trail the humans have placed around the site for tourists, but the rest, including the climb to the summit, will be up to you."

She motioned to the side and another gateway opened up. They could not see through it; it was opaque and lit in cool shades of blues and greens. *Damn*, Pete thought. *I really need to remember to suggest she put in a window one of these days when the shit isn't hitting the fan.* He watched as the others all went to and then through the light. Grey was the last to go, standing beside Pete. He nodded and both men went through together.

***

The sun was setting, giving what little light they had left a purple hue reflecting off the rocks, trees, and monolithic spire. It was now twice in less than a day that Grey had walked out from Harmony and into a scene from any sane person's version of Hell. Thousands of vampire demons were scattered about the landscape. Some roosted in trees like grotesque man-sized vultures. Other vampires stood hunched in clusters speaking in many languages. None of them had seen the seven souls come through Harmony's gateway. The demons were all gazing reverently up at the Tower as the moon, riding low in the dusky sky, crested its summit. Standing next to Grey, Pete started whispering to himself, over and over, "Damn it woman, you need to install a window."

All six of his charges turned in Grey's direction, all with the unspoken question of, *what the fuck do we do now?* to varying degrees of vulgarity upon their faces. The question was answered for him when a late-arriving vampire landed behind them. It looked from them to the Tower and back again several times in confusion, then it let out the tiniest of shrieks right before Lucifer lopped its head from its shoulders. It had been a small sound, no louder than the squeak of a mouse with laryngitis, but it had been loud enough. Every demonic vampire mien turned their way. There was a second's calm before the storm, then every demon shrieked, filling the air with a tangible weight of terror. A squirrel dropped from an overhead tree and lay twitching at Grey's feet. Raven laughed then said, "What is it with you and dead rodents falling from the sky?"

"Huh," Grey said when the vampire choir had quieted down enough for him to be heard, "Well people, I'd say we have ourselves a fight on our hands. Let's get to work," as the army of vampires charged them.

***

Metatron could not do much. As an angel he had more power than he did in a human guise, but it was still not something he could wield about like Lucifer and his flaming sword or any of the other Balance soldiers. At least, that was, if he wanted to stay a force for good. Power could corrupt, he knew that, but it was so very heady to swim in the ideas of doing more than protecting others. It was a fine treacherous line to swim and not drown. He did not want to do harm to random people he did not know. He would protect them yes, but he would much rather do so on his terms and how he saw fit. Holding a shield to protect the flanks of his allies was just not as satisfying as destroying those who had corrupted what he had been trying to accomplish. This failed attempt to reinvent what he had so skillfully cultivated with his Book of Enoch had left the bitter taste of resentment in the angel's mouth.

"Hey, Voltron!" Pete yelled intruding on Metatron's thoughts. "We didn't bring you along to daydream and think happy happy angel thoughts. I got – whoa shit!" he exclaimed as a pair of vampires leapt at him from different directions. Pete ducked and Zeus fried them both with bolts of orange lightning. "Damn it angel, get over here and watch our backs," Pete yelled again. "Andele! Andele! Move it, I have a hundred Grace Jones want-a-bes trying to chew on my ass over here."

Metatron let go of his negative thoughts and personal desires. He knew what it meant to be an angel, to stay on this earth within the same mind one was born with. He knew how to protect those that needed it, to deliver them from evil. So using all the power of love, kindness, and compassion he could muster, the ancient angel pushed all of that energy out into a shield, blocking any of the vampires from attacking these people whom he had thrown his lot in with. It did not matter if they were good, evil, or neutral. They were here as a result of his hubris. Good people, innocent people had already died as a result of his ego. It was time to repent.

"Stay together," Grey ordered, sending volleys of energy into the onrushing demons. "Metatron, guard the rear! Pete and Raven, watch the right flank. Gabe and Zeus, take the left. Alexander and I will lead the charge. We are going forward people! Don't fall behind and stay close."

There was no easy way to climb Devil's Tower unassisted, even with the flexibility of no longer being weighed down by gravity and the risks of mortal flesh. The monument's sides were sheer crumbling rock all three hundred and sixty degrees around. It is trying on a man physically, tiring and exhausting to climb with the assistance of harnesses and ropes. When the group had made it to the base, Pete looked up after popping a vampire like a five foot tall tick and said, "Jesus, Grey, I don't think I could climb that in the daylight, without the nosferatu nightmare nipping at my heels."

There were dozens of vampires clinging to the sheer sides, crawling insect-like toward them, readying to pounce down upon them like giant spiders in an arachnophobic's worst night terror. Grey forced a wave of energy up the side of Devil's Tower. It washed away any monster adhering to the edifice in one big push. He turned around, facing the others. Metatron was sustaining a powerful shield; a hemisphere sealing them away from the vampires and placing their backs up against the recently cleansed mountainside. Grey looked from face to face and said, "We can do this if we leapfrog around. Stay together and watch each other's backs. We have to…" Grey trailed off when he heard a young boy's voice screaming. He looked to Zeus, but before he could say anything Hank's voice shrieked, "Francis! Help me, Francis!"

Whatever weak and tenuous hold Zeus had been using to rein his sanity in snapped under the weight of his baby brother's voice calling to him for help. Grey had enough time to mutter, "Shit," before Zeus broke through Metatron's barrier and leapt like a gigantic hairy toad from ledge to ledge, quickly disappearing over the lip of the twelve hundred foot tall dead volcano.

"That God damned bitch!" Grey yelled. "Fine, Zeus just showed y'all how it's done people. On the count of three, Metatron, drop the shield and let's haul ass. One, two, three!"

Chapter 18

Soldiers can never leave Hell behind them. Once they see it - and believe me at some point every true soldier does, whether they are fighting for another man's cause or crusade, or for one of their own, they will see Hell - a soldier will never ever be able to leave it. A piece of them will always stay there, lost among the horrors they witnessed, propagated, or stopped. The eastern philosophies say Hell is a state of mind. I agree, because how can a soldier ever rectify mass murder, rape, and so many of the god awful actions that mankind - living and dead - foist upon their fellow sentient beings?

As a soldier I want to put this in terms those of you who may - and thank your lucky stars for it - go through life and afterlife having never seen Hell. At some point in your life you will see something that will brand itself into your mind. It may be sitting at a loved one's deathbed and watching them take their last breath. It may be a car doing ninety on the highway losing control and driving head on into a semi. It may be a man or woman so desperate to escape a fire that they hurtle themselves from a burning skyscraper.

Now magnify that by the hundreds or thousands of such instances that a soldier sees when Hell comes calling. Do you think you'd be able to disassociate from that? Could you sit down to Thanksgiving dinner with your family and not see the corpses from your past juxtaposed with Grandma's basted bird? Or watch some talking head on the television blathering on about the failings of a cause and country you fought for, had men you called brothers die for, and not want to lash out violently? Maybe the Dalai Lama could do that, but me, fuck no! When someone I love dies for a cause you better never, and I mean never, let me hear you talking about it in a flippant "I could have done better" tone of voice or contemptuous attitude.

I think there is only so much pain and suffering that the human mind can handle bearing witness to before it snaps. No matter how old the mind may be, there comes a time when too much is just too much. That is the reasoning behind the lack of sanity for any demon, I suppose. They aren't all crazy mind you, but nearly enough of them are to keep that label from being a stereotype. There is suffering and injustice that the mind can deal with and then there is that breaking point. We all have different thresholds for this. My body came to rest in what many consider to be the world's largest cemetery, where four million souls, hailing from twenty-four different countries, all found their final resting place in a tiny corner of nowhere in German occupied Poland.

The best any soldier can do is let Hell keep you company. No, do not let it twist you into a monster, but use it when and where you can. If Hell creeps up on you at odd times, and it will, see it, remember it, but don't follow that road back to Hell. Hover on the threshold, let the memory wash over you, but remember that for every Hell there has to be a Heaven somewhere, so look for it…………….

***

Raven leapt over the edge of gnarled rock that was the lip to the summit of Devil's Tower. Vampires were everywhere watching, waiting, talking, and playing. A pair of them was even tossing a white ball back and forth like a Sunday pickup game of catch. Dozens of them sat atop the struggling form of Zeus. Every few seconds two or three of them would be either hurled into the sky to plummet from the precipice by Zeus' might, or simply explode like overripe fruit cooked in a microwave oven. But, for every two that fell, four more would take their place, eagerly jumping onto the downed man.

The rest of her compatriots joined her, drawing the attention of the capering vampires. At center stage amidst the vampires Malign sat atop her throne of nothing once more. In a blood red evening dress, cut along the side and down the front to levels that would be considered pornographic if the fabric were to move but a centimeter in one direction or another. She bobbed her left foot up and down impatiently as she sat cross legged. Gabe spoke up from Raven's side, "I think this may be the first time ever that I don't want to see a *Basic Instinct* money shot."

Raven smiled, "They say there is a first time for everything."

"Aye," Gabe agreed, "who knew?"

"It's about time, Jasper," Malign said standing up from her throne. Half a dozen vampires slid into place to act as steps for her as she climbed down. "Don't you know it's rude to keep a lady waiting?"

"Well, when you see a lady be sure to point her out to me, you bitch," Grey said never missing a beat. "I wouldn't want to hurt a woman's feelings, now would I?"

Malign's movie star looks shifted slightly, elongating and taking on a simian quality when she grew angry. It passed in an eye blink and she was her typical calm, untouchable beauty once again when she said, "Oh, I have a lady right here. Allow me to make the introductions, because she only knows one of you."

Malign strode over to a thick cluster of vampires and trailing her hand Vanna White-like in passing, the demons parted to expose two people strapped to racks made of shadow. One was Hank, the boy was hanging limply and forlorn, with bright streaks of light running tear-like down his small cheeks. Raven could see that where the shadows had pierced his hands and feet they were twisting and squirming, wriggling like black worms in his spirit, wounding his soul. The other person was a young girl no older than her mid-twenties. She was dressed in the counter culture uniform of black on black. Her body was being invaded by the shadows in horrific and demeaning ways. The girl groaned and gasped in a mixture of pain and ecstasy. Metatron's voice was not something Raven was used to hearing, but he was the only one who could have yelled, "Maggie!" She looked over to see Lucifer holding the angel back, trying to calm him.

Malign grinned maliciously then purred, "See, Jasper, there is a lady present. You kept this poor lost little lamb waiting. She doesn't seem to mind at times." The shadows moved in counterpoint to Malign's dialogue, invading the young girl in very personal places, causing her to shudder. "But, then again," Malign continued and Maggie screamed in anguish as the shadows pushed their prodding too far.

"Let her go you monster!" Metatron bellowed. At a motion from Grey both Pete and Gabe had circled around the angel to help Lucifer hold him back if necessary. Malign laughed. "Oh, you funny little thing," she said, waving her hand at him in a shooing motion. "That's not how this is going to go, silly. Apparently you don't know who I am. Hello, I'm 'The Devil', duh. I'm not going to just let her go at the righteous tone of your voice, 'Get thee behind me devil and let the innocent victim go'. Honestly sweetheart, what do you think this is, a movie?"

A wickedly curved kris, black as a starless night, materialized in Malign's hand as she walked over to Maggie; she pulled the girl's hair back exposing her throat. She looked over at Metatron and said, "It just doesn't work that way in real life, sweets," and slit Maggie's throat open from ear to ear. Blood gushed over Malign's exposed arms, complementing her indiscrete ballroom gown with wet glistening maroon gloves.

The angel screamed, held back by a demon and two men whose charge was to keep the world balanced, and he started to fall.

***

Dante. The voice called to the spirit of the once mute road warrior as he sat next to his friend in the Las Vegas police department's holding cell. Bulldog was sitting on a worn and filthy cot, with his knees drawn up to his chin as he rocked away the built up sorrow. The monotonous motion gave his body a way to work out the extra energy racing through his system. The first inmate who had mistakenly made a remark about the biker's crying was now cradling a broken jaw, crouching in the farthest corner of the cell from Bulldog that he could reach. Dante watched his friend deal with loss and come to terms with concepts that had been forced on him in a very short period of time. The voice whispered again, *Dante.*

He looked around, but there was no one near him. No lights, no shadows, so he went back to his vigil. A woman of unspeakable beauty materialized next to him. Dante noticed her appear out of his peripheral vision. As he jumped off of the cot to face her he held his arms out, already channeling energy innately into a protective barrier. The woman smiled, her young features blushing with love and adoration, holding her hand out in a placatory gesture saying, "Dante, please do not be frightened. I mean you no harm."

"Who are you?" Dante asked. "Are...are you my mother?"

"That is not important right now. What is important is that I am the keeper of the Balance," Harmony said. "I am the Balance."

"Wait," Dante said, sitting back down next to his friend. "You're the lady who was with the cowboy outside of the pyramid. That was you, wasn't it? You look different, but I can see what you are - a woman, but not a woman. There's a blurring around the edges."

"Yes, Dante, that was me."

"Okay. Look I already told the cowboy I don't want to come work for you guys. Thanks for the offer and everything, but if I wait long enough I may be able to talk to my friends. Don't tell me I'm wrong; I've seen things, I know."

"Yes, Dante, I know everything about you. I know you were orphaned as an infant. I know how cruelly the world treated you," Harmony said drawing closer. She put her hand on Dante's wrist and looked him in the eyes. "And I know that Bulldog and the other Riders were the only people to treat you like family, giving you a place to belong. But, I truly need your help right now child, please. I made a promise to someone I care deeply for and I need your help to keep that promise."

Looking into Harmony's eyes Dante could see the answers to so many of the questions he had lived with his whole life. All he had to do was take her hand and go with her. It was a choice few men were given, to know or learn answers to every query he had ever made. He looked over at his oldest friend, a man he had never spoken to and shook his head, "I'm sorry, I can't."

Harmony smiled, "Yes, child, you can," she said and Dante felt power rush through his arm where she held his wrist. Power like no mortal man can ever know. He could feel weight returning to his limbs and the press of the sprung mattress pressing against his buttocks. When the frame creaked Bulldog looked over to see his friend sitting next to him. He jumped to his feet, startled at first, but when he realized it was Dante he wrapped his friend in a bear hug and laughed.

"God damn," Bulldog swore around his tears. "I knew it! I just knew it, if anybody I ever knew would become an angel it would be you brother."

Dante smiled and to Bulldog's astonishment spoke to his friend for the first and last time, "I love you brother. Thank you for everything. I have to go now, but we will meet again. Goodbye."

The handful of other prisoners that Bulldog had been sharing the cell with sat wide-eyed. Some made the sign of the cross and others swore quietly to themselves as the leather clad biker cried again, but this time with joy instead of sorrow.

Chapter 19

Have you ever done something that given the chance you would do just about anything to undo? Regret can burn you up inside. It may have been something you thought was right at the time, or maybe you still think it is right, but again, you regret it. I suppose that could be considered obsessing some, but we all do it. How many of you can't sleep at night? You lie in bed, wide awake, replaying the day's or week's or month's or year's actions that you might regret. I think sometimes that is the best part about being dead, no longer needing sleep. I could sleep if I felt the urge and I have on occasion, but shutting the mind off never happens. Wandjina may embody her people's beliefs, the Dreamtime as a connection to the Source, but my people believe sleep is a physiological process. The mind stays active on certain levels, even in sleep it is firing away, most often feeding your regrets.

Lots of people will say that the only real regrets you'll have are for the chances you didn't take. You'll regret not doing something, too? Jesus! We just can't win, can we? We'll regret something when we do it and fuck up, and we'll also regret it if we don't do it at all. So, by that logic the only time we won't regret something is if we do it and succeed, right? Oh yeah, that's a real healthy attitude there.

Sure, sure, I have plenty of regrets. But, I think that the regrets act as a measure to living. The more we regret the more we have lived. If you can look back over the years, scratch your head and say, "Well I'd do that whole damn thing over if I could," then congratulations! You've lived a full and interesting life.

Alexander has told me many tales over the years. I don't know if he does so just to get his kicks, if he has a real interest in me, or if he really needs a confidant and friend. I don't know. He told me once how he regretted his fall from the light into darkness. He said, "It made me sullen and unclean. Not to become a monster mind you, that is only a label and a paltry one at that. No, what left me with regret was that I had fallen out of stupidity, out of corruption from Malign and not because it was something I wanted."

And that is coming from the man, who by all accounts, may have been the greatest success in human history…So much for no regrets if you try and succeed, huh?

Not any of them: Alexander, Gabriel, Grey, Septemsab'aa, or any other spirit that has walked the earth for so long, angel, demon, or other doesn't matter; they all have more regrets than they can shake a stick at. That's just the price and reward for such longevity. You get to look back and be glad that you don't need to sleep anymore I guess, because you wouldn't be getting any anyway…………

***

"You sick sadistic bitch," Grey accused. Malign held a manicured hand to her ample chest in a mock *who me?* gesture. "Yeah, you," Grey continued. "This was your plan from the beginning. All this vampire nonsense was just a God damn cover, wasn't it?"

"Uh…Grey?" Pete asked standing next to the no longer struggling Metatron. The angel had fallen to the ground and was pulsing in a golden light that had threads of black shadow running through it. "Uh…Grey?" Pete said again. "I'm glad you figured out her dastardly plot and all. Evil white she-devil, on the Tower of power, with the vampire army, because I kept thinking it was *Colonel Mustard in the library with the candlestick*…but are you going to tell the rest of us what's going on?...because Voltron here isn't looking so good."

Metatron chose that moment to look up at Malign. Pete could see that his eyes had gone completely black, "Yeah, Grey, not good man!"

Grey walked over and crouched before the angel. "Don't do this, Metatron, she ain't worth it," he said trying to draw the angel's attention away from the demon and back to him. His efforts were in vain; Metatron stared at

Malign with his now pitch soulless eyes and yelled, "You killed her!"

"Why yes, silly," Malign said, taking the white ball from one of the nearby vampires. "Thank you for stating the obvious. I swear it never ceases to impress me how stupid you angels really are. Next you'll be telling everyone I'm an evil bitch like Jasper does. Yes, I believe we have firmly established this already."

Raven could see that what she had thought to be a ball, was actually a small dog. It was shaking and shivering as Malign stroked its coat, rubbing the blood from her hands into the dog's fur she said, "Now let me see, angel obvious. What do you think I have planned for your little halo polishing friend over here?" Malign walked, swaying hips back and forth pendulum-like, to stand next to the rack holding Hank. Zeus bellowed and bucked, tossing all of the vampires from him. "Hold that fool down!" Malign ordered, sensual voice colored with demonic menace, and dozens of vampires flocked to restrain the large man.

"Aw, fuck this shite!" Gabe yelled and started fighting the vampires away from Zeus. "Let the egotistical bastard go, Grey. I'm done. Let's help those what can be helped!"

"Will somebody please, tell me what the hell is going on?" Pete asked, looking around in exasperation.

He received his answer from Lucifer, "She wants to turn Metatron, Pete, just like she did me."

"The bitch wants herself another boy-toy," Grey elaborated.

"I'd settle for a man-toy, Jasper," Malign shouted over the now building battle. "But you've already established that you want nothing to do with me." She laughed and dropped the dog with a thud. She kicked at it as the dog scampered as far from her as it could go, and another shadowed kris appeared in her hands once more. "No matter what any of you fools do you'll never reach me in time to save the boy, and that puppet at your feet is already gone."

As she carried on, rubbing her victory in her foes faces, she did not see Dante's spirit materialize behind her. He grabbed hold of the shadowed rack keeping the angel prisoner and forced as much raw power into it as he could. The restraints buckled, exploding out and letting the boy fall limp. Malign spun around quickly, as shards of light grazed her back. She screamed, "No!" when she saw Dante wrap his arms around Hank and vanish.

Dante and Hank reappeared behind Grey. The cowboy smirked. He chuckled, running a hand along his jaw he said, "Well, that don't look like you planned for that, now did you?"

Ignoring Grey she screamed, "Kill them! Kill them all!" to what was left of her vampire army.

***

As the last of the demons charged them, Zeus had a quick moment to run over and check on Hank where Dante was sitting with him. "Hey, Hank, are you okay? She didn't hurt you too bad did she?" Zeus asked, rubbing the boy's head affectionately.

The little boy angel was smoothing his hands together, running them over his wounds like a Reiki master, healing the marks left by his prison. He said, "No, Francis, I'm fine. You don't look so good though." He reached out a small hand and started to sooth and heal some of the tiny wounds that the vampires had inflicted on his big brother. Zeus pushed his hand away saying, "I'm fine kiddo. Stay here behind us with Dante. This won't take long." The big man looked over at the Rider come Balance soldier and said, "Thank you."

After a lifetime of silence Dante had trouble realizing words were now there for him, so he only nodded as Zeus turned away frying a nearby demon with a bolt of lightning.

***

What was left of the angel Metatron stumbled from his crouch, moving slowly forward under his own power. Those that would have held him back were finally occupied elsewhere; the anger and rage running through his spirit were hot livid emotions that the angel had not felt since his first mortal life. He staggered over to the body of the young girl who had been his friend, his inspiration, his muse, and fell to his knees next to her corpse.

Malign had gone back to sit atop her throne. She watched, smiling maliciously at him as he reached out a hand to turn the girl's body over.

***

Raven was firing with zeal into any monster who stepped into her line of sight. Working back to back with Pete the two of them were quickly thinning the remaining ranks of vampires. Pete looked over to see Grey and Lucifer fighting side by side as well. *The devil and the cowboy,* Pete thought between blows to demons. *Sure, why not? That makes as good a genre crossover as any I guess.*

Zeus and Gabe were tearing into their share of demons as well. Now that his brother was safe Zeus was cutting lose and doing what he did best, carving large swaths of destruction. Chips of stone were being shot up into the night sky like shrapnel with every lightning strike as Zeus waded into the monsters laughing, "Bwaaa Ha ha!" for all he was worth.

Pete had been distracted watching his friends. He had not realized that Raven and he were down to just one vampire on their side of the battlefield. It sat on its knees, looking around as whatever hold Malign had over it evaporated, and the demon started begging for its life. Malign had gathered demons from all corners of the earth to do her bidding and it was obvious to Pete that this fellow was not from a country where English was their first language. It groveled at Raven's feet, stammering in a halting dialect, as she held one of her firearms leveled between its eyes. The vampire cried, "Mercy, mercy please, I implore."

"Oh, please!" Pete said drawing Raven's attention, "Please, please let me say it. How often do you get the chance for dramatic violent literary allusions? Please! Pretty please, with sugar on top."

Raven sighed, rolled her eyes, but said, "Alright, Pete, but just this once."

Pete pumped a victorious fist in the air, cleared his throat and said, "Quoth the Raven..."

Looking into the vampire's red glowing eyes Raven pulled the trigger. The demon's head exploded with a splatter. As she stepped over its dissolving body Raven whispered, "Nevermore."

***

Metatron reached out, placing his hand on Maggie's shoulder. When he started to pull her to him, Dolphie ran out from his hiding place behind a pile of rubble. Before Metatron could turn her body completely over the little white Bichon Frise bit his hand. Metatron glared at the dog in anger turning to surprise when it spoke in a heavily German accented voice saying, "Nein, you fool! It's her!"

Too late, Metatron drew back. Maggie's cold clammy hand grabbed his in a vice-like grip, twisting his wrist, digging cold talons of shadow into his spirit. As the cold raced up his arm Metatron pulled against the corpse, asking in shock, "What?"

Malign shot off her throne like liquid night. She grabbed the angel's other wrist and with her voice coming out of both her mouth and Maggie's she said, "You really are that arrogant, aren't you? You still don't get it, do you fool? This whole time you thought that it was your idea to bring some order to the masses like you did with your idiotic little tome centuries ago. It wasn't; it was my idea you pompous fool! All the death, all the strife was my idea, but you did your part in it, didn't you? What a silly stupid little angel you are."

What was left of the angel Metatron disappeared in a torrent of rage. The creature threw its head back and screamed in anger as Malign laughed.

Chapter 20

I'm not a very trusting person. I've met a few people who I love and would do anything for, but even them, with a few notable exceptions of course, at times I have trouble trusting them. Think about how often we have to take other people's words at face value, as the gospel truth so to speak. It's really scary when you think about it, having to trust people not to embellish with even the smallest hint of personal opinion.

I spent my life listening to my family, and my beliefs came from them, for a time. Eventually everybody starts to examine the things they are told. You can call it the age of reason if you like, but all that means is that you begin to think for yourself. Some people reach that point very late in life, if they reach it at all.

All our history books, all our recorded data, all our wives tales and traditions they're all subject to interpretation. We don't know, we weren't there. Look at how often people describe crimes and accidents in different ways, even though they all witnessed the same thing at the same time, and we're supposed to believe written historic documents that are centuries old? Or, scholars' interpretations of languages that have not been spoken for millennia, pardon me for sounding doubtful, but when your whole world gets swept away in the Third Reich you tend to lose your ability to trust.

There is one person in my life that has never lied to me. Oh, he will keep information from me, playing the "you aren't ready to know this, darlin'" card, but I trust Grey implicitly. Not just because he has lived through so much of what people term modern history - he was there and most times directly involved - but because he won't color the story to make himself look better. He won't purposely set out to hurt someone's feelings, but he isn't going to lie just to make them feel better about themselves either. If he tells me some hero out of history was a dick, then I believe him. I trust Pete not to lie to me either. I didn't want to like him, God knows I did everything I could at first to keep him at arm's length, but he is so hopelessly endearing in his emotions, he doesn't hide from the world. If he is scared you'll know it; if he is happy you'll know that too. That's why Grey and Pete complement each other so well. Grey is honest and true, but reserved. Pete is honest and true but extroverted. Zeus never lost his honesty. He has always been open, kind, and even naive at times. He died more than half a century before I did, so that's what Grey tells me. I obviously wasn't there, and that's as close to truth as you'll ever get.

Alexander or Lucifer, whichever name you want to call him, he is as confused about who he is as anyone I have ever met who has had as long a time to examine themselves as he has. Maybe that is the problem; he has existed so long. When a typical human psyche would naturally be drawn back to the Source by now, he has continued on and on, reinventing himself. He blames Malign for his fall. He says, "She seduced me, not just in the afterlife. No, she laid her seeds of betrayal long, long ago, back when I was but a young man, and she pretended to be human, a Macedonian girl of high nobility, my ass! It was bad enough that she bedded my father, but that wasn't enough for her. No, she had to flaunt it to those on this side of life by using the same human name twice in her exploits."

"We may not always get along, but I have much respect for your man Grey. If he had been around to curb Malign in her Cleopatra guises, I may have turned out to be a better man."

Can I trust any of what Lucifer has told me over the years? Can you trust the Devil? Is it better to trust the devil you know? But I've also seen times where you can't trust an angel either, so I suppose as long as you have a few close friends you can trust, you should consider yourself lucky and take the rest with a grain of salt...........

***

Devil's Tower rumbled as the angel Metatron transformed into Metatron the demon. Pieces of stone crumbled from the sides, cascading and crashing down from the summit to tear up any trees and brush that lay in their path, leaving a worn ring around the base, giving the appearance that the volcano had erupted once again and the rocks had cooled instantly.

Any of the demons left whole, who had gone along with the vampire guise and charade, had fled once Malign's control waned. Grey stood on the other side of the summit from the chaos, watching Malign create another monster. He looked over to Lucifer, who was staring fixedly at the struggling trio. Realization dawned on both men at the same time. Grey swore, "Fuck, that God damn crazy bitch!" at the same time Lucifer said something similar in a dialect no longer spoken among mankind.

"Come on!" Grey ordered the others who were looking around in confusion, as he sprinted across the flat-topped mountain toward the wrestling demons. No one questioned the order. They started to run after Grey, but Pete asked as they ran, "What are we doing, Grey? This looks like a demon on demon fight now. Isn't that out of our hands? I mean just last night you were willing to let Lucifer take out Mega-Bitch. Why are we interfering now?"

"Because," Lucifer answered instead, "last night I would have destroyed her if I could have and taken her place. She was lying to us earlier. She doesn't want a new toy. No, she will easily defeat that dandy Metatron - he was never a fighter. Then she will have all the power of a God damned she-devil and one of the oldest existing angels. Doesn't that sound like something that might tip the Balance to you, Pete?"

"Oh, yeah," Pete agreed. "That would be bad." As they were nearing the thrashing forms of shadow, Pete asked, "So, who does what?"

"Alexander and I will take on Malign," Grey said. "The rest of you hold Metatron back! He may have fallen, but maybe we can talk some sense into him before it's too late." Noticing that Hank and Dante had followed as well, Grey said, "You know him best Hank. See if you can break through to him once the others have him contained."

The small angel nodded his head and looked around wide-eyed as the others went to fight. Dante rested his hand on Hank's shoulder, watching in awe as Grey ran headlong into Malign, tackling her in an explosion of blue light. Using the force of impact to break Malign's grip on Metatron, Grey pulled her away as she screamed and thrashed. Lucifer did much the same with the human corpse version of the she-devil, who had called herself Maggie, only his explosive embrace was more shadow than light.

When the two powerful men had broken the demons apart the others rushed in to haul the demon Metatron away. The creature was no longer recognizable as the man or the angel he had been. It did not look like the typical animalistic demon form either. It still stood erect in a bipedal posture, but a second set of arms had sprung out from its sides, black as any demon. The arms were pushing and pulling at the creature, fighting it, instead of fighting for it.

Raven took charge yelling, "Quickly, force a shield around him. If those two can't keep that bitch off our backs, no one can."

The four of them circled the creature as it struggled with itself. A third set of arms had started to claw their way out of its back and were working their way up to its neck where they fastened their fingers around the creature's throat. The monster yowled in pain and tried to pry the fingers away, giving the other set of arms the opportunity to rip into the monster's chest. Sharp talons tore open a gaping wound where several more arms exploded out like a snake giving live birth. Pete wrinkled his nose up in disgust and looking across their circle at Zeus said, "Dude! This is gross. You ever see anything like this before, any of you?" He addressed the last to Raven and Gabe as well.

Raven said, "No, Pete. I haven't." Zeus shook his head while he chewed on his beard and drew his shaggy eyebrows down in concern. Gabe made dry retching sounds and placed the back of his hand to his mouth, but shook his head in negation to Pete's question. Looking around for some input from Grey, Pete could see that his friend had his hands full holding the demonic version of Malign back. Lucifer was having an equally hard time with Maggie. Pete was about to ask Harmony if what they were seeing with the creature Metatron was normal when Hank's quiet child's voice spoke up, "It's him. All those arms, all those creatures inside there are him. He has been so many people in his existence that he no longer knows who he is."

Hank walked up to the barrier's edge and placed his palms flat against the transparent energy shield. The creature continued to struggle with itself, but it stirred at the boy's presence. It started to pull itself toward the edge of the barrier and Zeus shouted, "Hank! Get away from there!"

The boy did not listen as he crouched down closer to the approaching monster. Pete glared over at the angel as he held his portion of the shield in place and said, "Damn it, this 'Frodo's in danger shit' is getting really old, really fast!"

"Drop the shield," Hank said to everyone in a resigned voice.

"No way!" Pete and Zeus yelled at the same time. Raven looked down at the angel who looked like a small boy, but was older than she was. Hank returned her glance and nodded his head with a sad smile saying, "Please, Raven. He does not deserve to have this be his end."

"Grey?" Raven yelled her question over her shoulder.

Pinning the thrashing and writhing form of Malign under his hips Grey looked up and shouted, "I'm a little busy over here darlin'. What is it?"

"Hank wants us to drop the shield," she answered.

"Why? Has he gotten through to Metatron?" Grey asked around a grapple that Malign turned into an action that would have been considered a courtship ritual in some cultures.

Raven looked back at Hank, raising her eyebrows in question. The angel turned his head back to the creature that had been his friend. Dozens of arms pummeled in and around the main body, some human, some demon, and one hand glowing slightly gold reached out and pressed its palm against Hank's. The boy looked back to Raven and shook his head in answer.

She yelled over her shoulder again, "No, Grey, he hasn't."

"God damn it, then why does he…aw shit kid," Grey said, understanding what Hank had planned. Pushing down hard on Malign to stop her thrashing and gain himself a moment's respite, Grey looked up to meet Hank's calm gaze. "Are you sure, boy? You don't have to."

"Have to what?" Zeus raged. "Have to what, Grey? I can't see him past the monster. What doesn't he have to do?"

Hank stood up and walked around to stand next to his older brother. He reached up, hugging the large man around his thick waist. Zeus looked down asking, "What don't you have to do, Hank?"

The small angel smiled up at his brother's concern saying, "He was my friend, Francis. I can't let him be taken over like that. It isn't right to the good man, the friend that he was."

Zeus' eyebrows pushed further down his forehead in concern. "What are you going to do, Hank?"

Hank hugged his brother again saying, "When you drop the shield, I'm going to pull whatever is left of my friend away from that creature. I will take all of us - the monsters, the men, and the angels - back to the Source where we can be what we were. He can be my friend again and not some twisted insane demon, lost to reason and humanity."

"No," Zeus said firmly. "I won't drop the shield and neither will the others if they know what's good for them," he yelled, meeting each of his friends' eyes in turn to make sure that they would not drop their share of the shield. Raven was crying, but she nodded that she would follow his lead. Pete and Gabe both nodded in support, too. When Zeus looked back down his brother had dropped to his knees again and was beckoning to the creature once more. This time the monster approached Hank under the intimidating shadow of the angel's big brother. Hank looked back up at Zeus saying, "Please, Francis, this isn't right. Look at him."

Zeus watched the creature pull itself along the crumpled rocks and debris. Once more Francis

Bancroft Ogelsbee stood over his little brother as a monster came to destroy him. Zeus looked down at his brother and the years of afterlife vanished, showing him Hank as a toddler again, just how he looked on the day they died. Zeus' lip quivered and his eyes watered as he said, "I-I c-can't, Hank, please…don't ask me to do this."

Hank stood up and hugged his brother once again. When he turned his face up to speak, Zeus could see tears of light rolling down the boy's cheeks. Hank said, "Please, Francis, it's okay, I'm ready. I'm not mad at mommy anymore."

Zeus started to shake. He could barely talk, but he managed to say, "But I still am, Hank."

"I know, Francis," the boy said. "It's okay; we'll be waiting for you when you're ready." Reaching up to grab hold of his brother's large hands with his small ones Hank continued, "Now, please, drop the shield."

Zeus did.

He grabbed hold of his baby brother one last time and as the monster came for him Zeus let go yelling, "I love you, Hank!"

"I love you too," Hank said and shot off like a comet, tearing around and through the creature that had been his friend. Zeus collapsed to the ground in a heap, sobbing. Raven ran over to hold him as his brother struggled with the monster. Wails of terror, anger, joy, love, and sadness in separate voices all issuing from the same throat called out. The creature had morphed into a pulsing mass of limbs. Hank was hovering around atop it. He was pulling on one angelic arm that was struggling to dislodge itself from the mass. The boy tugged at the arm and as whatever was holding it back let go the entire thing exploded in a cloud of light and shadow.

    Twice in the same night it looked as if Devil's Tower had erupted again, but instead of stone this time the volcano spewed light. The light shot into the dark sky like a geyser, illuminating the landscape for miles. When the eruption settled, the first hints of dawn were coloring the eastern horizon.

Chapter 21

God, loss hurts so badly doesn't it? When you lose someone you love it feels like a piece of you is gone forever. I'd personally rather lose a limb or eye over a person I love. Loss can be crippling in many ways. As we mature we learn, or at least we should, that losing objects and things just doesn't hold the same power as losing people. Anybody who has seen a child have a meltdown over its inability to find a favorite toy can understand that to that child it hurts as bad as any loss.

When we grow up and out of that material fixation we start to see the value in a person and what a true loss it is when someone moves on. Those that love them are all stuck behind yelling, "Come back," and having our own version of the toddler's meltdown.

This never really changes, no matter where you are in regards to life, afterlife, or moving back to the Source. There's got to be something past the Source when you think about it, change being the only constant if something is to remain stable or balanced. Then maybe we get recycled in the Source and sent back to earth. That could be another origin for the concept of reincarnation. Not just people seeing the animalistic creatures demons tend to devolve into, but that we come back again, only different. Physical life, then back to the Source for a bit, but before things can become too static there we run back through the turnstile for another ride on the rollercoaster of life. Maybe that's why people like me stay behind. We weren't ready to get off the ride the first time, so we keep going around. Another ghost sitting in the rear seat watching other people live their lives, while we clutch to what's left of ours, our grief?

They say we go through stages after we lose someone. You've heard that, I'm sure. The five stages of grief: denial, anger, bargaining, depression, and finally acceptance are how we are supposed to process the complexity of loss. They also say we can go through these stages differently depending on personality and our strengths and weaknesses.

I was not very good at begging. I never had much use for depression and I refuse to deny what I can plainly see. But, you know what? I've got no qualms with anger. I know you're surprised, right? Anger that someone I love was taken from me? Oh yeah, no problems there at all. Hey, does it count as acceptance if I accept that I'm going to go through life being a pissed off bitch from hell every time somebody I love is taken from me?..................

***

Grey glared down at the no longer struggling Malign. She smiled sweetly up at him. Grey's glare etched deeper as he asked, "Just what the hell are you smiling about? You lost. Game over."

"Oh, Jasper," Malign purred in her favorite condescending tone of voice. "I never lose. I'm an optimist." She gyrated her hips a bit beneath him and asked, "Are you going to let me up or not? I'm fine either way. Or maybe you want to spank me for being such a naughty girl?" She pouted her bottom lip out, batted her eyelashes, doing her best to look sullen and contrite.

Grey shook his head and let go of the demon. He walked away from her in disgust and went to check on his friend. Raven was doing her best to cradle the much larger Zeus. He had his head in her lap and she was stroking his hair. Pete and Gabe stood by, looking uncomfortable and awkward, not sure what to say or do. *Well, Hank*, Grey thought, *that's more than one miracle you performed today kid. I never thought I'd see those two struck silent by anything.*

Grey leaned down, placing his hand on Zeus' shaking shoulder he said, "I'm sorry son. I just don't know what else to say."

Raven and Grey startled, stepping back as Zeus sat bolt upright. "What to say? You don't know what to say?" Zeus asked glaring daggers at Grey. "You can tell me whether or not he succeeded, because I sure as shit don't know. How many times have you said it yourself, Grey? It's only a theory, we don't know of any angels who have actually done it. So, you tell me. Did Hank move on… or," Zeus struggled to finish his thought, "or is he gone?"

Grey closed his eyes and took a deep breath before saying, "I don't know son. I don't know."

"Harmony!" Zeus yelled, so loud that loose pebbles and scree, scattered about the mountaintop, vibrated at his voice. "Harmony! If Grey doesn't know, then you have to. Did he succeed?"

Harmony appeared and to Grey's sight she looked tired and upset as she walked over to speak with Zeus. Lucifer had let Maggie go and Grey watched the dead body lurch over to a pile of rocks and yank a small white dog out of its hiding place. The dog whimpered and whined as she carried it over to Malign. The girl slowly moved toward the demon and was absorbed back into the monster when she drew close enough. The merging was seamless and to all outward appearances it looked as if Malign had absorbed Maggie. The only change was that now the almost pornographically attired blond was holding the dog instead of the vanished corpse. She smiled at Grey when she realized he was watching her and blew him a kiss.

"No!" Zeus bellowed. "I don't believe it!" He stood up pointing a huge finger at Harmony and said, "You know…there is no way that you don't. You just won't tell me."

"Francis," Harmony pleaded, "please be reasonable. Even if I did know, I could not tell you. That is information from beyond this world. I could not give it to you even if it was mine to give. I…" She trailed off as Zeus stormed away from her. The Viking-esque man marched over to Malign where she stood, stroking Dolphie's blood matted fur. She smiled like sugar would not melt in her mouth with the big man towering over her and said, "Yes, can I help you?"

"Zeus," Grey warned, but the big man held up his hand, palm open in a *wait* gesture, never dropping his gaze from the demon. He growled down at her, "This, all of this, was your fault."

Malign sighed, "Why do I always have to deal with you morons. Yes, we established that earlier. All of this was my fault, duh." Her hand quickly shot out, reaching up to smack the big man's forehead for emphasis. "I like them big and dumb, but this is too much."

"Oh, shit," Pete added, wandering over to stand next to Grey.

To everyone's surprise Zeus turned his back on the demon and started walking away. Over his shoulder he said to her, "I'll be watching you."

"I do love a voyeur, sweetie," Malign cooed. "But that's all you're going to get to do. Look but no touch. You know your boss' rules; if I don't tip the Balance personally you can't do anything to me, silly."

Zeus had made it back to the others as they clustered around Harmony. He turned to look back at Malign and said, "Yeah…those are her rules." He hiked a thumb over his shoulder in Harmony's direction. "I got my own." Zeus reached into his chest, hand disappearing up to the wrist, and struggled for a moment before pulling out a shining bright sphere of purest silver. He grasped Harmony's small hands in his large paws and, turning them over, he placed the glowing sphere in her cupped palms saying, "I quit."

Everyone stared dumbly as their friend stomped away. When Zeus reached the lip of the mountain he yelled over his shoulder, "Remember, Malign, I'll be watching," and he stepped over the edge, vanishing.

***

Grey spun around to glare accusingly at Malign. He was fast, faster than most of the stories told about him could come close to accurately describing. Before he could swear, accuse, or denounce her in some way or she could smile and pretend that this was all part of her plan,

Grey saw fear in Malign's eyes. It was only there for a moment, but it was there. When Malign locked gazes with Grey, she was all beauty queen smiles again as she smirked saying, "See, Jasper, I'm an optimist. I didn't lose here. You did."

She waved bye-bye with saccharin sweetness, then disappeared.

The others turned as she vanished. Looking back and forth between where his friend had gone and where his enemy had been, Pete asked, "What just happened?"

Lucifer saw the wounded expression on Harmony's face and said, "She was right, you lost. It just did not happen in the way any of you, even her, intended it."

Grey wrapped one arm around Harmony as she bowed her head over the glowing sphere in her hands. He pulled Raven in with the other, resting his hand on her hip. She turned, pressing her face into his chest as she cried. Pete continued to look around, still not sure what to say or do. Finally giving voice to his frustration he said, "Well…that sucked."

***

"I thought I'd find you here," Raven said, sliding into the booth Grey was occupying at

Don's Eats diner. "The food isn't that good, Grey. You could always try something a bit more gourmet you know?"

"Nah," Grey said. "It'd just be wasted on me. I have simple tastes darlin'. The only cheeses I know are called *white* or *yellow* and with holes or without. That's as gourmet as I get." He chuckled, raised his soft drink to his lips and took a pull from the straw. Raven shook her head at the approaching waitress to let her know she did not want to order anything. It had been weeks since Zeus had walked away from his service to the Balance, from his friends, from everything. Grey had been, as Pete termed it, "sulking" for the better part of that time.

Raven smiled and reached across the table to touch Grey's hand asking, "Have you heard anything?" She did not need to say who or what she meant. Zeus' absence was on all their minds. His presence had been such an integral part to all of their days that they did not realize the size of the void he filled until he was gone.

Grey shook his head saying, "Just rumors. Nothin' I can pin down yet. There have been some sightings in Africa, but nothin' concrete."

Raven smiled sadly, "I just wish he'd let us help him. It doesn't have to be this way. Look at Alexander. Zeus could still help us, but not be one of us."

"I know," Grey agreed, "but darlin' that big old hairy brute has more heart than brains at times. He'll come around when he's ready. I prom-"

"Don't," Raven interrupted him. "No, we're past that. You can't, so don't you dare promise me, Grey. I can't take that."

"Fair enough darlin', fair enough."

Their booth was silent as the promise went unvoiced. Grey pointed out the booth's window and said, "Will you just tell Pete to get in here? He looks ridiculous standing out there in the rain, pretendin' he is waiting for a bus."

Raven turned around on her bench seat and tapped on the glass to get Pete's attention. He looked at her with raised eyebrows and mouthed "Are you sure he's not sulking anymore?" She nodded and exaggeratingly mouthed, "Yes," back. Pete started walking toward the diner's front door and ducked in. Before he reached their booth, Grey said to Raven, with a lopsided grin, "Ask Pete why he got kicked out of *Circus Circus*. He made a clown cry."

Pete slid into the booth next to Raven. As she choked down a laugh, and he asked, "What are you guys talking about? Have you heard anything, Grey?"

"No, Pete," Grey said. "I'm sorry. Even though I've been busy sulkin' all's I've heard are rumors."

"Damn," Pete said. "Harmony told me without her connection she doesn't know how to find him either, the big asshole. I'm sure Hank made it. I felt it, didn't you?"

"Mayhap, Pete," Grey said in reassurance.

Raven placed a comforting hand on Pete's shoulder saying, "Zeus will be alright, Pete. We just have to hold onto hope, I guess."

Pete nodded solemnly, "Yeah, I guess so."

"So," Raven asked in an overly dramatic baby voice, "what did that big mean old clown do to little Petey-Wheety? Did hims scare you?"

Pete glared across the table at Grey while his friend laughed, choking on his drink.

Epilogue

People wander in and out of your life, out of your afterlife, and for all I know that's what they keep doing no matter what phase of existence you are in. Faces that are welcoming and kind can turn bitter and cold, but looks of contempt can also turn to pity. That's just what it means to struggle along through sentience.

It is always hard to appreciate what you have while you have it. That's human nature isn't it? Companionship is important to all of us. People who go off into the wilds, claiming they want to be alone, are scared. Scared of living and losing, scared of what it means to connect to others. Sure, other people will let you down at times. They are human too; they have their weaknesses and breaking points. Maybe it's your turn to help pick up their pieces, so they can be there to pick up your pieces when they inevitably start crumbling off, too.

Of course, there comes a point in certain relationships where you realize that you're doing more of the janitorial work than the other person. Maybe that's because you are stronger than them, but it may also mean that they are taking advantage of your kindness. I'm not a big fan of being used myself, but some people are okay with it. Whatever floats your boat. But, always make sure when you fall apart, that you'd be willing to help those you are falling apart around when it is their turn to break.

If you don't, then you could end up all alone. It happens at times, all over the world. Souls are alone when they don't have to be. If they were just willing to give a little bit more of themselves and see other people as human beings with pain of their own. There is no need to stand alone when others are willing to watch your back. No need to be alone, no need to be a solitary soul standing out among the corpses, just another lonely raven.

About the Author

Nick Shamhart was born in Sandusky, Ohio on the winter solstice in the years before Americans started electing actors as President. He still lives in that mostly vowel state under protest from half of the voices in his head. The other half could care less where they reside, because they are too busy yammering on endlessly about everything from Sit-Com theme songs to theology and metaphysics. The voices help Nick write his books. If you like his books tell your friends all about them. The voices have many other stories yet to tell. They keep…*what?*…hold on please…*yes, I was just getting to that…no…no…look, do you want to do this?…well you can't…no…no…yes, alright.* The voices say thanks for reading.